CW01498539

*Emily: To strive, excel or rival*

**Meaning**


*Emily has the most beautiful eyes- once you see them you're trapped. She is always hiding what she really feels, and puts on a happy face. She can get very crazy sometimes and be the life of the party. Emilys are the cutest, nicest, most interesting, most gorgeous species known. She is exciting, adventurous, and outgoing. She might make some bad decisions, but she learns. Emilys are very rare, so if you catch one - hold on to her!*

**Urban Dictionary**


*Face of an angel: body built for sin.*

**Unknown**

**James**

1

The platform was all but empty on the damp January morning. The thick morning mist refused to lift and I could feel the droplets clinging to my skin, silently despairing over my hair. It was early, but it didn't feel early. I don't like sleep and I've never needed much. Apparently I was a nightmare when I was young, waking several times a night to come and have a frank and serious discussion at 2am. Usually about frogs. *I like frogs.*

Mum told me she occasionally booked a night alone in a hotel just to catch up on sleep. Now I'm older I wonder if she was alone but I'm not stupid enough to ask. *I should ask.*

A mean-spirited individual once compared me to Thatcher seeing as I have been known to survive on four hours a night and still been *compos mentis* enough to be a straight A student. Although, rather than the power suits and perms, I have a shock of thick, unmanageable, brown curls and - according to Nathan - my dress sense has much to be desired.

So essentially power suits and perms.

"You have to let me take you shopping."
"How many times...? I hate shopping. Why do you like shopping so much?"
"Why don't you like shopping?"
"Crowds; people; large clusters of persons; body odour; buggies..."
"That says more about you than you'd like to admit."

It was a long time ago I was the straight A student, heading straight to the top. I'd had my first existential crisis. Where am I going? What am I going to do with my life? Who am I really? All the philosophical questions that plague us all. I realised I was coasting through life and I needed to do something quickly. *Which is why I'm here in the cold.*

I shifted the weight of my backpack to the left shoulder, trying not to knock my rapidly cooling coffee in the process. I took a tentative sip and still managed to spill it over leaving a brown snail trail down the cup. My hands were sticky now.

"Damn." I cursed to myself and licked my fingers. A woman in a crisp, black dress looked in my direction and caught my eye. She smiled before returning to keep watch down the tracks for the train. I watched her stifle a yawn. Followed by another yawn in quick succession that struck her by surprise. I noted that, like this woman, the day was struggling to wake up: the night dragging on and the air freezing my lungs. My hands felt cold where the liquid had cooled.

I hoped from foot to foot in a lame attempt to warm up. My feet slipped slightly on the frost that turned this slippery station into an ice rink.

I coughed. *I really want a cigarette.* I quit a year ago but there were some situations where a cigarette would enhance the situation, such as standing on a cold, architecturally beautiful station, waiting for a train to take me to my new life. Like a scene from an old black and white movie. *What exciting lives we lead.*

*This is where I'm meant to be right now,* I mused silently. How beautiful the moment was. So yes, of course I choked on a gulp of my drink and split it down my coat.

As the train pulled into the station, I picked up the holdall, which was lying on my foot like a sleeping black Labrador and precariously carried my baggage onto the train. I tried (and failed) to look like a Seasoned Traveller, but I didn't trip over my own feet, so swings and roundabouts.

I picked a window seat near the luggage racks and made myself comfortable for the two-hour journey to Laaandan Taaan. I took one last look out the window and said goodbye to the grand ole City of York, choking on the rising lump in my throat.

The journey became increasingly uncomfortable as the crowds of commuters, families, students and other travellers got on. It was one of the new style trains but it still managed to lurch into the station. I sank into my book and tried to block out the noise and the waves of nausea, each bite of sandwich I chewed on took hours to swallow.

A grey haired bloke in a suit got on at the next station and sat next me talking loudly on his mobile. I tried really hard not to eavesdrop.

I muted my headphones so I could listen better.

"I understand that Julia but there is no reason they shouldn't accept our offer on the property."

Pause. *Must be his wife.*

"Yes, I understand but the house needs re-pointing and we need to get a landscaper in the garden."

Another pause.

"Stop. Stop. Stop! Listen. Go back to the Estate Agent and book them in to see me, then reschedule my 9am meeting tomorrow to 10.30. Damn it I'm getting that house." *Or not.*

I sank further into my book and peaked at his computer. He was typing furiously, fingers moving as intensely as his speech. His laptop screen revealed multiple tabs open: a Word document with a lot of text and charts; a news website (I couldn't work out which, looked heavy going though); a web page showing a lot of expensive looking jewellery - *How much for a necklace? That can't be a comma.* - and a website for jewellery and underwear.

I stared at the page and the words stopped making sense: I read the same sentence over and over again.

*"Deep in the human unconscious is a pervasive need for a logical universe that makes sense. But the real universe is always one step beyond logic."*

I gazed out the window. I felt lonely. I wasn't leaving a partner behind. It had been... too long since I had sex. Jimmy Boy was painfully single. Jimmy Boy was feeling it. I squirmed in my seat. I was **really** feeling. *I really need to sort that out. A new life, a new me, a new woman. I'll charm my way into someone's... heart.* My suppressed laughter came out as a snort. Grey Hair glared at me and went back to yelling at Julia.

We went through a tunnel and I took the opportunity to check out the other passengers in the mirror-like windows. I realised the woman from the platform was on the same carriage as me and I managed to make eye contact with. She smiled shyly and looked away. *That's a good thing right?*

If it's not blindingly obvious, but I'm not Nathan, so I don't have much in the way of an ego. I believed that I was always the nerdy friend, but I think I'm getting better with age. I think. However, still a little too pale, a little too stock and hair a little too thick and unruly. Since we decided that I should move, Nathan had insisted (made me) grow it into a decent style. He found me a hairdresser - rather than my traditional barbers - and I ended up a style that embraced my natural curls, but involved a lot of gel and took too long to style. It took longer than 30 seconds to style so it was certainly an adjustment.

"What the hell? I have a quiff!"

The hairdresser was not impressed with my reaction. Offense and regret flashed across his face.

"You look great."

"I look like Elvis."

"That's not a bad thing."

I maintained eye contact and silently drilling home my point. Nathan ignored me and continued.

"You're going to be in London! You need to relax that stuffy look otherwise you'll look like a tourist."

"What's wrong with looking like a tourist?" I'd protested, suddenly missing my old short back and sides.

"Never ask that again."

"I guess I'll adjust."

I heavily tipped the hairdresser for the obvious offense I caused.

A chill ran along the back of my neck snapped me out of my reverie. I shuddered and straightened up, unconsciously smoothed the downy hairs. I stretched up and craned my neck, working a crick out before it cramped up. My eyes settled on a passenger facing the opposite direction. My eyes were drawn to shoulder length hair shoulder length black hair, which caught the light and shone with a hint of brown. And a knee. I saw nothing else but hair and a knee. I pictured Cousin It.

Grey Hair was pretending not to stare at me. He watched me out of his periphery, then round the carriage; then back at me with a bemused look on his face. His credit card was in his hand, left hand frozen over his keyboard. *I bet he's sleeping with his PA.*

*Oh that's not nice.* Feeling suddenly guilty, as if he had heard my thought, I went back to (attempting) to read my book.

# Emily

## 1

*There's a man snoring in the seat behind me.* His heavy breathing is incredibly irritating and I can feel my blood pressure rising. I usually find the sway of a train soothing, but this one rumbled and bounced like it was about to come off the tracks and I sought solace in deep yoga breaths to calm my highly-strung nerves. I wondered whether a person could be strong enough to derail a train.

My eyes still closed I focused on the people around me and breathed in the sensations, I like trains. People relax on trains and their minds drift because there is nothing else they can do. I could feel tension, exhaustion and elation, quickly followed by a happy giggle by a girl typing furiously on a keyboard.

*Focus.*

*She's talking to her boyfriend.*

*That's obvious.*

*And that's not helping.*

*FOCUS.*

Eyes still closed I focused my will on the male voice yelling at the back of the train. It was a one-sided conversation so he was on his mobile. He bothered me. Phones weren't allowed in this carriage. *Breathe in... 2... 3... 4... Hold... 2... 3... 4... 5... 6... 7... Breathe out... 2... 3... 4... 5... 6... 7... 8...*

I tasted... something. It caught my attention like distant music or a smell on the breeze. His emotions snagged the bait and I reeled him in, focusing on pulling in part of his essence. I drank deep, feeling his energy running through my blood stream. There was lust and deceit. *He's having an affair.*

The longer I fed the quieter he became: I felt him grow tired and my energy levels picked up. I opened my eyes and drank the rest of my cold coffee, but something distracted me away from the bitter drink. Something else bitter: something that smelt/tasted my under ripe fruit, strawberries or oranges. Something... naïve?

My stomach suddenly twisted sending waves of nauseous through my body and ice spikes up my arms and down my legs. *I'm caught!*

Someone had sensed me. It was clumsy and faint: someone who didn't know what they were doing. I closed my eyes again and returned to my place of stillness, focusing my senses on the taste of citrus. It's like seeing someone in a fog and you can see them but they can't see you. I was trying to catch their attention. The smell/taste grew stronger and when I opened my eyes and saw a hand grip the headrest next to Cuckold. Subtly craning my neck I watched a head popped up like a meerkat, a head with messy brown hair and... I recoiled like I'd been stung, stomach flipping causing a wave of nausea to wash over me. Amazing eyes. Searching eyes that had a touch of craziness. Eyes like mine.

*So you've found an unawakened psychic vampire. What do you intend to do?*

*He might be awake.*

*You can't lie to me. I'm you.*

*I'm doing nothing.*

*Nothing?*

A muffled Northern accent interrupted my thoughts, announcing we were nearly home. The smog was already starting to twinge my nostrils and I could feel the thrum, the energy of the city getting stronger with each passing second. I took the distraction as a sign and started to prep to leave. I didn't feel like making any new friends and after this weekend I was ready for a day of nothing, before a week of hating the people I work with.

**James**

2

Once the train pulled into Kings Cross I waited until the carriage was nearly empty before I gathered my bags and fell into my new life. Literally.

I tripped over my feet as I stepped over the gap between the platform and the train. *FUCK!*

My bag skidded across the floor as I collided with the concrete and I came face to face - *face to knee?* - with a familiar knee. Then a pair of leather ankle boots as my chest and hands slammed into the platform. *Mind the gap between the train and the doors.* a female voice repeated in my head.

"Oh fuck." I murmured to the floor. My hands hurt.

Now the positives about slamming face first in front of a beautiful woman is that it made time seem to pass much slower than usual, so not only could I take the time to really appreciate the humiliation and pain, I could also fully appreciate every inch of her resplendent beauty. I let my eyes travel up the length of a tight pair of blue jeans, a black top showing underneath a black leather jacket, which strained over an obviously voluptuous bust, shoulder length, raven hair and...

My heart stopped in my chest and I gasped for air, I couldn't fill my lungs and for a moment I thought I might blackout. It could I was winded as my chest had collided with the concrete, or it could have been her eyes. Those beautiful dark, set into a heart shaped face and prominent cheekbones. Long eyelashes and too much eyeliner surrounded them and I the iris was so dark it could have been black. *Does she have black eyes?*

Light cascaded into the station, draping her like a cloak her and I saw her eyes were actually dark brown and her hair fell in loose curls, the type that look like it took a team of stylists a few hours, with a few hundred pounds of product to create. *Cost rather than weight, otherwise her neck would snap.*

*Why? Why does that come to mind now? Oh God, I'm still on the floor. I'm not moving.* I was still face down on the floor choking on floor dirt and my lungs. *How long have I been on the floor?*

The foot moved off my bag as I scrambled to my feet. My whole body started sweating from embarrassment and the blatant distain and amusement that radiated from her. The tightness of her jaw and the tendons that stood out on her clenched fist didn't detract from her beauty; instead it seemed to enhance it. I was reminded of Snow White's Step Mother or the Borg Queen.

Thankfully, out of the couple of dozen travellers who saw me slide across the floor none of them seemed to be recording me for YouTube stardom. I think. I may have seen someone unsubtly hold up their phone, but I could just be paranoid. They mostly glanced, smirked and rushed out the station. *I'm sure this won't end up on YouTube. This is going to end up on YouTube.*

As I pushed myself up I noticed her leather jacket sat at her hips, accentuating the curve and her legs looked stocky and muscular. She kicked over my backpack as I dusted myself off and I winced when I remembered my laptop was in there. She span on her heels and walked off before I had a chance to speak to her. I noted I must have been a head taller than her, even with the distance between us now and I listened to her footsteps long after she disappeared from sight. *Damn. I hope I see her again.*

The train was already being prepared to set out again and I was hurried out of the way by incoming and outgoing passengers. So I scurried off, trying to pull my tube map out of my pocket while checking my phone for scratches and cracks. *Please let my laptop be OK.*

**Emily**


**2**


I hate tubes: they make me uncomfortable. Something about travelling in a metal coffin, six feet underground, my nostrils being assaulted with the smell of other people. *I wonder what I smell like to others. Apparently Westerners smell like off milk to the Japanese.*

Some people hate flying: I hate tubes. But as I live in London and I'm not walking distance from work or any decent bars, and I'm not idiotic enough to own a car in central London, they're a necessary evil. It's surprising really, as I would have thought I would love them. All these people with their pheromones and emotions in an enclosed space, especially as emotions are heightened with the latest batch of attacks. I should be able to feed with ease, but I'm so nervous [*scared*] that I can't concentrate. Tubes scare me. My ex could feed enough in a 20-minute rush hour journey to sate her hunger for two days: I'm only satisfied like that from sex. *Bitch.*

*It's been a while, hasn't it?*

*Not now.*

I leaned my head against the glass and closed my eyes, overwhelmed by exhaustion from the hen weekend. Certainly not my hen party: it was… fun? But not my tastes. Too many party games and too much glitter. I hate glitter. Yes, that is completely due to Twilight for that. Since that fucking movie came out everyone thinks vampires sparkle and they are way too much in the public eye. Now if I dared confide in anyone what I was I would be a 'Goth / wannabe / freak / deluded'. Vampires don't sparkle; we don't live forever and not all of us feed on blood. Read a fucking book.

Great, I made myself angry now. *You wind yourself up.*

*I said not now. I wonder if everyone argues with themselves.*

Letting the vibrations lull me to my happy place I considered taking a nap when I got home. I let my mind wander back to my journey home. I like trains. Trains are safe. Trains have space and enough seats (*Ha, ha, ha, ha!*). If anything happens you can jump out of a train.

And it's not often an attractive person literally throws themselves at you.

I was getting off the train when I heard a splat and a thud behind. The sound of a flesh hitting concrete is a special one. When I turned round it was the cute boy from the train sprawled at my feet.

Occasionally you can feel the cogs of fate click into place. You can feel the bigger picture being built and the universe pushing you to the next step. I was going to help him up, laughing about this and then we were going to share a tube to our next destinations. Before he left I would give him my number and we would meet for coffee at the weekend. It was going to be amazing.

I felt my flesh burn as he looked at me. I could see him making a mental note of every lump, bump and curve. His attraction overpowered his embarrassment, which washed over like a tsunami when his eyes fixated on my chest.

I could feel him trying to engorge himself on me. His energy reaching out to meet mine. My blood pressure rose and the mound between my legs started to tingle. *No, he has no idea what he's doing. It's too much.*

I kicked his bag over to him and walked off, panting. I wasn't dealing with this. I could feel the fireworks forming and part of me was screaming to run. I was at a fork in a road. *You could help him.*

*No.*

*Go back!*

*NO!* My silent yell echoed in my head, louder than my footsteps through the station. I crashed through the barrier and ran down to the Tube, the sound of him zipping his bags and the wave of frustration and embarrassment following me like a nuclear blast.

**James**

**3**

Well that experience left me with nerves a more than a little shook and confidence truly battered. Although, my experience with the tube wasn't much better and it made me seriously doubt that I was cut out for this city. Two people crashed into me; three gave me evil looks and one tutted loudly at me as I collided, bumped and wobbled my way to West Hampstead station. I was running a little late but I couldn't be bothered to let Nathan know. He could wait. I was still distracted with my bruising and embarrassment.

I'd only been on a tube a few times before: school trips, day trips, drunken weeks and once to see Grease with Mum. Note: I hate musicals. But those times I wasn't in control, I just followed someone round like a little puppy and got on and off when I was told to: there wasn't any independent thought involved. Now I was trying to navigate my way through the bowels of The Capital: miles of escalators and steps; thousands of people and travelling in a big, metal coffin, six feet underground. I shuddered as I tried to shake the thought.

Enough people got off at Baker Street that I had room to sit down and I sat wondering whether I should have asked Nathan to meet me at King's Cross. These thoughts were interspersed with praying I didn't throw up on my bags. The early start, the lack of food and my jangled nerves had made me feel sick. *Or it could be because you're cramped into a stuffy, fast moving tin can of body odour and farts.*

*Thanks brain.*

I rubbed my head, trying to work out if I cracked it against the floor. My hands looked sore from the missing patches of skin. I pick a piece of grit from my palm and flicked it onto the floor.

Stepping out of the underground station into my new neighbourhood was one of those moments I will hold with me until I die. Another beautiful moment where there should have been no beauty. I breathed in the air, which rapidly cleared the sick feeling in the pit of my stomach and let me eyes adjust to the unusually bright morning. Londinium is vibrant, buzzing with life even though it was Tuesday morning and most people were at work. I couldn't wait to see my new home, with my readily prepared room.

I hoped that Nathan bought beer. I could do with a drink.

**4**

It should have been difficult making the decision to uproot my life: what was difficult was leaving my family, but it was the best option for us all. At 25 I had a half decent job [boring, but paid the bills], but I still lived at home: I was saving up a deposit to buy my own place. I also filled the archetypal 'older brother' role to my little brother and sister (15 and 10 respectively). My life wasn't exciting, but it was comfortable. *Rut.*

This all changed on a sunny Sunday in July when - over an elaborate breakfast of pancakes, bacon, eggs and sausages - Mum announced she was pregnant. She made the meal to soften the blow, but Dad still 'joked' that he knew he "should've had that vasectomy."

Obviously everyone was thrilled... Thrilled? Obviously everyone was happy... Happy? Obviously everyone was apprehensive, but Home is a good size but not huge. Detached, four bed, two bath family home, so comfortable for five, not so much for six. Although the baby would be with my parents for the first year, the decided that they needed to move and the discussion of moving costs were causing a lot of stress. Add Mum's hormones into the mix and... I was out of the house a lot. Her morning sickness was almost as bad as the outbursts and tears.

"Three Goddamn brats and it doesn't get any easier!" was heard screaming from the downstairs toilet most mornings.

"Why the hell do they call it morning sickness when it lasts all day?" was heard from the upstairs toilet most evenings.

As the eldest, the best thing for me to do would be to generously move out and give up my room. It was hard, but so as not to make them think it was due to them, I explained how I needed to "spread my wings and grow. There was so much I need to do and try."

Dad clapped me on my back (really hard) and looked away saying he'd "help with the boxes" in a quivering voice. Mum burst into tears, but she did that a lot these day.

*Definitely the hormones*, is what I told myself anyway.

It was on one of the many weekend trips down South to Nathan I was complaining about the problems of flat hunting and he suggested I move in with him. He said I needed to live the 'London Life'; experience Soho and Leicester Square; New Year's Eve at the Eye and some of the World's best food and culture.

I paraphrase, what he actually said was: "Dude, if you're going to waste your savings on rent, you might as well do it somewhere awesome."

"That would be awesome. Do you think they'd be OK with me moving away? I do help a lot around the house."

"Do you?"

"Yes!"

"He said unconvincingly. She has Mike [Dad] and the kids: she's not alone. And you won't be living there either way. You have to live your own life. You're young! Be wild and free before you settle down with a mortgage and responsibilities. You hate your job, so get one down here, the salaries are insane and we go drinking every night."

"That doesn't sound like a good thing you know." I stared at my beer, my family liked to drink and it had been passed onto me.

His shoulders sank as he glared at me, "That's not quite what I meant."

I'd reached a fork in the road of life. Shall I go for inevitable A) babies, a dead end job and boredom or B) The Mystery Box (London)? Granted B) might lead to A) anyway, but maybe not as quick.

So I started job hunting, had a few interviews and got a job as a Receptionist at a serviced office in Central London. There were 20 companies within the building and it had a security guard who let guests and staff through the reception security gates. It wasn't going to be the big career move but it paid enough to finance my new life and my savings funded the move and some new clothes, shoes, etc. I still kept some locked away in a contingency fund. You never know when you're going to need to drop everything and run away. I always wanted to join the circus. *Yes, I am a child.*

Nathan moved out of his current share house and we found a place that could accommodate us both. A huge turn of the 20th century townhouse was to be our new home. It had an amazing view from the roof - *Can you say roof parties? -;* it was in an area with decent bars and boutique shops and had an easy walk to and from the tube station. I had a large room at the top of the building across the hall from the landlord Andy. It was surprisingly well soundproofed, apparently, and Andy and [his existing tenant] Susan kept themselves to themselves.

Nathan moved in first due to my notice, but I went down to help him move and to decorate my new room. My framed Pulp Fiction and Deathproof posters; a lava lamp and a large, fabric piece of artwork I found at Camden market. I was going for the Shag Pad look. *Giggidy.*

I also bought a few overpriced items of clothing from Cyberdog for a club Nathan was going to take me to.

"Goth chicks in latex dude." He imitated Homer Simpson's drooling noise. He certainly earned his Hound Dog reputation: his brain was in his dick and he was ruled by his libido.

I was going to miss York though. There was so much history and as a city with two universities it had a great nightlife. I was born and raised here; I knew every inch of the city and everyone in it.

Still... London! Always seemed glamorous. Until you live here, then it loses it lustre pretty quick.

I refused to let my family see me away at the train station, preferring to say goodbye at home and shed my homesick tears in the taxi.

5

Nathan took the day off work to welcome me and to get drunk at midday on a weekday. *Hell, it's 5pm somewhere.*

He met me at the tube station and helped me with my bags on the short walk to our new home. There was a bottle of champagne, two kegs of warm looking real ale and two six-packs of Polish lager in the fridge. He handed me a can of the lager.

"I really need this." I drained half the can in one slug. I felt the knots in my shoulders loosening as I sighed and belched.

Nathan did the same: he was a hardened drinker also. His job in PR apparently required him to spend most of his time in client meetings drinking, or going for drinks after or drinking at networking events. I didn't even pretend that I understood what he did. It sounded like he paid to party but apparently he was the 'creative powerhouse' in his agency. I'm sure it was according to him alone.

I chose not tell him about my little incident at the station. I didn't want to give him any ammunition and I wanted to hold onto my chance to be a new James for as long as possible - cool, calm and collected. *Stop laughing!*

I found I was rubbing the back of my neck and Nathan was talking about something. *Christ, I haven't been listening.* I concentrated on nodding in the right places.

"You're not listening are you?"

"No."

The rest of the day was a blur of drinking, unpacking, drinking, researching gyms, drinking and preparing for my first day at my new job. And drinking. There was a lot of drinking. We polished off the beers and the bottle of champagne, but when Nathan pulled a bottle of red wine from... somewhere... I decided it was time for bed. Luckily, I was too busy for my nerves to get to me and I slept well thanks to the level of alcohol in my blood.

The next morning my body clock woke me up two hours before my alarm and five hours after I went to bed. And it was freezing. I snuggled further into my duvet in the dark room, a streetlight peeping through my curtains. I lay there processing my fading dream and thanking every deity I could think of that I didn't have a hangover, all whilst enjoying the sound of the silence. As silent as the busiest city in the U.K. can be: I could still hear traffic, dogs barking and people outside.

Finally, I managed to will myself out of bed enough to I jump into the shower to let the hot water wash over me, warming me to my core and soothing my nerves. Almost. My stomach had a knot that wouldn't unravel. I was feeling a little homesick.

Dressed in my new clothes - a grey suit, white shirt and thin black tie - I eyed my reflection, checking to see my shoes were suitably polished and congratulated myself on how good I looked. *Six foot of stocky, Northern lad scrubs up well.* I flexed, pulling a couple of body building poses and then breathed out with an audible groan. *Who am I kidding? I could do with a little more muscle and a little less pie.*

*"When you're younger you can eat what you like, drink what you like, and still climb into your 26" waist trousers and zip them closed. Then you reach that age, 24-25, your muscles give up, they wave a little white flag, and without any warning at all you're suddenly a fat bastard."*

Nathan and I ate our breakfast in silence, engrossed in our phones. I was looking at the news and Nathan was scrolling through Snapchat: he insisted on giving me a running commentary punctuated by showing me pictures and videos.

Andy came down the stairs in his tartan dressing gown and made us all a pot of coffee. *Don't think about what's under that. Don't think about what's under that. Don't... I wonder if he's nude? Damn!* Susan was still in bed. I tiptoed passed her room on the way downstairs. She's a tube driver and her shift ended late, or early depending on whether you'd been to sleep that night.

I felt very much the local as Nathan and I peacocked down the street in our matching brogues. This feeling was shot to shit when I had a happy little thrill as I waved my card over the terminal. Nathan noticed my grin at the gates opening and shook his head, laughing at me.

"Did you put your card in your glove?"

"No."

"You did. I saw you wave your hand over the pad."

"I didn't..." Tripping over my own feet I stumbled straight into a group of students, making me lose my train of thought. *Why isn't tube of thought a thing? Subway of thought? Underground of thought?*

They glared at me, swearing and yelling and as I backed away apologising I almost fell backwards to the escalators and had to be hauled up by a man in a business suit.

"Careful there."

This whole little misunderstanding became a scene and for the second time in two days, crowds of commuters were staring and filming.

"Why do people feel the need to document everything?" I muttered, shoving my hands in my pockets and sloped off towards Nathan, who - as my supportive friend - was documenting this for prosperity. He was laughing so much his phone was shaking.

"You're a dick sometimes, you know that right?" *There goes my dream of a new me. Same old James, a clumsy ass.* Granted, most of the time I'm not some sort of lame Mr Bean copy, but when I fuck up, I fuck up spectacularly.

I took the tube to Green Park and Nathan changed Bond Street and I was left to walk the short journey to my impressive looking, glass fronted, office building alone.

I was to be one of three Receptionists needed to cover the main Reception. The job wasn't difficult, but it was constant and demanding, so I had to be focused. It was surprisingly exhausting being polite and friendly to the suited people that came into the building to work and for meetings and appointments.

Gemma - engaged with short, brown hair - took me under her wing and showed me the ropes. I think she viewed me as her protégé, although the idea of spending my whole career here filled me with a strong sense of foreboding. With five years of service she had seniority over Alice - dating, but nothing serious and blonde - though neither of us directly reported into her. We only saw our boss, the Building Manager, Deborah (never Debs or Deb, only Deborah) about once a day.

My first day consisted of a tour, health and safety assessment and system training. I'm not computer whizz but I can usually blag that I know more than I do. The systems were a doddle. *This is going to be a cakewalk. Cakewalk! Cakewalk?* I got a uniform too. Not quite as nice as my new suit but they gave me a few different outfits to choose from and told me to make it last a year. As I changed in the men's toilets I looked down at my suit and figured it was clean enough to shove straight back in the cupboard. *I'll save it for my next date.*

*[Echoing laughter.]*

*I hate my head.*


Much to Nathan's annoyance I decided to spend my first three weekends visiting the tourist destinations, determined to get the sites out of the way before I became a proper local and didn't go because "it's too touristy." Nathan's words, not mine.

Although I had been the National Science Museum and the National Gallery on school trips, I wanted to see the Houses of Parliament, the Tate and take a trip on the London Eye. I even took a boat trip down the Thames, although that wasn't a fun trip alone: all couples and families.

Initially I found the size of the city and the amount of people daunting. It was never silent and yet no one spoke to each other. When I dared make eye contact with a stranger they would look away. God knows I certainly didn't try picking anyone up in that time. I found Londoners a little cold compared to the friendliness of York. Although that was just because I knew most people and they would always stop to see how I was. That and most people I passed were commuters or tourists, so they weren't cold, just busy.

It didn't take me long to adjust to the thrum of the city, the buzzing of traffic. A heartbeat so loud it vibrated through our bodies and we danced in time to its beat. *Ba bum. Ba bum. Ba bum.*

I was fascinated. I was in love. The mix of the old and new, the residential streets randomly interspersed between beautifully crafted glass office buildings. I found myself looking into the history of the city often. I love history. It's from I growing up in a city thousands of years old, where the streets smelt medieval and ran with the blood of the Romans and Vikings. Figuratively of course. Well... the smell was literal on the Sunday morning after graduation.


I became incredibly boring during the week: eating, sleeping, TV or reading - if I had the energy. I found all the extra walking exhausting and more than once I found myself drifting off at the kitchen table, only the smell of burning to wake me up. I was developing a taste for carbon.

On the rare occasions I had enough energy to try and do something productive I did push-ups and sit-ups in my room, watching my belly fat crease in the process. I had taken a look around one gym but I wasn't happy: everyone was so ripped, tanned and preened that I felt terribly out of place. The men had manicures. I have bitten stubs that occasionally bleed.

Work was... Work was work. What can I say? If I had a choice I wouldn't be there. But I don't. So I was. Every morning Gemma straightened my tie and Alice was obsessed with my (lack of) love life.

"One day you'll learn to dress yourself." Gemma.

"No he won't. He'll get a girlfriend and she'll dress him instead of you." Alice.

"I appreciate the sentiments but I'm very happy right now." I lied.

"Liar." They both laughed.

Alice kept trying to find out my type so she could set me up with one of her friends. During the quiet periods she would show me photos of her friends and ask my opinion.

I tried explaining that "although they are very attractive [not my type] I don't have a type" and I thanked her for the sentiment but she "really, **really** didn't have to do that." But she was insistent: some would call her pushy. I would be one of them.

I'd developed a people watching game with my ex and I decided this would be the perfect job for playing it. The office got very quiet on Friday afternoons and with the big glass doors we could sit and watch the world go by. The rules were:

1. Judging people by their appearance along and you had 30 seconds to come up with their back-stories.

2. Additional points for creativity.

3. You could win if you have the most fantastic and believable. E.g. you couldn't say: "they're a spy" unless you could prove it: gadget, shifty conversations or witness a dead drop.

4. Outright win if you could prove that you were right.

I was really good at it, if I do say so myself.

On my fourth Friday a woman walked in dressed in purple tights, a purple wraparound dress with a purple handbag. Her hair was a deep purple, cropped short and pointing in every direction. She looked about early 20s, but it was hard to tell because the nose ring made her look young. She stood by the door, tablet in the crook of her arm with fingers flying over the screen. She frowned at the screen and I noticed some crinkles around her eyes.

"She's a struggling writer here to see the Publisher's on the top floor, looking for her big break." Gemma hissed, she was under her desk fiddling with the cables and peaked up just long enough to get a good look

"Nope, she's stunning, so she's a model here for a casting call. That agency had just moved in on level two."

"You're both wrong, she's from a finance magazine, she's here to interview the investor's on the third floor."

"You're joking? Looking like that, no chance. Have you met Mr. Gregory yet? He's a snob." Alice exclaimed incredulously and far too loud because Purple Girl's head snapped up before going back to her tablet, grinning to herself. Alice blushed and became suddenly fascinated with the papers on her desk. I directed their gazes to the diary on my screen.

"There is only one person with an appointment at 3.30pm." I pointed at the clock that said 15:15. "They have a female name and this is the only woman who has walked in, in the last half an hour."

They stifled a giggle as she walked up and proved me right. I blew the end of both of my index fingers and gave them the finger guns.

"Ladies. Drinks on you tonight."

# Emily

## 3

I swirled my drink around my glass, concentrating on it to make sure it didn't slosh over the sides and ignored the man next to me who was trying to make eye contact.

"May I sit here?"

He was alone and I could tell how the conversation would go. He was going to try and start talking to me, to form a connection and potentially get my number. I parted my lips baring my teeth at him in some semblance of a smile. It didn't reach my eyes, which I darkened to show my displeasure. My red lipstick made my teeth look particularly white.

"Sure."

I downed my drink and went to the bar for another leaving him to watch me in disappointment. *It doesn't mean I'm truly smiling just because I show you my teeth.*

**James**

6

The rain was light, but it was that irritating kind that soaks you to the skin when you're moving but you can barely feel it when stationary. We attempted to huddle under one umbrella as we walked down to our local pub/cocktail bar/gastro pub [delete as find applicable. I call it a pub, apparently it's not]. But with me being about six inches taller than both Alice and Gemma meant they kept jabbing me in the head with the spines and running water down the back of my neck. I shuddered and accepting my fate I stepped into the rain; and stepped straight into a puddle. *Fuck.* Wet socks are a horrible feeling. Nathan had insisted on meeting us there after I'd shown him Facebook photos of my new work colleagues. He'd set his sights on Alice and taken to salivating over her Instagram.

"Please don't have sex with my with my co-worker. You know it will be awkward when she eventually finds out what a douchebag you really are."

Nathan gasped and pressed his hand to his chest in mock offense. "You Sir have offended my honour! I am the perfect gentleman."

"Cad more like."

He raised an eyebrow. "You sound like something out a 1930s movie. Who says 'cad'?"

I pulled out my phone. "Cad. Noun. A man who behaves dishonourably, especially towards a woman. I could call you a dog if you'd prefer but that would be offensive to the animal."

He howled.

We were sat in the dining room eating the spaghetti carbonara that I made: I was becoming quite the chef.

"James, it will be fine." I ignored him and focused on trying not to spill my food.

"James. James. James. James. James. James. JAMES!"

"WHAT?" I snapped: he could be so irritating.

"I'm going to tap that and she is going to scream my name." He grinned and added a shoulder-shimmy.

I couldn't stand Nathan sometimes. Lovely bloke and as loyal as a Staffordshire bull terrier but he was a teenage boy at heart and only thought about sex. What made it worse was that he was sexy and he knew it - *I'm sexy and I know... I'm sexy and I know it.* - and I would agree with him he is very attractive, from a bloke's point of view. I'm not on any kind of homo/pan/bi-sexual spectrum, I am very much a straight man that can appreciate another man's good looks: bright blue eyes and perfectly styled, golden blonde hair, he could wrap any woman round his finger. *I'm not jealous. Really! OK, maybe a little.*

Now he was sat next to Alice as she giggled and twirled her hair in her fingers, enthralled in his every word and judging by the way his eyes scanned from her hair, to her waspish waist and back to her handful of a chest, he was as attracted to her as she obviously was to him. *Subtle as a brick Nathan.*

Gemma and I shared a knowing glance and excused ourselves to the bar for fourth pitcher of Porn Star Martinis, which were going down entirely way too well: my head was swimming and I could hear Alice's giggle from across the room.

"She has a distinctive laugh when she's been drinking."

I nodded in agreement. Distinctive was not the word. Glass-shattering? Abrasive?

The bar was chaotic, full of workers relaxing after a long week - the smell aftershave, perfume and stale cigarette smoke oozed from their clothes. There was electricity in the air and you could almost taste the pheromones. I leaned against the bar and breathed in deeply, savouring the air like a wine: a chill ran down my spine and my taste buds tingled. *I feel alive.*

"You have to excuse Nathan, his brain is very much lodged in his..." I watched two more people run in from the rain and shake themselves like dogs trying to get dry. "I guess it's not letting up."

"Nah, he's not worse than Alice is. He seems polite enough and he's certainly made me feel relaxed, even though he only has made it clear he eyes for her." She wiggled the fingers on her left hand, which was accentuated by the light catching her large, diamond engagement ring. "Which is a good thing I suppose, he knows the. And as long as he isn't dangerous?" There was an inflection at the end that indicated a question.

I shook my head and pulled a face. "Nah, he's a kitten but he thinks he's tough."

"If you don't mind me asking, you two grew up together, so why doesn't he have the same accent as you?"

"I honestly have no idea. His parents are originally from Surrey so I'm guessing it's because there was no Yorkshire dialect in his family home. I have noticed that he has a tendency to correct himself when the colloquialisms slip out: I think that he thinks it hinders him at work. I can't imagine it would look good if I referred to one of the female clients as 'Lass'."

"I wouldn't mind if you called me 'Lass': I think your accent is adorable." A clipped and high-pitched voice chirped up behind me.

I jumped and turned and found myself face to face with a pair of large dark eyes, long eyelashes and a lot of eyeliner. *Why do I always notice her eyeliner?*

*Not now!* Now wasn't the time to be arguing with myself. I was face to face with the woman from the train. I held her burning gaze for a moment or two before I was drawn to her beautiful mouth and those lips, which conjured a hundred filthy thoughts. They parted and I saw the tip of her tongue.

I squirmed. *Oh fuck me; I wonder what that would feel like running up me.* She grinned wickedly her eyes exaggeratedly travelled up and down my body. I tensed the muscles in my legs and rubbed my neck as the blood rushed away from my head... to my other head. I stood dumbfounded, jaw slack and tongue practically on the floor. *Breathe. Breathe. Breathe.*

*SAY SOMETHING!*

The barman slid a Martini glass over to her and I watched her walk away - still smiling for me - those beautiful Jessica Rabbit curves clad in a tight black shift dress had my legs feeling like they were going to buckle under my weight. *Go after her!*

Gemma coughed and her laughing drew me back to reality. She was staring at me and obviously waiting for an answer to a question I hadn't heard. I needed to pretend I had been listening.

"Huh?" I grunted. *Smooth.*

"I said: do you know her?"

"Not really." My response came out as a croak. The internal me was kicking and screaming for not speaking to her and still contemplated running after her, but she was long gone. *Damn it!* I couldn't see her at all.

**Emily**

**4**

So it wasn't a complete accident that I was in the same bar, but you can't blame a girl for chasing an attractive boy. How often do you meet a man who is willing to throw himself at your feet? I mean I was going for an after work drink anyway, I needed to unwind and just because I happened to follow him to the bar he was heading towards... I mean that's not stalking, it's just... a happy, planned accident? I mean it was an accident that I saw him, just not an accident that I followed him.

I left the bar quickly after seeing him. The chase is thrilling and I wasn't ready to give it up yet. I wanted to make him really want me and I didn't want to get bored. I get bored easily. I'm a child, I want a toy when I don't have it.

**James**

7

We were nicely drunk, the lights sparkled invitingly and under the cry of: "The night is young and so are we!" - *Thank you Alice.* - we headed onto the next bar, one that Nathan recommended.

"We had a client take us here for lunch." He kissed his fingers like a chef. "So good."

This was a hotel bar and much classier spot than the last and I felt completely out of place. The clientele looked like they earned in a day what I earned in a month. I was surround by amazing suits: there was a woman in Saville Row suit. Yes, even I know about Saville Row suits.

We commandeered a section of sofas and chairs and a nervous laugh escaped my lips as I sloshed the round of cocktails over their glasses as I clonked them on the table. The noise was loud to me but no one looked over. Alice and Nathan were too enthralled with each other to notice. The alcohol had enhanced their feelings for each other and I had a feeling someone was going to get laid tonight. And it wouldn't be me. *Jealous?*

Alice had her very long legs - *Why haven't I noticed that before?* - draped around Nathan's and Nathan had his fingers underneath in Alice's hair. He was massaging her neck. I collapsed into a leather chair with an audible squash and was washed with a wave of exhaustion. The week had been long, the alcohol was relaxing and all I wanted to do was sleep. My eyelids closed slowly in a dangerously long blink. I was dozing off. Gemma obviously felt the same, judging by the way her eyes were drooping and her conversation was faltering also. She made a 'leaving' gesture with her hands and her eyes flittered to the door and back. We silently agreed that we were going to head to the tube station.

"Slash." I mouthed and she nodded and turned to the love birds to inform them of our departure - I could hear their protests as I wandered off, concentrating on putting one foot in front of the over and not tripping and sliding across the floor. *Marble? Can't be too expensive. Though this is an expensive place.*

*Concentrate.*

*They definitely polish the floor*

*Concentrate.*

*Why would they polish the floor? Do you want broken necks? Because that's how you get broken necks.* I glanced around the reception at the beautiful suits, dresses and expensive shoes gliding across the floor. *Why don't they struggle to...? What's that?*

An oddly familiar *tap-tap-tap* crept into my awareness. As it increased in volume and I (and I swear the rest of people in the lobby) looked up to watch a pair of bare, muscular legs; a rather impressive chest that was precariously balanced on what looked like an impossibly small waist; clad in a black dress making their way from the lifts at the back of the room. *Can't be her again. How drunk am I?* Her dark eyes were cast downwards under heavily shadowed lids as she rapped across the room. A slight smile on her face, she seemed to be basking in the adoration of the people around her, aware of every pair of eyes watching. Her hips seemed to swing deeper until everyone had at least looked at her, if not openly staring like me.

That's how I perceived it, seeing as when I broke my gaze long enough to look around the room, no one seemed to be staring like I was. There were throngs of drinkers and guests still engrossed in their conversations and I had stopped mid-step to watch her and stare like a creeper. *I should speak to her. She must have a room here, or she is a hooker. Hooker is unlikely. Isn't it? She hasn't noticed me. Perhaps she'll notice me. Should I wave? I shouldn't wave.* My thoughts tumbled over each other in my alcohol haze and my mouth opened, dry and words unable to form.

I was holding my breath. She stopped. Her head swivelled in my direction. She smiled. She started walking towards me. My heart stopped beating. I wasn't breathing. *Is this a heart attack?* My arm wasn't tingling. *I'm going to be sick.* I was blushing. I was hot. I felt like I was stepping into a warm bath and my head was held underneath the water. Until she made eye contact then I felt like was falling into her eyes and her eyes were a sauna.

I coughed. My lungs hurt as I filled them with oxygen again. *So it's not a heart attack, I'm just really fucking then. Oh Christ.* The fact she stopped a foot away from my nose, completely invading my personal space was made all the more awkward by the amount I was sweating.

"We need to stop running into each other like this." Her voice was quite high pitched and soaked in intent.

I coughed again. Choking on my own saliva. "A paranoid man would think you are following him." *James? What the hell was that?*

"Well, only the paranoid survive after all. Maybe I am following you."

"Should I be concerned? Do you want to murder me? A gender swapped Jack the Ripper." *So I'm going to go, you don't seem to be listening to me.* My brain walked out and the sound of a door slamming echoed through my head.

"You're a whore?" One eyebrow raised in amusement.

"That's ironic I was just thinking the same thing about you."

Her eyes darkened, but still sparkled wickedly. There might have been a chance I was charming her. Maybe she found my dark humour entertaining. *No!* Echoed from a distance.

"Why?"

"I... I..." I stammered trying to realign my thoughts. I felt the alcohol in my stomach churning and bit back the rising nausea. "I was wondering if you had a room here and I mean..."

"So I'm either a murderer or a whore?"

"Neither!" *Where is that accent from? Not as posh as some Southern accents but it certainly not Northern. Midlands? Isn't that Brummy?* Distracted by her accent it dawned on me that I should have continued explaining myself. I recognised the distain from the train station as it crept into her eyes.

"You don't need to worry. I'm neither a whore nor a murderer. The fact that you're asking me where I sleep makes me wonder if you want to kill me."

"No! I just..."

"I will admit that I'm a little offended that your first thought was that I would want to kill you, rather than buy you a drink. Am I that scary?"

"No! **No**! Not that... I thought... It's just... I... I shouldn't really have anything else to drink anyway."

"That is apparent. Nice to meet you." She went to turn away.

"Wait! Oh God James screw it. This couldn't have gone any worse anyway." She turned back to listen to my external internal monologue with an amused look on her face. "OK, you saw I'm a klutz and I'm not particularly confident talking to women, let alone beautiful women. Both times I saw you I didn't have the guts to speak, so let me buy you a drink, as an apology at least. You don't have to drink it with me, but I feel like I have offended you. Calling you a murderer. And a whore."

"That was surprisingly honest and I appreciate the gesture..."

"But you have a partner or you're married." My shoulders sank. *Chalk this up to experience on how not to pick up a beautiful woman.*

*I thought you left.*

"You really should learn to never assume. I have a prior engagement but hopefully we'll bump in to each other soon. In fact I'm sure of it, after all, you owe me a drink." And once again, she turned and disappeared into the crowd, only the sound of her *tap-tap-tap* remaining.

**Emily**

**4**

*Fuck, I'm late!* I tottered across the hotel lobby at speed, footsteps clattering round the room and making me feel incredibly self-conscious. Like the White Rabbit in a skin-tight dress and heels, although it was like Alice chased a Playboy Bunny down the rabbit hole. That would be one hell of a different story.

*Fucking shoes.* I'd worn my Fuck Me Shoes and they were an example of torture devices designed by men to appease their sexual appetites. Granted, so were bras, dresses, any item of footwear, clothing or cosmetics that annoyed me at the time.

Truth be told I'd wanted to make an impression on Lee. I was looking forward to drinks and the things that would follow drinks that warranted me wearing these God-awful shoes and paying for this hotel room. He was incredibly sexy, not too tall or too loud, but had wicked dark eyes, with a glint that implied there was more to him than he let on. When I took the chance to read him he tasted sweet and bitter like 80% cocoa dark chocolate. And the best part, I could tell he wanted to try and hurt me, in the best possible way.

I shivered with anticipation, body tingling and skin on fire. After my pre-drinks and teasing that boy, I was all pitched and ready to seduce Lee. *You should stop engaging with married men.*

*After tonight.*

*Yeah, yeah...* Then Fate once again threw me off track and shattered my façade. I felt hot; skin burning and ears burning like someone was talking about me. I stopped dead in my tracks and breathed in deep, smelling something new but unnervingly familiar...

Fate and I do not get on. She likes me to play by her rules, I make my own. I hate her. Have I said that already? I believe that coincidence is a great word for people that don't want to believe there is anything guiding us. We're all one big accident. Heaven forbid we are rats in a lab for something else.

I made eye contact with that boy. He was wobbling a little, quite drunk now and very nervous to see me. *Fine. Fine. We'll play it your way.* I spun on my heels, instantly regretting it because spinning on stilettos is stupid. There is a smell centre of gravity on those shoes anyway and removing the balls of your feet... I managed to recover my balance without him seeing, I hope.

"We need to stop running into each other like this..."

**James**

**8**

"EEUUUUUGGGHHH!" I woke up groaning loudly. Every time I moved my head the world whirled like a Waltzer. Slumping back against the pillow I stared longingly at the glass of squash on my bedside cabinet. Tiny droplets of condensation had formed on the glass, leaving water droplets racing each other to the pool of water where the base reached the wood. The thirst was almost unbearable: I needed to rehydrate but moving was impossible, so I lay there recalling my dreams. They were vivid and feverish, Technicolor at the time but fading quickly.

I was chasing after someone through the streets of Italy - what I imagine they would look like because I've never been to Italy. In fact, it may not have been Italy. The roads were steep and bathed in golden light. The path was lined with small cottage-like houses with doors that opened right onto the street. I hurriedly walked and ran following the scent of a musky perfume. I must have caught them as I was starting the wake up because then it was just sensations: the smell of hair and perfume; the warmth of skin against skin; the pressure against my lips and between my legs.

I started squirming in bed, painfully aware of my frustrations, but feeling too queasy and drained to satisfy them.

My mouth felt weird, like I had been licking a cat. I giggled at the juvenile thought that crossed my mind - *Giggidy* - and forcing myself I rose up onto my elbows to down my drink in one.

The hangover did not secede and I surrendered to my own aching head and muscles, spending the rest of the day watching Family Guy DVDs and dozing in and out of consciousness. As the day went on I decided I was alive enough to try eating. As I waited for my dinner to arrive, I certainly wasn't going to cook, I decided to message a few old friends and call Mum.

She managed to bring back my headache in less than ten minutes. She was mad. Really mad. She used words like 'disappointed'. I had only called a couple of times since I moved and on Wednesday I received a voicemail from Mum that I was only just responding to. I don't remember most of the phone call - I phased out reading an article about dream meanings - but I know I grunted in the right places because she sounded happy when she hung up, and the ball of guilt and homesickness alleviated slightly.

I spent Sunday in the same state, as I had no pressing matters to attend to, but I still slept badly that night. In fact, I slept badly almost every night from then on. Every night after my sleep was broken and my dreams were chaotic and sexual, although I could never remember exactly what happened or whom I was with. Every morning I woke dripping in sweat, frustrated and/or angry. It had been embarrassingly long since I'd had sex and I couldn't get - *Fuck! I didn't ask her name!* - the woman with dark eyes out of my head. She'd become the focal point of my fantasies.

It didn't help that Alice took Nathan home, which should have saved me the pain of possibly hearing their fucking (we hadn't tested out quite how well the soundproofing was), but instead meant I got to hear all about it on Monday in graphic detail.

No man needs to know this much about his best mate.

Have I mentioned that I have a vivid imagination?

"He had me pinned up against the wall: the shelves were shaking. We broke a vase! Oh James he's the best! Thank you so much!" *Jealous?*

*Oh my fucking God yes!*

"You're welcome, but as a sign of gratitude would you mind sparing me the literal ins and outs of your night?" I paused as Alice's eyes turned into angry slits in her face. The tone of my voice made that sound bitter: resentment and disgust dripping from every word. "Also, when you inevitably come over to ours, would you mind warning me so I can make sure I'm out?"

Alice radiated hurt and huffing turned back to type furiously.

"Just because you're tired, there is no need to be rude! What has gotten into you? Keep going Alice." Gemma encouraged.

Did you know it only takes 48 hours of insomnia before you start to hallucinate and disrupted sleep is as bad as none at all? The bags under my eyes had formed into black suitcases and I managed to button my shirt incorrectly that morning. If Nathan hadn't pointed it out I would have ended up at work with two different shoes on.

*Worst. Monday. Ever.*

"You said it yourself, I'm tired. I haven't slept properly since Thursday night and now it's really starting to take its toll."

"Buy some sleeping tablets and stop your whinging. Alice, go. What happened?"

Alice continued her rather graphic sexscapade, apparently Nathan's sharp tongue wasn't literal and he was keen to show her what he could do with it. *Why weren't we busier? Dear God why can't I stick my headphones in when it's quiet?* I phased out and started thinking about Dark Eyes again: I needed to find out her name. *Hootie McBoobyTits? Tits Mcgee?*

*STOP!*

I daydreamed about surprising her with a dozen red roses and whisking her off a beautiful restaurant. She would be so enamoured with my charming repertoire - *HA!* - and dashing good looks - *HAHA!* - she would swoon into my arms. I would kiss her in the elevator on the way to her hotel room and would tumble on the bed and fuck like rabbits all night. *For the love of God, STOP!* I shifted in my chair, uncomfortable with my rising arousal and berated myself for pointless fantasies. She had become the background noise in my head: my first and last thoughts of the day. It was insane. A stupid crush. A teenage crush.

Why was I obsessing over a woman I had bumped into three times? Fascinated, enthralled, addicted and I didn't even know her name. I felt like a stalker, but without the benefit of being able to look at her. *Benefit? Wow, I need to get my head straight. Maybe if I knew her name I could contact the hotel. No, wait, that is definitely stalking.*

*Or is it romantic?*

*Nope, stalking.*

Yawning, I mused why I couldn't survive like I could before on such little sleep. This city was exhausting and I had taken to surviving on coffee during the day and whisky at night to help me sleep. I had really developed a taste for whisky.

Taking Gemma's advice, during lunch I wandered to the chemist to pick up some sleeping tablets and was slapped in the face by St. Valentine. Every restaurant seemed to have a 'Valentine's Day Special'; even some pubs had boards out stating it was a ticket only night. Roses, chocolates, teddy bears and heart-shaped trinkets seemed to litter every store I passed. I picked up a box of chocolates for the girls. I'm just that charming.

The remainder of the day went by in a blur - Alice (and me) in daydream land and Gemma actively avoiding speaking to me, which I thought was rude seeing as I bought them chocolates. What more do they want? I apologised!

When I left work I saw I had a missed call and ten emails from Mum and Dad, I downloaded the photos when I got home. I'm not exaggerating when I say there were about 50 - five on each email, each about a 1mb big.

**Hi Jim,**

You're a big brother... again. We tried to call but guessed you're at work. Grace was born at 1.09am and was a healthy 8lbs 6oz. Oh God Jim she is utterly beautiful. I've attached some pictures, when are you going to come and see her?

We do miss you and we hope you're keeping well and you're not drinking too much. Stay away from drugs! And always use a condom - sorry Son that was Mum jumping in there. She's still a little emotional.

Write soon. Love you xxxxx

I typed up a response.

Hi Mum, Hi Dad,

Oh God I'm so sorry. I got your voicemail. She's beautiful! I can't wait to meet her, let me try to get a week off work and I'll come up and visit properly.

Love you both xxx

I stared at my computer screen sipping on my reasonably priced whisky thinking, and contemplating my response. My mother had just had a baby. She'd brought life into the world and here I was chasing after someone who might as well be a figment of my imagination, considering I had no idea who she was in a city of 8 million. The first and last time I managed to force myself to speak to her, I insulted her. Now she could think I'm clumsily charming - *[Cue laughter]* - or she will avoid me in the unlikely chance we meet again. Although we have met three times already, what are the chances? *I can calculate them but you won't like them.*

*You're not that smart.*

Sometimes I worry that I have two-way conversations with myself. I asked my ex about it once but she assured me it was normal.

I swirled my drink around in my glass wondering what the chances of meeting her again would be, and what I would say when I saw her. When I realised I'd lost 15 minutes daydreaming I berated myself and re-typed my email. My family needed me: my fantasy woman didn't.

Hi Mum, Hi Dad,

She's beautiful! I can't wait to meet her: in fact, you better set me up a bed as I'm going to try to get next week off work. See you soon. I'll let you know tomorrow. If I can't get the week off I'll definitely be down at the weekend.

Love you and miss you both xxx

## 9

Deborah understood when I explained that Mum had finally given birth and I should really go home and visit. I asked for the Monday and Tuesday off, but she was nice enough to give me the full week "if [I] need[ed] it."

Remembering my last phone conversation with Mum... "I need it, thank you."

She even went as far as suggestion locations for excellent (and expensive) gifts. Did you know that apparently Harrods have some wonderful gift baskets? I still don't, I saw the price and went to Boots instead. And Aldi.

Carting my weight in nappies on a peak time train from London to York was not fun. It's amazing how many commuters ask you: "How old is your child?"/"Do you have any photos?"/"Do you want to see mine?.". No. The answer is always no.

For once, Nathan didn't whine about me being unavailable as he had other things on his... mind. He and Alice were bunking on the regular now. Only now did he decide to mention that he'd arranged to have Alice round on the Saturday night. Part of me thought that he hadn't mentioned it after what I said to Alice, although there is a good chance I'm paranoid. Either way it was a lucky escape from me. Alice's voice carried at the best of times and I really, **really** did not need to hear them going at it.

"She's a screamer dude."

"Yep, I could have guessed that."

"I'm taking her to that fancy steak restaurant, I managed to wangle a table through work. It was their last one."

"So you really like her." It was a statement rather than a question, he never made this much of an effort with women he wasn't bothered about. He never made this much effort with anything really.

He paused, looking contemplatively at the ceiling, but his fair skin couldn't hide the blushes. "I really like parts of her."

"I'll believe you: many wouldn't."

**Emily**

**5**

I awoke in the night, bed soaked with sweat and my skin with burning. I could feel him thinking about me. My head span and I realised I was panting. The Son of Bitch didn't know what he was doing, so I just lay there, seething, digging my nails into my palms and biting the inside of my cheek until it bled. It's not his fault, but I was still angry that this stranger could have this effect on me.

On the other hand I could just be crazy. This could be all in my head and he's not thinking about me or… *I'm not giving him what he wants.* I don't know why everything was a battle with him, but it was. I regretted speaking to him. I sensed it would be dangerous if we got together and I wasn't dealing with that.

Lee was lying in the bed next to me, facing away and snoring. Delicious as he was he no longer satisfying and I was getting hungry. My skin looked dull, I was always tired, irritable and I was craving someone else.

**James**

**10**

The hallucinations began after the eighth night without a solid or satisfying night's sleep. I found myself tossing and turning, plagued by chasing and being chased; blackness; fights and monsters. In one I was being thrown across a room and I woke up... making some sort of noise. I thought it was snarling but it could have been squealing. My throat hurt either way.

The sleeping tablets hadn't worked, they had just made me groggier.

I felt like I was pulling apart at the seams. Although, It seemed like everyone was exhausted. I started noticing purple rings around eyes, pallid skin and patches of spots that were the symptoms. But their tiredness hadn't almost killed them on more than one occasion. Someone had to catch me when I tripped at the top of the escalators and I was almost hit by a taxi crossing Oxford Street. Both times were when I was staring at women I was certain were Dark Eyes.

Neither of them were, of course.

I had also managed to smash a mug at work and two glasses and a plate at home.

I was losing grip on reality. *I need to sleep.*

Needing an outside opinion I caved and spoke to Nathan. It was the night before I travelled home and we were watching the latest Godzilla movie in the living room. We had the house to ourselves so we cranked the surround sound up to 11.

"So I like this girl..." I blurted out. I didn't move my eyes from the screen and I didn't lower the volume. Even out of my periphery I saw his eyes widen and he turned away from the TV.

"Well that's a new one Jim. Who is she? Is it Gemma? Don't shit where you live dude."

"It is 'don't shit where you eat or eat where you shit' and you're shitting where I eat."

"That's different."

"It's not." I paused. "And no, it's not Gemma. I don't know her name."

I could feel his eyes burning into me. He raised an eyebrow. "OK then...? So how do you know her?"

"We've bumped into each other a couple of times."

"And?"

"And that's it."

"That's it?"

"But I can't get her off my mind."

"You sure she exists?" I didn't answer. I wasn't sure of anything these days. I sat up the other night researching insomnia and it's amazing the effects the lack of sleep can have:

- An inability to concentrate
- Decreased productivity
- Irritability
- Feelings of unhappiness, frustration and confusion
- Shortness of breath
- Sluggish movements
- Muscle weakness
- Frequent yawning - *obviously.*
- Increased sensitivity to pain

It has been getting steadily worse due to the worry. It was a vicious cycle, I couldn't sleep and it made me worry and then I was thinking so much I couldn't sleep. The coffee and alcohol cycle was spinning faster.

"You realise you sound like a stalker?"

"How is it stalking if I don't know who she is?"

"You're obsessing over someone you've never met! It's worse than falling in love with a celebrity, at least you know their name and something about them. You're infatuated with an image, her personality might be terrible, which might be fine for a one-night thing but I know you, that's not what you had in mind. Is that why you've been moping around looking dog rough for days?"

"No, I just haven't been sleeping."

"Lovesick."

"No! You know me, usually I don't need a lot of sleep, but the past week I feel like I've been living in a dream - like I am a small man in the driving seat of this massive robot. I told you I almost fell down the stairs right?"

"Lovesickness causes exhaustion, I know the signs. Now, do you have any idea how many people pass through London every day? Let alone the people who live here? You have no chance."

I said "But I saw her twice in one night." and then automatically regretted it.

"And? Maybe she was on a pub-crawl. You need to let it go. Look, when you're back we'll have a lad's night on the pull. While you're home maybe, hook up with an old girlfriend. Sarah was always been into you and from what I heard you're a bit of a tiger."

"How? Why? When?"

"You know Sarah and I are friends. We got drunk and asked questions about you." I stared at him intently knowing what Nathan's 'friends' mean, especially when he's drinking with them. "Genuine friends. I never went there, I wouldn't and you know it."

"OK, fine." I took a swig of my beer. "So I shouldn't keep thinking about that woman?" I knew the answer.

"No. Now drink you beer, watch the movie and for the love of God get some sleep! You'll feel better for it."


## 11


It was surreal making the journey back to York: in only a few short weeks I had undergone a metamorphosis into a seasoned traveller. The daily tube commute had made me cynical, silent and invisible to most. *I'm a proper Londoner now.*

*Well that's not nice now is it?*

I headed to the train station straight from work and the platform was packed full of tired looking passengers - mostly in suits - travelling home.

The station was warm and it felt much later than it was: the sky was dark and my eyes were heavy. Yawning, I shifted the weight of my backpack to the left shoulder, trying not to knock my rapidly cooling coffee in the process. My eyes were cast downward to avoid eye contact, I was watching a pair of uncomfortable looking black shoes waltz in front of me, the clacking of heel on marble echoed through my head. I overheard a few conversations of people complaining about their bosses before I put my headphones in. Their voices were annoying me and I was afraid I would crack and start yelling.

The robotic sounding female voice barked over the speakers that my train had arrived and I turned the volume up until the vibration was almost painful. I needed a protective bubble. I picked up the holdall I was guarding from the mob, and slouched my way onto the train, draining my drink in the process. I burnt my tongue.

I managed to grab a window seat near the luggage racks and amused myself at the juxtaposition of fully grown, suited, professionals sitting cross-legged on the floor like children. *Of course the train is oversold.* As the train pulled out the station I made eye contact with a man who promptly averted my gaze. I was pleased that the sour look etched into my face made me look suitably unapproachable.

The journey became increasingly uncomfortable and yet I still managed to fall asleep, although the repeated banging of my head against the glass gave me a headache. The pain was surprisingly soothing and helped me refocus my thoughts. I wiped the drool from my mouth and settled myself back onto the window to continue my snooze, through the rhythmic thrumming against my head.

It was either the nap of the crisp, clear Yorkshire air, but once I stepped off the train I felt a dozen times better. I started to feel like myself again. The London smog must have been clogging up my lungs - it certainly clogged up my nose. Black snot is not fun and it freaks you out the first time you see it.

I felt the fog start to lift from my head. I suddenly felt very hungry. *I still need a decent night's kip.* My reverie was interrupted by my mother's voice yelling at me.

"JIMMY!" Her voice was already cracking. I was surprised - and touched - to see my watery-eyed family, even my own eyes started streaming. Obviously I was missed much more than I realised. Mum squeezed me tight to her and my new baby sister started fussing in Dad's arms.

"Who is this absolute heart breaker then?" I cradled her in my arms and looked into the face of an angel. *Is that cliché?*

*Yes.* I made a mental note to see whether it was crazy to have conversations with yourself. I was almost certain it wasn't but I needed to make sure.

She had a head of brown hair and the tiniest hands that curled round the finger I was wiggling on her nose. "This is Grace, let's go home and I can formally introduce you. I've been baking." Mum sniffed.

Dad wiped his eyes when he thought no one was looking. *Big softie.*

## 12

It was nice to be home: the pace slower, much more peaceful. Strangers smiled at me again and I found I was no longer avoiding their eye contact. I was a little apprehensive about no longer having a room, but my parents had anticipated that.

"Wow, you work fast." My room was now painted a pale yellow with pictures hanging on the walls. There was a wardrobe, sofa, changing table and... "No crib?"

"It's in our room and that…" Mum pointed at a new looking sofa. '…is a pull out sofa bed. You will always have a bed here." I saw her eyes glistening as she moved in for another hugged. I welled up Mum gave me another hug and I welled up again. I still had space and privacy and I couldn't thank them enough for that. I thought I was going to have the sofa… In the living room, not the sofa in a bedroom.

I dropped my bag and ran downstairs to gorge and relax. I felt my shoulders unknotting as I ate Mum's home cooking and drank Dad's stash of good whisky.

"When did you start drinking whisky?"

"I've always liked whiskey."

"No you haven't."

I ignored him. "It's good." Draining my second glass and enjoying the warm tipsy feeling, in familiar surroundings, I beat off the barrage of questions from Matt and Ollie about my 'glamorous' new life. "I breathe in a lot of smog, I ride a lot of tubes and I drink a lot of cocktails. It's not particularly…"

"You do what now?" Mum interjected.

"I ride a lot of tubes."

She just stared at me. I maintained eye contact even though Grace was feeding. It was horribly hard not to look at Mum's breasts but I really didn't want to be that creepy. *Eyes up top. Eyes up top. Eyes up top. Oh God I looked!*

"Well, not a lot of cocktails…"

"You did drink that very quickly." She didn't bother to withhold the disapproving tone from her voice. I took a swig from my refilled glass and gasped with satisfaction. Mum couldn't drink while breast-feeding and she loved a glass of wine or eight.

"You're just jealous. How long has it been now?" I won't repeat what she said to me.


It was either the food, the exhaustion or the drink, but I slept better than I had done in days. Heavy, dreamless and woke up groggy, but relaxed. The sofa bed was comfortable. I awoke stretching like a cat and watching the light that filtered in through the curtains. Making a happy noise I (literally) rolled out of bed and (figuratively) crawled downstairs.

"Jim, what happened to your voice?"

I frowned at Olivia who was pushing her bacon around her plate. "I just woke up." Yawning to demonstrate my point.

"Oh… You sound different."

"Do I?" I looked at Dad for clarification.

"You do have a Southern pansy twang."

"Yeah whatever. It hasn't been long enough for me to pick up a new accent."

Mum looked at Grace with a look of wistful sadness. "I'm not used to you being so far so for so long."

I got up and wrapped my arms round her. "I'm sorry, I promise I'll call more. You know how it is when you just get caught up."

"You have to live your life." She smiled, then wagged her finger at the little 'uns. "You two better not disappear like this one." Matthew and Olivia, who looked and each and started laughing in a rather disconcerting manner. *The Children of the Corn! I wonder what they've planned.*

"So your plans while you're back?"

"I thought we could go for lunch somewhere today, my treat and then I was thinking about catching up with Robert and Sarah."

"Sarah?" Dad.

"Yeah. She knows I'm back and I said I would buy her a drink." I stated matter of factually, subtlety implying that I wanted this conversation to end. Sarah was a difficult/painful/in-depth (delete as applicable) subject.

**13**

Mum and I went for lunch at a tearoom with stunning art deco architecture and deliciously handcrafted cakes and sandwiches. Dad took the kids to the cinema to see... Something. I wasn't paying attention. The tearoom was so quaint it was almost twee, but I did scoff myself on sugary treats. I really had an appetite at the moment.

"You're really putting them away."

"Yeah I don't know what wrong with me."

"You slept long as well last night." I grunted in agreement with a mouthful of Victoria Sponge. "It's nice here and it's nice to be out the house. I was housebound for the first six months when I had you. Though after four you think I would have this 'Mother' thing down by now."

"How was the labour?"

"A breeze. They had to wake me up when it was over." Dripping in sarcasm. *Ah how I missed this.* Mum's quick wit always kept me on my toes and I had inherited none of it. "I thought it was going to be more difficult, starting over when I should be starting to slow

down. Having my fourth at 45. We're still adjusting, but I wouldn't have it any other way."
Still sleeping Grace squeaked in agreement. "Come on then City Boy, tell me everything."

I chewed quickly and swallowed loudly the massive mouthful of scone (pronounced sc-on, not sc-own for those that wondered) and told her (almost) everything. Job; Gemma and Alice; Alice and Nathan; Susan and Andy. I even delicately broached Dark Eyes. *I need to forget about her or find out her name.* And I instantly regretted my decision.

"You've never properly met and you have no way of finding her?" She paused before the laughter brought her to literal tears. "You need to forget about her or find out her name." *Like mother, like son.* "So you're not holding out for Sarah then?"

*Inhale.* "No."

"But you're meeting her tonight?"

I shoved another mouthful of food in. I was so hungry.

"But you're not interested in her."

I made a non-committal head movement.

"So where are you taking her?"

"Dunno yet. We're going for dinner."

"And you're not interested in her?"

I took a swig of my drink and made a non-committal head movement.

"And there is no one else?"

*Exhale.* I love my mother's line of questioning. She could give the Spanish Inquisition a run for their money. She could be part of them! No one would ever expect that. "The women seem a little... unapproachable."

"All the millions of women? Every single one?"

*Inhale.* "Be nice."

"Anyway, as long as you know that while you're back you don't have to spend every night with us. It's nice to have you home."

"Stop worrying. I came to see you... And her." I mumbled through a mouthful of half chewed up smoked salmon sandwich, while pointing at the tiny, sleeping baby. "I missed my family."

Mum looked like she was going to cry. "You do realise I'm not expecting you to come home monthly? It's nice of you to come for Grace but you do need to live your life. I'm not going to hold you back."

"I know Mum." I took her hand. "Thank you"

"We missed you too."

"I love you. Now, another round of cakes? I'm starving."

**14**

It's not that I wasn't interested in seeing Sarah, of course I was very interested. I was very interested in seeing every part of her again. *Dat ass though.*

Sarah was an ex-girlfriend. She was **the** ex-girlfriend: my first love and the girl I lost it to. We were only together for about 18 months between 17 and 18 and the sex was still the best I ever had. Intensely passionate, but we burned so bright we died out quickly. We were still friends. Mostly through the in-depth interaction of Facebook likes and comments. And even after all this time I couldn't deny the attraction. *Low-hanging fruit?*

*No! She's stunning.* Tall and slender, she was only two inches shorter than me. You could see her ribs when she was naked, and her clothes always fell like a dressmaker's dummy, or a coat hanger. She'd been asked a few times if she modelled but she had no interest in it, not for any reason she could explain: "I just don't want to. The same way I never want to go fishing."

"Damn goes my perfect date." was the joke I always followed with.

Her ginger hair fell just below her shoulders and her piercing green eyes always looked a little wet, like she was about to cry. More than once I thought she might have been a wood nymph: a delicate member of the fae that danced amongst the trees.

However, this was shot to pieces when she inevitably spilled her drink, tripped over her feet or dropped something breakable. She was clumsier than me, attributed to her long limbs.

She must have grown into them since I last saw her as she glided across the Mexican restaurant floor in shoes that made her taller than me, which looked like they could kill me. We reminisced over tapas, hibiscus mojitos and Tequila shots.

"You're looking good you know, London has done wonders for you."

I loved the attention. I was very relaxed and enjoying the obvious flirtation. I'd never noticed how long her fingers were, which were elegantly playing with her wine glass. She kept flicking her fringe from her eyes, which seemed to accentuate the curve of her neck and the scent of her skin.

Man, did her skin smell good.

My stomach growled: I was hungry. "You're not looking too bad yourself. Come on, let me get the bill and I'll buy you a cocktail."

"No, we'll go Dutch."

I'd eaten nine out of the twelve courses of tapas, there was no way I could let her pay. I placed my hand over hers and stared deep into her eyes. "I wouldn't hear of it."

"Where has this confidence come from? You're like a different person, has someone been teaching you about women?" There was an unmistakable twang of jealousy.

I shook my head, but my vision moved too fast and I felt a little woozy.

*Inhale.*

*Exhale.*

*Inhale.*

It wasn't going. I excused myself to the bathroom and tried not to trip over the other diners on the way. I was sweating. Somehow I was struggling to recognise my reflection. I had a weird moment of déjà vu where I flashed back to my dreams and my stomach growled again. *Why am I so hungry? Maybe I could grab some crisps. I can't have been eating properly and now I'm relaxed so I am. Or my hormones. Perhaps I'm pregnant.*

*I'm not funny.*

Shaking it off and splashing some cold water on my face I strode confidently back to our table. "Come on, we should go."

We sat next to each other on a sofa in the cocktail bar, music so loud we were shouting directly into each other's ears. I had my hand on her thigh and she intertwined her fingers with mine, rocking her knee backwards and forwards coquettishly. The cocktails had dropped our barriers nicely and we were discussing everything. And for once I think (hope) I was being witty, charming and funny. I hadn't even called her a murderer or a hooker.

*Focus on Sarah. She's real.*

Her hair fell in front of her eyes again and she chewed on her thumb knuckle. I could sense how nervous she was so I, so I took that hand out of her mouth and kissed the red knuckle, just once. I took her happy gasp as a cue and held her gaze as I looked up and leaned into her lips.

This time she made a soft, little whimper as my tongue sort hers, my hands moving towards her hips, pulling them closer to me, sliding her across the sofa.

I suddenly knew what I was hungry for. *Oh God I need this, I need her.*

She pushed me away panting. "Did you want a night cap? I have a one of the new flats above the mini-supermarket."

"Back to yours for coffee?" I flashed a grin at her and she giggled as she stood, a little off balance and swaying slightly from the alcohol swirling through her blood stream. Although, I like to think it was the effect I had on her.

The flats were impressive: amazing location, finished to a high standard and incredibly warm. Annoyingly warm. I started sweating as soon as I entered. I could feel the beads of sweat pricking my forehead and nose, a droplet formed at my shoulder blades and ran down my back, tracing a river down my spine.

"I love the location and it's so cheap. Surprisingly well soundproofed as well." Sarah giggled as she fixed me a drink, her eyes met mine with a wicked glint. As I watched her hips gyrate across the kitchen my head swam again, and I had to put my hand on the worktop to steady myself. I felt like I was falling and vision grew hazy. I could smell her perfume: I thought I could even smell her skin. I ached and readjusted myself, a little ashamed of how hard I was already.

Sarah handed me a glass, which I threw to the floor and pinned her up against the cupboards, holding her hands behind her back with my hands and grinding up against her hips. The need was too much.

I kissed her so hard I could tell I was bruising her lips, I heard say: 'Ow', but she was squashed up against my lips so it was muffled. I didn't care anyway, tonight she was mine and she would know it. She tried to push me away when I went to kiss her neck but as my lips found her collar bone she melted like butter and I carried her to the bedroom, walking over the shattered glass and the sticky pool of whisky that had formed on the tiles.

I barely remember that night: I didn't feel like me, it felt like a wild animal was released from deep inside me. An insatiable beast. *All the pent up frustration: all those months without release.*

I wanted her satisfied before I even began. She tried to protest, to kiss me slowly and undress me slower still, but I pushed her down and - literally - ripped her shirt from her chest. The fear in eyes only enhanced my lust and I buried my face between her legs licking and sucking until she bucked underneath me, calling out in pleasure and smacking my face with her pelvis.

Then she was putty.

I plunged myself until her sopping wet mound. We went on for hours until she was sore and told me to stop.

I awoke with a feeling of unease and I tried to recollect the night before. It can't have been me that pinned her arms above her head and pressed down until bruises formed around her wrists and she complained I was hurting her. Or that threw her onto her stomach and ploughed into her until she was holding the headboard and chewing on the pillow, as I pulled her hips into mine and wrapped my hand around her throat so when she came it was so much harder.

I never fucked anyone like that before. And my God was it satisfying.

Until the next morning.

"What the hell James! I look like I've been in a fight!"

"You weren't complaining last night."

"And there is glass all over my kitchen floor, for fuck's sake the whiskey is all sticky and a tile has been chipped. There goes my deposit." She threw her hands up in exasperation as she turn to get a cloth.

"I can help you clean it up."

She looked at me and for the first time I saw the marks properly: her lips were purple and there were handprints around her wrists and her neck. "That was fun but..." she paused and looked away "...but I think you should go. I have to go to work. I'll call you."

What I heard was: "That was scary. I can't handle what you did to me and you need to go have a long hard think about your mental state. You violent nutter." I left without another words, still smelling of sex and stale alcohol.

*I really want a cigarette.*

Mum stifled a giggle as I completed my Walk of Shame home. "Good night?" Dad was already at work and the kids were at school. "Your face!" My lips were also purple and the top lip was slightly swollen from Sarah's pelvic bone. "So... Sarah or...?"

"Do you mind if we don't talk about it?"

"Why?"

"I still don't feel comfortable discussing... sex with my mum."

"Oh for goodness sake, I have four kids, how do you think you were born?"

"Seriously, can we not? I think I'm just going to hang around the house today and watch TV, maybe catch up on some reading."

"With a face like that I recommend it. Here." She tossed a packet of frozen peas from the freezer. "You'll almost be back to 'normal' tomorrow if I keep you topped up on fluids." She did the air quotes around 'normal'.

*Ladies and gentlemen, introducing my mother: the comedienne*

**Emily**

**6**

Last night I dreamt about watching a woman pole dance in a church to Bring Me The Horizon. She had long, blonde hair that was partially pinned up with a jewel-encrusted clip and she made prolonged eye contact with me during every spin. She wore a blue, bejewelled lingerie set. The pole was where the cross should be and I was watching from the pews.

I don't know what it means. I don't think I want to know.

James

8

The rest of my trip flew by. It was so relaxing, I never thought I would miss my parents nagging but I suppose you don't know what you've got 'til it's gone. It went by without further... incidents as well, thank God. I couldn't handle any more bruises.

Although, on Thursday night I went out with Robert, we went to a couple of pubs and he mentioned about my "new swagger". Especially when I walked back from the bar waving a napkin with the barmaid's number.

"You have a mobile?"

"Yes?"

"It's on you?"

"Yes?"

"Then why did she write her number on a napkin? This isn't the 1970s." I stared blankly for a moment, my ego deflating round my feet. "I'm busting your balls. Good on ya, you going to call her?"

"Shut up and drink your beer. I want to head to a club."

We hit the local rock 'club'. We refer to it fondly as a club when it is basically a pub with a dance floor, which smells of sweat, artificial smoke from a machine smoke and the faintest smell of vomit. I never thought I would be nostalgic for the days where cigarette smoke washed away everything else.

I got talking to a tattooist in a leather mini-skirt and a rose tattooed on her neck. Her name was Rachel and she had a slim face, thick thighs and a big butt. I think Mum calls them 'Birthing Hips'; Nathan calls it a booty you can bounce on; all I knew was I wanted to sink my teeth into them. She had a body you wanted to touch and hold and she feigned coquettishness as she licked her lips and looked me up and down. I was obsessed with her lips. They were full and pouty and were the colour of black cherries.

"I bet you're good with those lips."

I felt like I was having an out of body experience, there was another man in my body chatting to Rachel and encouraging her to take me back to hers. I was just watching. She giggled seductively and planted a long, slow kiss on my lips when I promised her a night she would never forget.

"You better not welsh on that debt." She ran her fingertips along my collarbone and I felt a stirring in my jeans. I promised her that I'd get her down to London. Although, I believe my particular wording was: 'I'm going to get you to go down in London.'

Robert dragged me away at that point, bored as soon as he realised that I was the one with all the luck with the ladies tonight. "It's a first and I would say make the most of it but what the hell is wrong with you?"

I'd been staring at Rachel from across the room and I'd been wondering where else was tattooed and what she had pierced. "What do you mean?" I was still staring.

"Nathan is a bad influence on you. I thought you were seeing Sarah tomorrow? I thought you **saw** her the other night."

I looked at him when I heard him emphasise 'saw'. "Yeah, we are meeting for coffee." I couldn't tell him what I did to her and I hoped she hadn't told him. *She could have done, they are friends. Anyway, she was into it at the time.* I didn't want to talk about it. "Let me buy you a drink."

I took Sarah for coffee: her bruises were fading but still looked sore - red welts rather than purple fingerprints. She nervously played with the cuffs of her dark grey jumper, pulling the sleeves over her hands and avoided looking at my eyes except when she thought I wasn't looking. Then she kept staring at me inquisitively.

The conversation was boring - polite, small talk, like you have with a stranger in a queue. It was nothing compared to Monday night. When we parted it was with a curt kiss and a hug where our bodies didn't touch. I got the feeling I wasn't going to hear from her in a while.

On Saturday, once again I bid a tearful farewell to my family and reluctantly headed back down South. The trip home was exactly what I needed I felt human. I felt better than my human, life was in 4K now and I accepted what a handsome man I was becoming. When did this happen? Why hadn't I seen this before I moved? *Because you weren't this successful with the ladies.*

The platform was all but empty on a sunny February afternoon and spring was threatening winter for dominance: a clash of Gods and York was the battleground. There were shoots poking through and it was warm in the sun, but still freezing in the cold. I was positive about the future, though I couldn't face the exhaustion again and vowed to stay healthy and get plenty of sleep. The dreams had completely stopped and apart from a (couple of) rather disconcerting body experience(s) - which I decided to attribute to alcohol consumption - I felt great.

This time, rather than attempting to read I decided to people-watch the day trippers, shoppers, families and couples on weekend breaks looking excitedly out the window and talking animatedly to the people sitting opposite them. There was a young couple with similar brown haircuts chatting to the train guard in the seats opposite. After a few minutes the guard moved on and I could see them trying to make eye contact. And it was then I decided reading was the best option, even I shoving my headphones in my ears for added effect. I didn't feel like making any new friends and I certainly didn't want to make small talk with strangers.

I started thinking about Rachel, staring out the window and daydreaming about her thighs. The reflection of the window showed the couple whispering to each other and making furtive glances in my direction. Luckily, it was quite bright and I could concentrate on the fields. I'd been texting Rachel since last night and I'd gone straight into talking to her about when she would be free for me to wine and dine her. *I really am becoming quite the Lothario.* I was quite feeling positive when the train pulled into Kings Cross, when that all went out the window

"Fancy meeting you here." said a family husky voice as I walked towards the Underground. I span round and saw the back of Dark Eyes' head jogging towards St Pancreas and somehow I knew she was smiling. *Damn it, just as she was out of my system.* I was almost certain that she was following me now and I didn't know whether to be flattered or scared.

**Emily**

6

A bead of sweat trickled down my back. I was tempted to rub it away, but I let it trace down my spine and pool at the top of my butt. I could smell the body odour of the man who was stood **way** too close to me. I sent out negative energy and he stepped back nervously.

I sipped my coffee and tried not to spill it further down the front of top. Luckily I had just pulled my jacket on to hide the stain when I bumped into him. My heart skipped and beat and my skin prickled with nerves. Pin pricks up my arms like acupuncture, which dissipated as soon as they arrived.

"Hi, good to see you again. I guess we both have friends out of the city then, seeing as we keep meeting at the train station." is what I wanted to say.

"Fancy meeting you here." is the ridiculously cheesy line that came out. I wanted to say more, but nerves got the better of me and I ran away to my tube. Plus I really wanted to get home. I'd had a long weekend.

I don't know why we ran into each other again. I wish I did. It seemed highly unlikely to the point that I would think he was following me, but that is... improbable. I blame Fate. There are so many serendipitous events every day that people pass off as 'coincidence'. Some say it's one God or another, when it's actually the universe guiding us. Fate is a bitch and so is her sister Karma.

Yes, I understand I'm meant to meet this boy. Yes, I probably am cutting my nose off to spite my face. I don't care: who needs noses anyway?

James

9

I arrived home ready for a wild night in front of the TV. The journey took it out of me and now I had the time to reflect on the trip with a nice, cold beer and some bad, trash TV. Celebrity Big Brother was on: I've lost count what season and I didn't recognise anyone in there, apart from the sister of that major Hollywood Director who's name I don't know. My head was spinning with my encounters with women and what they meant. I knew it was mostly because of seeing Dark Eyes again, but I was attempting not to think about her. *I'd probably never see her again. Probably.*

   *Hopefully?*

Aimlessly flicking through channels distracted me from the static hum inside my head: it was soothing. Then Nathan bounced into the living room and started tugging at my arm like a puppy wanting to go for a walk.

   "We're going to Soho."

   "Sounds fun. Who with?" I settled lower into the sofa in an attempt to avoid his response. *Please read my body language.*

   Unfortunately Nathan chose to ignore it. "We are. Come on." I let him pull me off the sofa - literally, I ended up on the floor - and we left. I decided not to bother changing from my long sleeve T-shirt and jeans: black on black looks smart enough.

   We talked about my family during the first drinks; during the second he updated me about how things were going with Alice, including a disturbingly graphic description of her blowjob technique. By the third drink I was feeling relaxed enough to fill him in on my success with the Rachel, the barmaid's number and Sarah. It was after the first round of shots I hinted about her bruises ("She had a few marks...").

   I am sure I saw a flicker of concern in his eyes, only for a moment. "Some women like it rough. Anyway dude, you don't quit when you're on a winning streak, let's go get you a Southern Belle." I won't try and imitate his awful Texas drawl, which ended up sounding more Russian than anything else.

   I let him take me to club. The crowded dance floor smelt of perfume and aftershave and I felt underdressed, but it was still fun. The pounding, commercial dance music vibrated through my body and ended up yelling in the face of the barman as I tried to order my drinks.

The artificial smoke flooded my nostrils and almost overpowered the CK One from the bloke standing next to me. His name was Paul and he was incredibly friendly... Uncomfortably so. He was way too chatty. He invited me along to the Chelsea match next Saturday (I declined). He also offered me a line of cocaine in the toilets, but I politely declined.

Although it was a good night I couldn't escape the static hum, the background noise in my head. I found myself thinking about Dark Eyes whenever I wasn't in conversation and sometimes phasing out during, trying to decide whether to say anything to Nathan. He wouldn't believe me. *I don't believe me.*


Gemma and Alice were pleased to have me back. I don't think Alice would be too pleased to know that I know she has no gag reflex and the ability to swallow a banana whole. I was tempted to tell her I knew that about her.

They were fascinated by my stories about Rachel, Sarah and The Barmaid. Gemma playfully punched me on the arm. "You utter dog." The respect I was receiving disappointed me, which was a shock. Part of me was enjoying feeling like a Lothario, but the other part realised that I was actually being a bit of a bastard. I had no intention of getting in touch with The Barmaid.

What I couldn't understand was what had happened. It appeared to me that the more I was a bastard, the more women who were interested in me. Even The Girls were treating me more favourably. It could be an increase in testosterone or pheromones (science isn't my strong point) or it could be because I was no longer a grumpy sod. *I'm over thinking.*

My temperament had improved because I was sleeping through the night and because Rachel and I had been in near constant communication for a week. Messaging first thing in the morning with our Outfit of the Day; chatting at lunch about what we were eating and messaging each other all night before wishing each other sweet dreams. It would be an understatement if I said it got a little racy a few times. We exchanged pictures, voice messages and videos.

I had tried to reach out to Sarah, but it wasn't worth the effort. Sarah had responded to my messages politely but concisely, asking nothing about me and making it abundantly clear she wanted nothing to do with me. The last message I received was on the following Wednesday and it just said: "I don't know you anymore". I sat and stared at my phone trying to decide whether to respond, then my phone beeped with a photo of Rachel in a compromising position and Sarah went completely out of my mind.

Rachel was coming to stay a week on Saturday and I couldn't wait. I spent the time impatiently waiting, detoxing and working out. I had nearly two weeks and I wanted to look my best. I was also busy cleaning, stocking up on champagne (which Nathan and Alice drank and I had to restock) and nice foods and planning restaurants, lunch places, bars and clubs. I was going to give her the weekend of her life. I even picked up a dozen roses to surprise her with at the station.

I stood in the entrance of the station dressed to impress and waiting for her to walk through the gates, ready to take her for her first drink at the champagne bar. With it's faux traditional décor and chandeliers it was a great place for a first impression.

I think she was pleased to see me the way she planted a big kiss on my lips and wrapped her arms around my neck. She looked amazing, dressed in a black, micro-mini, skater dress and a pair of black heels: she had a killer pair of legs underneath some tights with stockings painted on. She had roses tattooed on her forearms that matched the one on her neck. They stuck out underneath her military jacket and were revealed when she pushed up her sleeves. Her black hair was piled on top of her head and either her perfume, her hair or skin smelt of strawberries. I struggled not to bury my face into her neck and inhale deeply. *I want to taste you.* I could feel my libido rising when she wrapped her arms round me and squeezed.

"Come on then City Boy, are you going to show a simple country gal how the other half live?"

"We're both from York: I'm hardly a traditional City Boy." She pouted and looked disappointed. "But shall we start the weekend with champagne cocktails m'lady?" She jumped up and down clapping excitedly like a five-year-old meeting Santa and hooked her arm in mine as we walked to the bar.

Rachel tasted her champagne cocktail and made an approving noise. "What was it that attracted you to me? I can't be your usual type of girl, you look so 'normal'." She even did the air quotes before draining her glass and nodded towards the bar. "You ready for another?" She got up and went to the bar before I could answer either question, protest or offer to pay.

When she sat back down, she placed two more champagne cocktails in front of us. "You have a lot of energy then?" I finished my first and started on the second, the bubbles already going to be head. *I knew I should have had more than just cereal.*

"Yeah, I'm jittery most of the time. On the plus side, it means I have the constitution of an ox and I don't put on weight easily. I don't lose it easily though either." She patted her stomach. "What were we talking about?"

"You have an amazing figure. That's not what we were talking about but you do have an amazing figure."

She flushed and wiped her hair from her eyes. "That was it, your type."

"I don't have a type. I find you fascinating: I'm attracted to eyes and personality - your eyes are beautiful and I want to talk to you all day and night."

She waggled her eyebrows at me giggling. "Just talk all night?" *Someone's getting tipsy.*

"Well not just talk - not talk at all - but a gentleman doesn't make assumptions of a lady."

"Well shucks, don't you know all the right things to say? Come on, boring date questions. Favourite colour?"

"Blue."

"Favourite book?"

"I don't read as often as I should. I've been trying to get through Dune for about two months now but I just haven't had the concentration. I like Science Fiction books or Horror when I do read."

"Sound like you need some Spice." I grinned at her reference. "Favourite movie?"

"I'm a Tarantino fan so Pulp Fiction or Deathproof."

"I love those movies!"

"Come on then, same questions to you."

"Black, obviously." She gestured towards her outfit and hair. "The Picture of Dorian Gray and - don't judge me! - Mean Girls."

I choked on my drink. "Seriously?"

"It's a good film!" She punched me lightly in the arm. *What is it with women punching me?* "Shall we go dump my stuff at yours? What do you have planned for tonight then Mr. Big?"

"You wait and see."

I took her by her hand and led her to the Underground. Our journey was crowded and we were pressed against each other in such a way I had to force myself thinking about everything but the situation. Very difficult when she was purposely pushing her arse into me.

We sauntered back to mine as I told her amusing anecdotes of my area, including where I almost knocked a group of students down the escalators.

I bumped into Andy as we entered the house, which proved more awkward than thought, trying to explain who she is. I decided not to bother.

"Whoops, sorry James, I was just sticking some washing on. Do you have any that you want to shove in mine?"

"No, it's fine, but thank you. This is Rachel."

Rachel shook Andy's hand: I saw her struggling not to stare at him, who had just returned from the gym and was walking around topless and dripping wet from the shower. The man had abs of steel and biceps you could crack a walnut in. Her eyes almost popped out of her head. "He seems… nice."

I carried her bag upstairs like the gentleman I am. *Ha!* "Yeah, he's a good bloke. I'm pretty sure he's gay, I've seen him looking cosy with a couple of guys on the sofa, who were then making breakfast in the morning."

"I would assume so then."

"But then I've seen him getting cosy with a woman."

Rachel looked at me looking slightly annoyed. "You realise sexuality is a spectrum right? It is probably best if you stop worrying about it." She pulled me in close and kissed me. Her lip-gloss was slick on my lips and her tongue was delicate and tentatively sought after mine. "Today has been fun so far, so where are we heading and where can I freshen up?"

"Would it be corny if I said you were fresh enough already?" I pulled her close and kissed her again, this time with a little more urgency and a lot more laughter as she giggled at my atrocious chat up line.

We almost didn't make it out of the house, ending up semi-naked and rolling around the bed, panting. I was in the process of pulling off her tights when I remembered the dinner reservations and we quickly dressed and ran out the house, against the joint protests of our loins.

**10**

I gazed at Rachel as she sucked olive oil from her fingers. It spilled down her wrist and she unceremoniously licked it up. She obviously enjoyed her food - she enjoyed life - and didn't care who knew.

*God I'm aching right now.* The effect she was having on me must have been written all over my face because she giggled and sucked on her index finger long and slow. The candlelight reflected off her hair and cast shadows across her face: the Merlot we were drinking had the colour of blood in the obscured light.

"This is fun." Rachel had a beautiful energy about her and a wonderful outlook on life; everything was an opportunity to have fun.

"Come on then, we've had a few drinks, we're feeling a little tipsy, tell me your most embarrassing secret?"

I raised my eyebrows in disbelief. "Really? On our first date?" She nodded and popped another olive into her mouth and signalled toward the bowl, offering me the final few. "No thank you, you finish them. OK, well I know I come across as cool, calm and collected."

Rachel stifled another giggle. "Fake it 'til you make it, eh boy?"

"Oh shut it, drink your wine. Well, when I first got off the train when I moved down here, I tripped as I got off the train."

"That's it?"

"You don't understand, it was a total wipe-out, I slid across the platform on my chest, dropped my bags, almost breaking my phone and ended up faced down on a pair of shoes."

"That's brilliant!"

"Oh no, the best bit, the shoes belonged to this gorgeous woman who looked at me like she just trod in something."

"She did. You." She laughed heartily at her own joke

"Didn't I tell you to drink your wine? I ended up lying on the floor for what felt like hours when she kicked my bag over to me, which hit me in the face. As if I couldn't get any lower. Literally." A slight embellishment, but exaggerating never hurt anyone.

"It didn't hit you in the face." said a voice behind me. I jumped, cracking me knees on the table and clanking the glasses together in the process. Dark Eyes. She wasn't as tall as I thought she was, but glancing down I realised she was wearing a pair of flat boots.

"I'm certain you're following me now."

The anger resonated from her instantly and I felt a wave of heat like a nuclear blast. She bared her teeth in a fake smile, the rest of her face a mask in front of cold eyes. "I'm starting to get offended by that statement."

"Maybe if you didn't keep appearing…"

"This city isn't as big as you obviously think it is." She interrupted, her voice pitched slightly higher and coming out as a hiss. Other tables were looking now as I realised that this could be perceived as an argument in the middle of a packed restaurant on a Saturday night, in front of my date. "I wanted to introduce myself as we keep running into each other. I didn't want you to think that I'm avoiding you. I'm Emily."

She held out her hand, I stared at it. *That's not as exotic a name as I thought it would be.* She raised an eyebrow inquisitively and if I wasn't mistaken, her pupils had dilated. *Did she just hear that?* I took her hand and shook it; she had quite a grip and her hands were freezing cold, but incredibly soft. My head swam and my legs felt weak.

"James."

"Well, I'll leave you to your…" She paused looking Rachel up and down in obvious assessment and disapproval. "'Date.'" The words dripped with venom as she looked over Rachel. "Nice to make your acquaintance." She sneered before smirking and walking away.

Rachel had finished off her wine and she gripped the stem between her fingertips, waving it back and forth. "Christ she's brazen." Her eyes didn't leave her back as Emily - *Emily?* - walked away. "Still trying to decide whether to go after her."

"And do what?"

"I dunno. Slap her a couple of times? Push that smug face in a plate full of pasta?" I laughed and poured her another glass. "So that will be the look of distain she gave you then? I see what you mean about it making you feel low. Is she really following you?" She'd polished off the olives and was thumbing through the wine list. "Shall we get something fizzy?"

"Sounds like a good idea." I downed my drink and made eye contact with the waiter, who was already watching me after that scene. "London has 8 million people in it, not including the people that come through everyday for work or for the airports, etc. The chances of seeing the same stranger twice are slim to none. This is the fifth time I've seen her and the fourth she's spoken to me. In fact, twice she has involved herself in my conversation with someone else."

"She likes you. That is obvious." Rachel brows knitted together as she played with the menu.

"If I'm being honest I find her creepy and rude."

"She's gorgeous."

"She was rude to you."

"She tried to pick you up while you're on a date. Credit where credit is due, the woman has balls."

"I don't like my women to have balls."

"Ha. Funny man. I can handle myself and I think you're exaggerating... again." She winked. "She's probably not stalking you."

"Probably?"

"Anyway, she looked pissed so I don't think you'll be seeing her again. Which will be a shame as you obviously like her."

"I... I ... I... don't!" I protested, stuttering, the old anxiety coming flooding back as I realised the table next to ours was listening in on our conversation. I made eye contact with them and they went back to their food.

"It's cool dude, we're not an item. We're both adults; let's just see how things go. Now, you drink your wine and I'll tell you about the time I skidded across the floor of the office I was temping at and ended up sliding into a meeting room."

The rest of the night continued without a hitch and we didn't discuss Emily again. I did my best to keep her out of my mind and we were halfway through the bottle of pink champagne when I realised I was quite drunk. Rachel was also, so it wasn't a problem. Although not surprising since we started the day with champagne cocktails and were ending it with the same. I tried not to work out the amount of alcohol I had consumed - the nausea was getting quite real and I contemplated a tactical chunder before getting her home.

Continuing on with the theme of Rachel making the first move she jumped me in the taxi on the way home. Literally. She straddled me on the back seat. I discovered she wasn't wearing knickers, even though I was certain she had them on when we left mine earlier, and I made full advantage of this, finding her wet already. Her happy moans drowning out the protests by the cabbie. *She still smells of strawberries. I wonder if she tastes of strawberries too?*

It was midnight when we fell in through the front door, giggling and loudly shushing each. We barely made it in through my bedroom door before she was ripping my shirt off. I lost three buttons off a brand new shirt.

Unlike with Sarah this night was clear as day, maybe because Rachel had more passion about her: it was stimulating, awakening.

I was pleased to find out she did have the faint taste of fresh strawberries, as I licked, sucked and nibbled every inch of her beautiful body. I buried my face into her she pulled on my hair, pushing me further into her, grinding against my mouth until she screamed and called out my name. My tongue ached and my jaw was stiff when she pulled my face up to kiss me, smearing her face with her own juices. She was flushed, panting and looked happy.

She pushed me on my back, pulling her hair off her face as she inched further down my body. Taking me in her mouth it was a beautiful agony. Relief and tension washed over my body in spasms, until I was pulsating and aching for release...

Then she stopped, almost at the point of no return. She had a wicked grin on her face. *She knows what she is doing.*

I pulled her head back down to me by her hair and growled: "I recommend you finish me off."

"Oh but then you'll need to refill." She purred as she climbed on top of me sliding, slowly, down the length of my shaft, her head sliding back in pure, abject pleasure.

"I'm not going to last much longer if you keep doing that..." My head fell back in a moan as I let the waves of pleasure take over my body. Through half closed eyes I saw an aura of light around her. Her head was flung back and her fringe plastered to her head forehead with sweat. Her eyes were closed and she looked... delicious.

I pulled her down harder onto me as I thrust up, causing her to yelp and squeal in pleasure and surprise. I slammed harder and harder into her. The world spinning; lights flickering; her aura growing then...

Then it was 4am and I was on top, Rachel was on her front, her back bleeding with long nail marks down it and her arse was red raw with sore looking handprints.

*CRACK!* I slapped her with my right hand, my left hand round her neck as I ploughed into her, the rhythmic slapping on my hips on her behind.

*CRACK!* The back of her neck was trickling with blood. *Bite marks?* They were definitely mouth shaped and it looked like teeth indentations under the little pools of blood.

*CRACK!* I slammed into her again and her cries rang out: she was screaming my name. I felt blood tricking down my back, pooling in the crack of my arse.

*CRACK!* Rachel started bucking and shaking as her orgasm started rolling through her body. She was gasping for air, both hands were round her throat now. "More..." She said breathlessly. "Harder..."

She was clawing at my hands: I could feel the pressure building, I couldn't stop if I wanted to. "Oh God..."

"YES!" She screamed. Then...

*Le petit mort.*

Heavy breathing.

Sleep.

## 11

I could feel the warmth of the sun cascading across my naked back and the damp sheets wrapped tightly around my legs. My eyelids flickered open and I saw Rachel's dark hair scattered across my pillow and I smiled through my half-sleep and listened to her happy, snuffling, little snores. Running my fingers down her arm I leaned across a placed a kiss on her forehead and pulled her close to me, falling back to sleep as we snuggled in close.

"I think we pissed off your housemates." Rachel whispered loudly while shaking me. She was struggling to control her giggling and it gave off the impression she was hyperventilating: her shoulders shook.

"What?" I groaned sleepily. *Why isn't she still next to me?* She was pink with a beige towel on her head and my shirt clinging to her damp skin. She'd washed off the smell of sex and smelt like strawberries again.

I wanted to kiss her. To play. Aching, I rolled onto my hip to try to show her how much I wanted her again. She pushed me away, escaped wet hair tickling my face as she struggled to keep the too small towel on her head.

Hurt, I looked at her. "What?"

She stared at me disparagingly. "I think we pissed off your housemates." She repeated.

"How? Why?"

"Why do you think?"

"Were we loud?"

"Really? You're really asking me that? What do you think City Boy?" She kissed my forehead, even though I'd reached for her lips. I reached up and twisted her face towards mine, maybe a little too rough because I was annoyed with her distance. I saw her wince. She sunk into my arms as she surrendered to the kiss.

Her shirt - my shirt - fell away from her as we rolled across the bed so I was on top of her, planting delicate kisses and playful nips across her face and neck, whilst running my fingertips the length of her body, making her squirm and giggle with pleasure.

She protested and rolled on top of me, pressing my already rigid erection into my stomach. "Mmm, come on, they're already mad, they can't get madder."

"No, but I have a train to catch."

I craned my neck to look at the clock. "It's only 9am, we have all day. Let me play with you." I purred and slipped my fingers between her legs, the moisture already spilling down her thighs, proving she wanted me as much as I ached for her.

"Babe, I can't miss my train." She got out of bed and started getting dressed.

The pang of rejection split through my chest and I felt very exposed lying there naked and wanting. "What time is your train?"

"There is one at 10.30. I have a couple of designs I still need to draw up for tomorrow." She threw my shirt at me. "Get up and get dressed, you can buy me breakfast." She teased, smiling cheekily, but you could cut the tension with a knife, things were different today and I was in two minds whether to probe. *Should I be honest or aloof?* I was told to play hard to get but that is possibly the worst piece of dating advice I have ever received. I pulled my jeans on while mulled this over: I needed thinking time.

"So what happened? Why are my, sorry, why do you think my housemates are mad at us?"

"Well I got up and grabbed a shower about half an hour ago and I bumped into... Who's the woman? Long brown hair and blue eyes."

"Susan." I was lacing up my trainers and the rejection merged with the sinking feeling in my stomach. Nathan and Andy I could handle, I'd heard them have sex before, but there was that rule about Susan: we let her sleep. Rotating shifts were hard enough without being rudely awakened in the middle of the night. She liked her sleep and we were good at letting her have it.

"She was stood in the doorway to what I guess was her room." *Oh God...* She was downstairs and across the hall, the bathroom was next door to her room, the pit in my stomach got deeper. "She just glared at me and said 'So you must be James's friend' and walked into the bathroom after me." She made air quotes with her fingers with the word 'friend'.

"Did you do the air quotes?"

"She used the air quotes." *Great.* She sounded properly pissed, so we must have woken her up. Or worse, kept her sleeping in the first place.

"OK. OK. OK. Let me think." I was pulling on my jeans and pacing the floor looking for a clean T-shirt. *Should I shower?* I could smell sweat, sex and dried blood radiating from my skin. "She's on a day shift today then. I'll pick up some flowers and maybe a big bar of chocolate."

Rachel stood in a tight pair of blue jeans and a T-shirt with 'Combichrist' emblazoned across it. I noticed the scratch marks peeking out above her neckline. She was pulled her hair into a ponytail and checking her neck for something. "Combichrist?" I said to her back.

"EDM band. Not your type. Dude?" She waved her wrists at me, which had big purple welts on. *Oh no, not again.* "And what the hell?" She gestured to her neck, which looked sore: the bite marks had pierced the flesh.

I ran my tongue around my mouth. I could taste copper. "Sorry." I said disingenuously.

"It's fine, guess I'll be wearing long sleeved, polo necks for a while." She laughed, kissing me again before shoving the rest of her clothes into her bag. Her face was completely free of make up and she looked cute. Younger. "I need a massive pint of coffee and I feel like something sugary, a big muffin or pastry. Come on." She really seemed eager to go, standing by the door checking her phone.

9.30am. I had planned out a day for us. "I was going to cook." I nonchalantly smoothed my hair in the mirror, trying to keep the neediness out of my voice. *Might as well shower later.* "You want sweet, how about pancakes? We have maple syrup." I cooed.

She didn't look up from her phone, fingers still flying over the screen. "I should really head back. I'll come back soon." She lied.

*She is taking the marks better than Sarah but she is definitely being distant. Maybe it's the hangover? I hurt her more than I hurt Sarah though.*

"Sure, let me know when you're free next and I'll check my diary. Come on, I'll take you back to Kings Cross, we'll grab something there." I tried to ignore the nausea rising from the mix of emotions.

"YOU UTTER LEGEND!" The cry that greeted me as I slumped through the door on my return.

The nausea was very real now. I knew I wasn't going to be sick, but I really want to crawl into a dark place and feel sorry for myself. Rachel had given me a hug and a tender kiss at the station - a goodbye kiss - I could still taste and smell her and yet I knew I wasn't going to see her again. I needed to not think about that right now.

Nathan cracked me on the back so hard I almost dropped the large bouquet of pink and purple roses, carnations and assortment of other flowers, plus the box of dark chocolates, I had picked up on the way back. Set me back a few bob so I was keen to keep then in good condition to give to Susan.

Nathan dragged me to the kitchen where Alice was eating pancakes: the bottle of maple syrup I bought sat on the table. That made me feel worse, I was going to make Rachel those pancakes.

I decided it was the hangover that was making me feel sick, tired and low and busied myself putting the flowers in a vase and writing out a note for Susan for when she got home this evening. Unfortunately Nathan's excited chattering buzzed around me and he managed to add embarrassment to the tempest of emotions.

"Help yourself to pancakes, you're going to need to energy." Nathan grinned and pointed towards the used pan and the jug of batter.

"I thought you weren't here last night." *If anyone is up there looking out for me, they didn't hear anything last night.*

"Change of plans."

"Why?"

I saw Alice and Nathan exchange glances." We went for dinner round the corner and it made sense to come back here." So Alice wanted to snoop on Rachel.

*Oh God I'm going to have to ask...* "So you were here all night then? When did you get in?

"Stop pussyfooting, we heard fucking everything, you utter Porn Star! Never pegged you for a screamer boy and Christ they were some noises she was making. I've never been so proud."

*I'm in hell. I'm going to kill them both.* I could feel anger rising above all the other emotions. *They wanted this.*

*1... 2...*

I couldn't look at them so I turned back to the cooker and made some pancakes with the leftover batter. I wasn't hungry, but it was a distraction, especially flipping the pancakes. I love flipping pancakes.

"I think we woke Susan." I nodded towards the gifts on the side. "You weren't up early enough to spy on Rachel of course."

"Of course not!" Alice said an octave too high, too fast and too loud.

"You're a terrible liar Alice."

"Why did she leave so early?"

"She had a train to catch."

"At least we know she's definitely real. Unlike…" He paused to swallow his mouthful of food. Nathan is such a wanker sometimes. "Did you ever find out her name?"

"Emily." Sitting down at the table I poured way too much syrup on my stack. I couldn't help but imagine Gemma's face when Alice told her everything tomorrow, that's if she hadn't already text her.

Nathan persisted. "So how was yesterday?"

Between bites of my food I told them about our day, leaving out all the gory details seeing as they already knew them and I'm not one to kiss and tell. "So when are you seeing her again?"

"I don't know. Hopefully soon."

"Judging by her screams, I bet it will be next weekend." Nathan beamed with pride. "You're the man I always hoped you would become." He wiped away a fake tear and clutched his hands to his chest, mimicking a proud parent.

He was wrong though and unfortunately it meant that I was right. I never saw Rachel again. I was understandably paranoid: both times I had blackouts - granted both times I had been drinking - and Rachel and Sarah had ended up bruised and/or bleeding. This never happened to me before I moved. What was going on with me?

Rachel text me when she got home to tell me what a lovely time she had and we still spoke every day for about a week - sending me photos of her artwork and the designs she had tattooed on others.

She'd even got a new tattoo herself, a green cartoon character on her foot and laughed when I said I had no idea what it was, "but it's adorable". Then the she started taking longer to reply and her messages had become less personal. A day or two would go by and I'd get a flippant, chatty reply. Nothing like the conversations we'd had previously.

After the second week I got a message saying she was seeing someone and "of course it wouldn't be right if we kept talking. You're a lovely guy and all but…" *blah, blah, blah*. I didn't hear from her again after that. Obviously I hadn't heard from Sarah and curiosity got the better of me. I gave up and text Robert, in two minds as to whether I hoped he had herd from her.

**Dude, random question but have you heard from Sarah?**

**Yeah I saw her on Saturday, she was out with a group of mates. Why?**

**Just wondered. I hadn't heard from her in a while.**

**Oh.**

**Oh? What do you mean Oh?**

**Nothing.**

**What?**

**Leave it Jim. Give her some time.**

**Why?**

I was getting really pissed off now. I knew why he was being evasive but he was my friend first!

**We met for lunch about a week ago. She wanted to talk about you. Look I don't know what happened and I don't want to get involved. Let's just leave it.**

*1… 2… 3…* I was struggling to keep calm now. *What the fuck has she said?*

**What did she say? You owe me that.**

**I owe you nothing. She said you're different, you're not the James she used to know and she doesn't know if she likes the new you. Just leave her alone for a while.**


Part of me thought they were dating, but I wouldn't care if they were. I knew it was me. I couldn't believe I had hurt her that much. That's not me. *Isn't it?*

*But she enjoyed it at the time.*

*Did she?* I asked myself.


**12**


On the 7<sup>th</sup> of April Gemma and Alice dragged me out after work: Nathan was working late and would catch up after. Gemma pushed a pint across the table to me and I stared at the condensation running down the outside of the glass, barely hearing their chatter about Gemma's wedding and Alice's birthday plans. I waited until they'd almost finished their drinks before I downed mine in one and signalled I would get the next round in. I didn't know why I was there, I kept re-reading the messages from Robert, replaying York over and over in my head. *I'm sure she enjoyed it.* I didn't care about Rachel, after all, I was a one-night stand for her.

When I came back to the table Gemma took my hand before I could take a sip of my drink. "We're worried about you."

"I'm fine."

Alice lightly touched my other arm. "Stop lying. We know it's about these women, it's obvious." I suddenly felt very tired and with all the worry I folded, needing a woman's perspective.

I told them about Rachel and Sarah, I even touched on Emily, although, I left out the literal ins and outs and some of the more bloody details. I stuttered and stumbled my way through and my drink was empty by the time I finished. Their glasses barely touched. Faces a mask of concern and apprehension.

Alice got the third round in, she could afford to miss some details as Nathan had told her about Emily. They were getting way too close for comfort.

"What is wrong with me?" The alcohol made me feel all the more melancholy. *This wasn't a good idea.* I sipped the drink anyway. I saw them looking at each in the periphery of my vision.

"Maybe it's them?" Gemma.

"Maybe you should see a doctor." Alice.

"I'm not crazy!"

"You're hurting these women and you don't seem to remember doing it." Gemma.

"They enjoyed at the time."

"You remember that?" Gemma.

"Actually yes. There are just parts I don't remember."

"I'm just saying before you hurt anyone else." Gemma.

"You make me sound like a psychopath."

"I'm not saying that..." Gemma.

I sat bolt upright and I focused on my breathing. I could feel my pulse racing, which was quite common these days. "I can't believe you are accusing me of hurting them on purpose."

"I think what Gemma means is..." Alice.

"I think I know what Gemma means."

"No you don't. I'm not saying on purpose, maybe you couldn't help yourself. Either way you need help." Gemma.

"I'm not like that."

"I know. It's just you did hurt them." Gemma. She had a faint look of disgust in her eyes, or maybe I was projecting my own fears onto her. Either way I felt sick.

"Maybe you should see a doctor." Alice repeated. I looked at Gemma again. I knew her well enough now to know she won't leave this alone now and I knew Alice well enough to know this whole conversation is going to get back to Nathan. "It sounds like you hurt them, possibly scared them and they no longer feel safe around you. Look, you have to be more understanding of other people's feelings. Women don't usually like to be hurt during sex. You're supposed to make them feel special, wanted, not have them wake up with bruises."

I could barely hear her rhetoric over the sound of rushing blood in my ears. I wanted some advice from friends and now they're suggesting I was a danger and should be committed? "I'm not dangerous! I didn't hurt them and you weren't there, they did enjoy it!"

"Doesn't sound like it." Gemma continued quietly.

"You're really that naïve that you think people couldn't enjoy a little pain?"

Gemma ignored my question. "Look, Alice is right, just talk to your doctor, it's probably nothing and then I'll set you up with my friend Soph. She's really sweet, quite shy so you'll have to be delicate with her."

*1... 2... 3...*

My vision grew hazy, darkness creeping in at the edges. My head swam and I was leaning hard on the table to steady myself: my chair no longer feeling stable enough to support my weight. "No thank you. I can find my own dates."

*5... 6...*

"Well obviously you can't, you haven't been out with anyone from London." Alice's time to chime in now, sipping on her white wine.

*7... 8... 9...*

"Let us set you up. Honestly I've met Soph and she's such a doll."

*10.*

There was no blackout, everything was completely clear, but it felt like I wasn't in control of my actions. Rage coursed through me and it felt like the passion from sex, I finally understood crimes of passion. *Which isn't a good thing.* I was going to enjoy every moment of the scene I was about to cause. But it wasn't me. Not the me I knew anyway. I could have been the me that Sarah and Rachel knew.

I knocked back my drink and slammed the glass onto the table making them jump and the surrounding tables turn to look at me. "You know what?" I didn't recognise my voice. "How about you keep your fucking noses out of my sex life? I was wrong to involve you, but how about you stop asking questions, stop poking around and you..." I jabbed my index finger at Alice. "...stop changing your plans to spy on the women I bring home.

"I'm sorry I asked for your help but you've made me out to be some sort of monster. What I enjoy sexually is nothing to do with you. Maybe I don't want some simpering girl. Maybe I want a woman. Not some pathetic..." I paused, suddenly painfully aware of the eyes on me from the hushed drinkers. "...slip of a thing who I have to be delicate with. I want a WOMAN who wants to be thrown around and fucked by a MAN. Thanks for the drink." I stormed out into the fresh spring air.

My internal monologue clapped slowly. *Well done, that is how you make a scene.* I really wanted a cigarette now, which is what I decided to do next. I decided to go and buy a packet of cigarettes, but as I started to walk away I could hear the swoosh of a door opening violently and the *clack-clack-clack* of two sets of heels running across stone and concrete.

"Wait! James!" I still faced away, but I recognised Alice's voice. "Look I'm sorry. We were just trying to help, as friends. If we're being totally honest I think Rachel was seeing the guy she dumped you for, but we're just concerned."

Gemma's voice followed. It sounded like she was shivering. "You're not the man we met only a couple of months ago." I froze, why couldn't she understand that I didn't want to talk about this?

"You haven't seemed yourself and Nathan is worried about you." I turned round then and Alice stepped back with a sharp intake of breath. They stood next to each other, both without coats but Gemma was visibly shaking. "You've changed, really bloody fast as well. We worry."

"Look," I stepped towards them and Gemma stepped back. Fear? "I'm fine, but I need you all to keep your nose out of my business, I shouldn't have confided in you, but can you please stop asking me questions?"

"Have you taken something?"

"Sorry what?" *Talk about a tangent.*

"Are you on drugs? Your pupils are huge."

"It's dark. You know I don't do drugs and you're really testing my patience. Now, I'm going home, I'm sorry I yelled and I'll see you at work tomorrow."

## 13

The bar we were drinking at was only a short tube journey from home, but it was an hour's walk away. Still, I decided to walk home, I needed the unseasonably warm air to clear my head. Andy insisted I didn't walk through the streets of London alone: he was worried that a "delicate soul" such as myself would get attacked, mugged, murdered or raped.

The stars were bright and the moon hung low and lazy in the sky, stealing the sun's red glow: the nights were getting shorter. I was looking forward to summer. My vision brightened and my lungs felt lighter as I walked, but I still avoided eye contact with the passing crowds of people. I had to concentrate on putting one foot in front of the other without stumbling. My head was still spinning, which I attributed to the adrenaline still coursing through my body from the fit I just threw and/or the drinks I had been downing.

I was going to get it from Nathan when I got home, he was protective over Alice these days: they seemed to be getting serious quite quickly. That was no way to behave, especially toward women, let alone women who were looking out for me and I did offer them up the information. Maybe it's my fault: I hadn't been myself for a while now.

The dreams had returned, although the exhaustion had abated, so I didn't think it was a problem. I was enjoying them and last night's was wonderful, so vivid and full of the tastes and smells of a woman; the feel of fingertips running over my face and nails over my back.

I stopped and looked at my reflection in the darkened window of a closed clothes shop. I knew I looked different - for the better - but I could see why Alice had stepped back. My eyes were angry, crazy almost. I leaned closer and looked at my pupils, but I couldn't quite make them out. I knew I wasn't on drugs and I hadn't been spiked, so any dilatation would be because of the dark. A couple walked passed me staring. *I must look wasted though.* I took in a few deep breaths and let the rapidly cooling air sooth my nerves.

My walk was calm and peaceful and it gave me a chance to clear my head. The time gave Nathan and Andy the chance to sit and seethe though. They let me have both barrels when I got in. I was an idiot for walking home alone and I was a rude douchebag for yelling at Alice and Gemma.

I stood in the hallway in silence, staring at the floor and wondering why I was letting them speak to me like this, until they finally stormed off, exasperated. *I feel like a child.*

I went to bed late and had a deep, dreamless sleep that night, waking in a good mood and vowing to be the old me. Or at least faking it so I no longer bothered anyone. *I don't know why you care.* I will make a conscious effort to be the happy James everyone knew and loved. *Why?*

I ignored my own questioning. I needed to make it up to everyone and I must call Mum and Dad. I didn't know what was going on with me, but there was no need for me to take it out on the people I care about. To start out on the right foot I made a pot of coffee for the house; tidied the kitchen and even quickly ran round tidying up the living room. I left a note against the coffee machine:

**Morning all!**

**Help yourself and I'm cooking dinner tonight, text me and let me know if you're going to be about so I know how much to make. They'll be leftovers if you can't make it. I'll pick up dessert as well.**

**Have a good day.**

N


The sun was shining and I even started whistling as I walked to the tube station, all I needed was a bluebird to land on the end of my finger and I was Snow White. Only with shorter hair. And male. And real. So nothing like Snow White.

I even made eye contact with strangers on the tube who smiled back at me: I think I should get a prize for that alone. Competition time! Make a Londoner smile and win a brand new car! *I might do the lottery.*

Knowing I would make it to work before Gemma and Alice I stopped on the way to pick up coffee and pastries to have before the doors opened. I don't know what they were more surprised about, the fact I had beaten them both to work, the complete 180 on my mood or the treats. Out the corner of my eye I saw them exchanging looks and mouthing something I couldn't make it. People talking behind my back irritated me, the fact they were doing it in front of me made it worse. *How disrespectful? Breathe. Come on man breathe through it.* I chose to ignore it and not let them ruin my faked good mood.

Things seemed to be going well. The awkwardness faded after I apologised for my outburst and the day went quickly as I planned what I would cook this evening during the quiet periods. Even the clientele coming into the building were polite and friendly - the second best kind of clientele. The best type were the absent ones, but that wasn't going to happen today: it was quite a busy day.

Then she walked in.

I was in the middle of checking Mr. James in to see the solicitors on the first floor when I instantly recognised her *tap-tap-tap* coming in through the front door. My head shot up, one half hoping I was wrong and the other half desperately wanting to see her again. My heart stopped and my mouth filled with cotton, which was immensely inconvenient considering I was mid-sentence.

"I've let them know you're here if you just wan...t... to... go... thr...uuuurrrrgghh..." Emily stood behind him smiling, making eye contact for a few seconds too long, so Mr. James had time to turn around to see who I was gawping at. He looked at Emily who politely smiled and inclined her head, blinking slowly. Or time slowed, one or the other. When he turned back to me he was grinning in a vaguely patronising manner at my slack jaw. He laughed as he walked through the security gate. *Sod.*

Gathering my nerves I greeted Emily. *Keep it together boy, she's not here for you. She didn't know you work here.* "Good afternoon, how can I help?" I said curtly with only a slight tremor in my voice, which I hope she didn't notice.

"You know I said we should stop meeting like this?" She said abruptly. *Rachel was right: she is brazen.* I nodded, I remembered every moment of our interactions in minute detail. "I changed my mind. I think we should meet more often. I'd like to buy you dinner." She spoke in choppy and sharp sentences. "Here's my number. Text me and let me know when you're free." She commanded. "I won't keep you now. You have a queue forming." She turned to leave and stride passed the couple in business suits that had walked in behind her, who smiled at her confidence

"Emily!" I stood as I called after her and she turned around looking a little stunned. I obviously ruined her exit. "What are you doing tomorrow night? Let me take you out instead. It's the least I can do after..." I trailed off, not wanting to admit what I said in front of all these people. The three people in the queue all smiled at each other knowingly. We had an audience now. *Why do people keep entering?*

"Sounds perfect. 7pm. Text me a place." Once she left the building, three of the four people in the queue started whooping and cheering and the fourth that just joined looked incredibly confused.

I was going on a date with Emily. I wanted to sing or pinch myself. *I must be dreaming.*

*"It's a beautiful day and I can't stop myself from smiling / If we're drinking, then I'm buying / And I know there's no denying / It's a beautiful day, the sun is up, the music's playing."*

*I'm definitely going to get a lottery ticket.*

**Emily**

**7**

*Breathe. Breathe. Breathe.* I paced up and down the street corner, the muggy air choking me slightly. My bag was chaffing my shoulders and I realised I was rubbing my hands together, trying to calm myself down. With a quick check to make sure I wasn't in eye line, I jumped up and down and shook myself a couple of times. Pumping myself up like Rocky.

"Come on girl, you know what his answer will be." I glanced round the corner, the entrance to his work obscured from view, mind racing with all possible situations. *What if he is still seeing that girl? I mean I know I'm more interesting than her. What am I saying? I know he's no longer seeing her.*

Closing my eyes to focus I stretched out my senses and I could feel his mood. Positive, but tinged with doubt and sadness. Something was bothering him. Rejection! That's it, he feels rejected. *Well not anymore. Go get him girl!*

Three deep breathes and I was ready. *Don't forget to breathe when you're in there.*

"Here we go…"

**James**

**14**

I skipped the drinks that night, I had a meal to cook and a certain blonde man's nose to rub. I skipped home, almost literally, and greeted Nathan with:

"AAHHH HAAAA! Not only does she exist, I'm going on a date with her tomorrow night!"

"Sorry, what?"

"Emily!"

He stared blankly at me before reaching into the fridge and throwing a beer at me, which narrowly missed hitting me in the head. "Yeeeeaahhh. I have no idea who or what you're talking about. Drink that and repeat. What?"

I told him what happened whilst I started cooking. Susan looked suitable impressed with the story and more so with the cake I picked up from the French patisserie around the corner: she dug out a chunk of cream with her finger, tasting and making an approving noise before she and Andy dove in with forks, against my protests that they'll ruin their appetites.

"So are you planning on bringing this one home as well? I'm not working on Sunday." Susan sniggered.

I didn't turn round from the cooker, not wanting her to see my blushes. "Erm, no."

"This is the one you were obsessing over." You could hear the penny drop for Nathan.

"I wasn't obsessed."

"You were though."

"I'm not arguing with you.  Make yourself useful and make sure that doesn't burn while I go get changed."

Of course I didn't sleep well that night (Sod's Law). I know I slept because I remember dreaming, but I couldn't get comfortable, tossing and turning from the nerves. I assumed it was nervous, I wanted to impress Emily but I knew nothing about her. Other than the fact she knew how to make me weak at the knees.

I'd spent the evening looking for a nice restaurant near Berkeley Square, assuming that she must live or work near there as that's where I kept seeing her. I text her the address and all I got as a response was:

**I'll see you there. E x**


No matter, I'm sure she wouldn't stand me up because she had asked me out: she was definitely interested. I would have to remember to ask her how she found out where I worked: she must have walked passed the building and seen me at Reception. Or walked passed me walking in, but there was a nagging feeling I just couldn't shake. One that kept me awake for most of the night. I lay in bed staring at a crack that was forming in the ceiling, going over all the odd things that had happened since I moved:

- We met at the train station and I fell over in front of her, which isn't too strange because I'm clumsy.

- Then she approached me in the bar and swiftly disappeared, which is plausible as she was trying to be aloof and mysterious.

- That same night she found me in the hotel and disappeared again - this is slightly stranger.

- After that night I started getting the blackouts, mostly happening at heights of passion when my adrenaline was pumping. This is easily allocated to the amount of alcohol I had been drinking recently, certainly a lot more than when I lived in York. I glanced over at my nightstand that had an empty glass of whiskey on it. There was an empty bottle on the floor.

- Then she'd been at King's Cross when I arrived home.

- She'd interrupted my date with Rachel - that was very odd. *Who does that?*

- Finally she'd found out where I worked and asked me out on a date.

I mulled over the theory she had been following me, although I preferred to think of it as fate.

My biggest worry was the blackouts. I realised I that I was worried they were connected to Emily somehow. *You're paranoid and that's ridiculous.* Although the weirdest thing of all was the strange conversations I'd been having with myself. My internal monologue had started answering me back. *Like now.* Like now.

"You're nuts!" I sat up in bed talking to the darkness. "You drink too much. You worry too much! You need to cut that out and stop the drinking before bed. It's not healthy." I switched on the light in my room - it was 3am - deciding to watch some videos on my laptop and needing to watch something light hearted.


I fell asleep not long after and woke up with the laptop still on my bed and the battery dead. I felt better, it was obviously nerves that had rattled me last night, plus I didn't think I was good enough for this beautiful woman. Tonight was the big night, the one chance to wow her. Like a job interview for a dream position, except I don't feel I'm suitable. So just like a job interview.

I really had no idea why this woman is interested in me, but I needed to stop questioning it.

I'd spent the day cleaning my room and preparing myself. Not that I thought she would be coming home with me, I felt better knowing that I wasn't slovenly in any aspect of my life, but I couldn't shake the nagging doubts. I decided to share them with Nathan, arguing with myself wasn't doing any good: I ended up going round in circles with my head spinning.

"I have no idea why she asked me out. Do you think I should ask her?" I confided in Nathan as I had a drink with him to calm my nerves.

"For peat's sake," Nathan almost spat out his beer. "Of course you shouldn't ask her! Why would you do such a thing?"

"Why not? Surely it's a compliment? Why would a beautiful woman like Emily be interested in..." I waved my free hand in front of my body. "This?"

"It makes you look weak."

"Sorry?"

"And stop that, you're too apologetic. Look dude I don't want to sound..." He did a derogatory finger wangle with his free hand. Andy looked at him and glared.

"Over-emotional is what I think this unenlightened child is trying to say."

"Ahem, yes, well, thanks Andy. I don't want to sound over-emotional, but you're a good bloke. You're fun to be around and you're clever. Not bad looking too according to Alice."

"She said that?"

"You have a lot to offer." He continued without clarification. "And I think you need to think more of yourself. You've been a bit odd lately but you've had a lot to adjust to. Go out there and be yourself and if she doesn't like that, then screw her. I mean fuck her. Wait..."

"I get what you mean." I interjected and raised my can to toast. "Thank you. Here's to a good night."

**Emily**

**8**

*Well… I fucking blew that, didn't I?*

**James**

**15**

I could count on one hand how many first dates I had been on. I'm not usually the 'dating' type; a lot of my exes have started off as friends. So I don't have much comparison, but even I know that my date with Emily wasn't normal.

Emily herself was… not odd… eccentric? Not normal. But normal is boring. She is confusing, but utterly enthralling and it was one of the strangest interactions I'd ever had. I have no other words to describe it.

I met her outside of this beautiful (and expensive) Japanese restaurant. I had some money saved up from cutting down on my nights down the pub and eating out after work - Nathan having a girlfriend was amazing for my bank balance - so I decided to spend it on Emily.

I arrived at 6.45pm pleased it was dry if not a little chilly, as there wasn't a covering above the door. I thought I would wait outside, so she wouldn't feel nervous walking in alone, I know it can be a bit daunting walking in and worrying that your date might not arrive. Plus, if she did stand me up no one but me would know.

"They found her body face down dead in the rain." She was singing and her voice carried on the breeze, accompanied by her signature *tap-tap-tap*. I took a deep breath to try and settle my frazzled nerves. I'd been waiting in the cold for more than half an hour and dark clouds were gathering threatening to break. *15 more minutes and I'll leave. Or 15 more minutes and I'll text her. Please don't rain.* I really didn't want to be stood up in the rain, how pathetic would that be? I had already run through every possible scenario for her delay and had just about made peace with the fact she had stood me up.

All thoughts and concerns were thrown out of the window when I saw what she was wearing. I let my jaw hang loose not caring for how gormless I looked. *Stunning.* My eyes travelled up the length of her body, from her insanely high and dangerous looking stilettos, to her bare legs exposed through a long, purple, high slit skirt, revealing a black and white portrait tattooed on the front of her right leg: her leather jacket that was zipped up to the neck so I couldn't see what was on her top half.

She was oozing confidence and sex appeal and she smiled as we made eye contact. "Such a shame."

"Excuse me?" I looked down at my clothing thinking she must be ashamed of me.

"No of course it's not you. It was the song I was singing, I've had it stuck in my head for days. I forget sometimes that I'm singing aloud and people can hear me. You look marvellous." *I love the way she says that.* She paused studying my face. "Do I have something on my face or in my teeth?" She sucked on her teeth and lightly brushed her cheek with her hand.

"No? No. Why?" I managed to stutter out.

"Nice to know I give a good first impression then. You're catching flies." I closed my mouth quickly and blushed. She leaned in with her hand on my chest: the contact made my pulse race even faster and she gave me a polite kiss on the check. Her perfume was musky and reminded me of the smell of those hippy shops, the ones that sells smoking paraphernalia and incense. *Sandalwood. That's it, Sandalwood.* When her lips brushed the flushed part of my face my mouth started watering. *Delicious.*

Beads of sweat pricking on my forehead as I held the door open that I tried to subtly brush away. "You look wonderful. Nice to know I'm worth making an effort for."

"Thank you." When she removed her jacket it revealed a white, long sleeved blouse, with a purple corset at her waist, which accentuated her bust. I tried not to look. I failed. She looked like a fashionable pirate wench. "I don't go to all this trouble for just anyone you know." She assured me as I went to seat her - like the gentleman I am - but the waiter got there first.

"Ma'am. Sir. I will be your servant... server this evening." The young waiter winked as he sat us. I would have been more offended at the outrage of him flirting with someone who was quite obviously my date, but I think he winked at me.

The service was impeccable all night; she had a way with the waiter, batting those long eyelashes at him to get the highest quality sake to start our meal. Although, I'm not certain it made the blindest bit of difference. I'm not a small man, so I will admit that I was a little jealous at the attention she gave him, but those feelings melted as the sake hit my bloodstream. By the second bottle I was certain it was me he was flirting with, pouring my drink first and barely look glancing at Emily.

I tried to ignore the wink the waiter gave me as we ordered our dishes ("Excellent choice sir, a personal favourite, you obviously have excellent taste.") and I turned the Emily, struggling for topics of conversation to fill the ever increasing, awkward silence. "So tell me about yourself."

What I really wanted to ask is: "Why me? Why would a woman like you be interested in a spud like me?" But I kept my cool and my mouth shut. I'm cool as a cucumber. A sweating cucumber.

"Have you noticed it's an automatic human reaction to fill any silences with speech? More so in the Western world but it's still incredibly common. It's like the silence scares us. We're terrified we might talk about something important to us. Something honest and true." She sipped her sake and studied the glass; only looking at me after she'd finished talking, just in time to watch my jaw slam into the table. I didn't know how to respond and she laughed at my dumbfounded expression. "Don't look so frightened, I work in HR so I'm used to having to read people. It's amazing how many people think they can get away with obvious lies during a disciplinary or a job interview. What about you? What do you like about your current role? I'm guessing you work on Reception?"

"I'm a Receptionist." *Crap, of course she knows that.*

"Yes."

"Oh of course, sorry." *Shut up James.* Nathan's words were ringing in my ears. *'You apologise too much: it makes you look weak.'* "It's interesting meeting the different people that come in."

"And?"

"It can be quite challenging, sometimes we get some real… interesting characters."

"Twats, wankers or dickheads dear, we're both adults."

"Excuse me?"

"You swear. I swear. It's fine."

"How do you know I swear?"

"Call it a hunch." She took a sip of her wine again.

We chatted for a little while about work and what we hated about it as we nibbled on our sashimi and sushi rolls. The small talk was even irritating me now, although that could have been the cutlery. This wasn't my first time eating sushi but I wasn't very skilled with chopsticks.

She worked for a large charity and it seemed to be rewarding, but you could cut the tension with a knife; a bubble was forming, which Emily seemed eager to pop.

"So what happened with that girl I saw you with?" Bang. She lit the dynamite and ran away. Of course she would have known that I didn't want to discuss Rachel. Of course it hasn't gone well seeing as I was on a date with her not long after.

"Oh, not a lot, you know how it is."

"I don't. Tell me." I thought she sounded annoyed, though that could be my paranoia talking again. I knew I was being unnecessarily vague, but I found that question too personal for the first course of a first date.

I gave up with the chopsticks and started using my fingers, staring at the food to get a break from her penetrating eyes. I could feel a droplet of sweat running down the length of my back. *I wonder if I can change the subject?* "What about you? I'm guessing you're not seeing anyone."

I sucked soy sauce from my fingers as she topped up my glass, which was still half full. "Drink that."

"I'm OK."

"Drink it." She ordered. Her behaviour was confrontational and it was baffling me.

I sat back in my chair with my shoulders squared. I was getting defensive. "Why?"

"It was the Marquis de Sade who said: 'Conversation, like certain portions of the anatomy, always run more smoothly when lubricated.' And I can tell how tense you are."

I picked up my drink, swilling it round and watched the liquid make little rivulets and rivers whilst Emily finished the rest of her dish silence. Frowning, she expertly waved her chopsticks between her fingers. Faint lines creased her forehead and around her eyes. *How old is she?*

I opened my mouth to speak, but she interjected. "I'm sorry." I almost choked on my drink; she looked at me with watery, puppy dog eyes and a sad smile on her face. I melted. "I hate small talk and I want to be honest from the start." *Start of what?* "I can be intense and but I want to know all about you. Music that makes you move; your flaws; fond memories; your childhood; what keeps you up at night; your insecurities and fears..."

Now I topped up her wine, this is the first time she'd appeared fallible and human. "She started seeing someone else. I guess wasn't her type, I don't have any tattoos and I'm clean-shaven. To be honest, I found her a little patronising for not understanding some of her bands and movie references."

"I understand, sometimes opposites attract, but you need to have a common ground. My ex was the polar opposite of me and in the end we just couldn't see eye to eye."

Our mains came out with another round of sushi.

"Sounds serious, did you split up recently?"

"Oh no, this was a while ago now, I still hear from her time to time." Another long silence followed, in which I finished my drink. This whole evening the conversation was stop start and punctuated with a lot of drinking. *Don't get drunk. Don't get drunk. I might be drunk already, love drunk! Oh God, I am drunk. Fuck it I'm going to ask.* The alcohol had made me brazen and I'm sure she looked up at me as I thought it. I let the silence drag on a little longer, just to make sure she had a mouth full of food before, I looked her in the eyes - holding her eye contact for long enough until I could see her getting concerned - and said:

"Why have you been following me?" It was her turn to choke now and I saw the shield slip again, only this time she looked panicked. "I knew it!" I exclaimed a little too loud, a family at the next table turned round to look at us. "You have been following me." I hissed in a whisper.

"I haven't."

"You're blushing."

"I've been drinking and I'm warm. You have to admit that you're hot."

"Well..."

"Temperature!" That already familiar disdain crept back into her eyes. *And I've blown it.* "I haven't been following you, but I am attracted to you so I couldn't resist the opportunities to... make sure you remembered me. First impressions are everything and after you quite literally threw yourself at me..."

"I tripped off the train."

"I know! I know."

"But how did you find me? You knew where I work."

"I recognised your uniform from an interview I had once in the building. For the Property Developers on the top floor."

"There isn't a Prop..."

"There used to be a Property Developer on the top floor." She sounded exasperated. "You were wearing it in the bar and hotel remember?" She was right, I started to feel incredibly stupid and as if she sensed my embarrassment she started stroking my hand. "Let's get another bottle, make that waiter work even harder for his tip tonight and I think he'd do anything for you." She smiled and I suddenly felt very safe. It's like my life clicked into place at that point, like two cogs slotting together.

Time crept by and it was just Emily and I, with her caressing my fingertips and gazing at me: the other diners become nothing but colours and noise, like bad reception on a poor quality TV I could barely make them out. *This is where I'm supposed to be.* This was the first time I become aware that Emily had a way of upsetting, and securing my world in a matter of moments.

Time slowly started to speed up. "Kings of Leon." I blurted out still staring at her hand, she blinked at me looking confused and I was back in this reality again. "Kings of Leon, it's what I'm listening to at the moment. Music that makes me move. Your turn."

She laughed a loud and genuine laugh and we spent the rest of the evening chatting about movies, music, books and TV. We both liked action movies, though she preferred horror; she reads a lot and doesn't watch a lot of TV and we both have the same eclectic taste in music - although Country and Western is included for her and I can't stand it.

"It's whiny."

"It's emotional, you don't like Johnny Cash or Dolly Parton?"

"No."

"A Boy Named Sue or 9 to 5?"

"No."

"Cretin. You're wrong." We both laughed as she pretended to sulk. *Adorable.*


She seemed to have fun - after the initial awkwardness and defensiveness - but we parted at the restaurant door after almost being kicked out by the restaurant staff. We had managed to commandeer our table for four hours, so I left a 20% tip as a thank you and an apology. The night was glorious and I didn't want to part from her, so I suggested a nightcap.

"Another time. I promise." She gave me a soft kiss on the lips: she tasted delicious. I wanted more. I pulled her into me hungrily, feeling her stumble and giggle as my tongue sort hers.

Time refused to follow a normal pattern tonight, because hours seemed to pass as our lips met and our bodies intertwined for the first time. I could feel the blackness taking me, my temperature rising and my head was swimming. I tried to slow my breathing: I was losing control, our passion was building and. I needed her: I needed to be inside her.

Thankfully, she pushed me away before I blacked out completely and ripped her clothes off in the middle of the street. She filled my senses: her perfume, her taste, and the softness of her skin, which seemed to sparkle in the lights of the restaurant. The sounds and smells of our surroundings came rushing back as we detached. I heard a couple giggling at us and whisper about 'young love' and 'getting a room'. "I promise."

"Emily." I growled and pulled her into me again, finding her lips and running my hands through her hair. She felt so small and fragile as she melted again, making a happy little moan as she warmed her hands underneath my jacket. I felt her struggle to regain her composure.

"James, I mean it." She pushed me away forcefully and stared at the floor panting. *Why isn't she looking at me?* When she - finally - looked up her pupils had dilated and there was a wild look she was barely keeping under control. "I want to get to know you better, I want you to know me." There was a strange emphasis on the 'know'. "Text me tomorrow. It's my turn to take you out. I owe you dinner now." The coldness and distance had returned: her sentences choppy and blunt.

And she was gone.

**Emily**

**9**

I stared into my glass of wine, half empty bottle on the table in front of me, and my laptop playing the latest episode of... Whatever I had put on. I couldn't see it. My head was on my arms, chin folding in on itself uncomfortably. The background noise was soothing as I contemplated why I struggle to hold a decent conversation. I can read emotions, I can sense peoples' feelings, I understand most people better than they understand themselves, and yet faced with the simple task of a first date, I blow it.

I'd spent the day meditating and doing yoga to calm my nerves. I hadn't slept well the night before - unsurprisingly. The remotest modicum of calm was shattered when I ripped the dress I had picked out, apparently I've put on weight, and resulted to old faithful - a toned down version of my steampunk cosplay outfit.

I was late. Of course I was late. Of course I missed my tube. Perhaps if I'd picked shoes I could walk in I wouldn't have missed it. We met outside of a Japanese restaurant that he picked. It was nice. But it was cold. I was cold. And I was late. *These are great omens.*

*Not now!*

My mood was darkening and I was irritated when I saw him loitering outside the restaurant.

*Why didn't he go in?* I took my headphones out my ears, begrudgingly sinking back into reality, although perking up slightly at his expression. He looked amazing. He'd styled his hair and wore a suit that fitted perfectly. His black brogues complimented his outfit and looked freshly polished.

I was sweating profusely when I let the waiter take my coat. I was pleased with what I had ended up wearing. I love heavy fabrics: they don't show sweat marks. I tried to surreptitiously pat my forehead and the waiter nodded at me, acknowledging my nerves and helping me calm down. I saw him winking at James, a man-to-man sign that he should be confident. I don't think James took it as that.

I was drowning in my own emotions and my heart was thumping so hard he would have seen it if it looked at my chest for any length of time. Not just the furtive glances when he thought I wasn't looking. I couldn't focus on what he was saying and certainly couldn't toy with him. I struggled to sound happy and keep my happy face on. I could tell I was being blunt, pretentious and obtrusive, but I couldn't collect my thoughts. I need quiet, just for a moment. I needed him to shut the hell up.

"Have you noticed it's an automatic human reaction to fill any silences with speech? More so in the Western world, but it's still incredibly common. It's like the silence scares us. We're terrified we might talk about something important to us. Something honest and true."

He sat in stunned silence and I sipped my drink, letting the potent alcohol calm my nerves. The spinning abated and the ache in my Solar Plexus Chakra lessened long enough to take a few deep breaths.

I continued to talk and tried to get him to open up a bit, he seemed like he was at a job interview and it irritated me. I pushed his buttons, tried to make him annoyed and tried to get him drunk. He fought me at every turn, but when I asked about the other girl I thought he was going to walk out. I was sure I had blown it so I told him the truth, after all, he suspected what I was doing.

"I'm sorry. I hate small talk and I want to be honest from the start." *FUCK! What if he picks up on that? It's one date. The start of what? We don't know what it is.*

*OK, breathe, stay with it. You don't know what these feelings are. Just because he makes you feel like…*

*NO! Not now.* I was still talking. My lips were moving and words were coming out but I didn't know what they were.

He was talking now. I picked up the tail end. "…don't have any tattoos and I'm clean-shaven." The evening picked up from there.

However… I almost walked out when he called me a stalker. I mean just because I vaguely recognised his uniform and then calculated from the bars I saw him into to the location of that building that it was probably his work place; then went back there (a few times) to take a look and make sure that's where he worked, that doesn't make me a stalker. Right? That's just a normal crush. Isn't it?

There's that horrible sinking feeling when you think you've been caught. I suppose when you're used to social media stalking, there isn't a massive jump to real life. *Except one is unhealthy and the other is illegal and they're both wrong.*

Lifting my head from my arms I emptied the bottle into the glass and replayed the last episode. I did want to see this, but I couldn't focus my attention. It was coming up to midnight. *Maybe I should just go to bed.*

I clunked my head down, continuing the post-mortem. The rest of the night seemed to go well and he even kissed me as we left, which was after closing. But what if he can't get over the previous display of crazy? Or the fact we don't like some of the same music. *I mean I know I'm being stupid, especially after that kiss.*

That kiss.

That fucking kiss.

I felt our souls connect, his aura reaching mine and creating fireworks. Our skin sparked wherever it touched and he manipulated my energy without knowing what he was doing. He tasted naïve and malleable, and it made me hungry. All my previous emotions were washed away and I wanted to devour him. I felt a growl rising in my throat and my adrenaline thudding. His ardour matched mine and a simple goodnight kiss was about to turn into something a whole lot less wholesome and much more suitable to adult eyes only.

I pushed him away. I couldn't. I wanted to make him wait. I closed my eyes and breathed deeply, pushing that side down and away. He was delicious and my hunger was quenched off one kissed, but my appetite was wide-awake. So was his. He forced himself towards me my resolve weakened. He has no idea how sexy he was it he was intoxicating. Awesome. There was so much latent energy within him. He's wild. So much passion waiting to tear through his chest.

I wanted to feel his hands on my throat.

I pushed him away again. I knew I needed to wait. I didn't want to give this up yet and I love the chase.

I picked up my phone. Perhaps I should text him. I've never believed in the three-day rule, in fact if my head hadn't been all over the place I would have taken him home. I wanted to. Why didn't I? It seemed so stupid now.

I restarted the episode again, realising I had missed half of it again. *What am I watching?*

I drained my glass and realised I was drunk. Very drunk. The alcohol sloshed uncomfortably around in my stomach and regretted letting my nerves get the better of me: I barely ate that day and large amounts of wine and sushi was making my stomach churn.

**James**

**16**

I stood there with my head spinning, dripping with sweat and more energy than I knew what to do with. My erection throbbed uncomfortably in my boxers. As I walked to the tube station I just about made out a shooting star streaking across the skyline, not quite hidden by the light pollution from the Capital. *Tonight was magical.*

I may or may not have heard a warning crash of thunder before the heavens opened. I started a light jog, along with the other 'bright, young things' that ran screaming and giggling, fearing that the storm would ruin their carefully put together outfits and perfectly coiffed hair. I decided to let the rain ruin my suit and tried to let it clear my head and calm me down in the process.

I saw the world for the first time, but I also felt exhausted from the inquisition that I received over dinner. The sushi wasn't sitting right either. Or - more likely - I didn't know how the date went and I was feeling a little queasy from nerves now my passion had been drenched. *Had I been too forceful? What if I scared her away?* Judging the way she kissed me, I think it went well, but there were a lot of silences. A LOT of silences.

It felt like my first rainfall. The first time I had the cool rain running over my skin and it was beautiful. I could feel the quizzical looks from the people running past me for cover. I slowed my pace to a leisurely walk to savour the feeling. A flash of lightening split the sky in two and I stopped in the street to listen to the thunder before a rather hulking mass of a man barrelled into me swearing. "Get out of the fucking way freak!" he yelled as he ran past me, clipping me with his shoulder on the way.

My senses were alive: this must be what drugs feel like. *Or could I...?* At the very least I cared for Emily. *She's fascinating, odd, intense, but fascinating. I want to know all about her.* Now I was confident she wasn't stalking me and I was just paranoid, I definitely wanted to keep seeing her. Although, the large amount of paranoia I was now experiencing was concerning.

I turned into the tube station; cautious not to slip on the tiled floor as my shoes were soaked, but I found myself striding across the station and run down the stairs without a problem, leaving a trail of footprints and drips. *I can't do this sober and dry!*

I stood on the tube, so I didn't soak the seats and contemplated texting her when I got home. *Would it be too soon? I suppose so.* I was always told to play it cool, but why? If you like someone shouldn't you let him or her know, rather than playing games with their emotions? I was musing over the predicament when I saw two young women in jeans and matching coloured coats giggling at me.

"Ladies." I doffed my non-existent cap and they laughed harder. Nothing could ruin my mood, even coming back to see Alice mounting Nathan on the sofa and kissing in a way that should have been reserved for the bedroom. She was topless and I got a great view of her assets as she tried to pull her shirt back on. She had a wonderful... pair of eyes.

"You alone then?" Nathan grinned at me, the pig was proud he had been caught.

"How was it?" Alice tried to act nonchalant as she rearranged herself.

"Yes, I am alone and it was good thank you, but I'll talk in the morning." I held my arms out in a T shape and shook some drips into the puddle forming at my feet. "I need to change."

"No brolly?"

"Of course not."

Alice tutted. "You've ruined that suit."

I raised my eyebrows at her. "Sorry Mother! I probably have, but you know what? I don't care." I broke into song as I ran up the stair and jumped in the shower, scolding my freezing skin. The hot water was a stark contrast to the rainwater, but both ran rivers down my back and thighs. I traced the patterns with my fingers, I wasn't trying to get clean I was showering to warm my body: I was a lot colder than I realised.

When I snuggled into bed I took one last look at my phone, deciding to text Emily, but I'd already received a message from her. I realised that I could have damaged my phone in that rain and thanked God that it wasn't.

**I had fun. Next Saturday? My treat. E x x**

I responded, hoping she wasn't asleep yet: it was coming up to one in the morning.

**Of course, you name the time and place. James x x**

*Definitely should have bought that lottery ticket.*

**Emily**

**10**

When I woke up in the morning, with a dry mouth and uncomfortable ache in my temples I realised I had text him. And he had text back. *I have a second date!* It was almost enough to make me feel less hungover. *Now who says drunk texting is bad for you?*

James

17

That night I dreamt about her. We were walking towards each other in a crowded room, she in a long flowing dress and I barefoot and in a suit. We kissed when we met and the scene around us exploded becoming fire, colour, light, molecules and atoms. We were in the middle of a scene in a summer blockbuster film. It was so vivid and I was lucid, so I looked her in the eyes and asked if I was dead. "No, of course you're not, I'll always protect you."

When I woke up I could smell her perfume, I could taste her and feel the bruising on my lips from our kisses. *Oh no. Oh no. Oh no. I love her.* I was utterly certain that I loved Emily and in a way I never have - and never would - love anyone and I was terrified. One date and I loved her? *What if she didn't love me back? It would break me.* I couldn't think like that. I couldn't think about it at all!

Thank God for Nathan. Nathan is always a wonderful and welcome distraction: I got a dressing down for texting her straight back, apparently my first thought was correct and I should have played hard to get. I pointed out the fact that he never played hard to get.

"It's different for me because I don't struggle to pull. Anyway, what do you mean? I play it cool. I am cool."

"But you're not hard to get."

"What are you trying to say?"

"It's easier to name the women you haven't slept with." His face pinched. "I have, in fact, ordered the paperwork for you to change your name to Bike." His scowl deepened. "Because everyone's had a ride on you."

"Yes, I got your joke. Very funny." My reflexes must be awesome because I managed to catch the cup he lobbed at my head before it smashed against the wall - or maybe he's not a very good shot. He skulked back upstairs to Alice, they were spending Sunday in bed, *I swear they do nothing but eat and rut.* Jealous? Me?

He did look offended, but he needed bring down a peg or two acting like I knew nothing about women. *You know nothing about women. That's not the point.* I argued with myself whilst I fixed Susan a mug of coffee. She'd plonked herself at the table with her head in her arms, making pretend snoring noises. Poor girl had a difficult night, the union was discussing strike action again and she was in two minds about whether or not she supported the strikes. She supported her colleagues but she didn't know if she believed in the reasons to strike. We were discussing the pros and cons for the majority of an hour, but in the end I had to hold my hands up in surrender.

"I haven't lived here nearly long enough or have enough information to comment. You do what you think is right and I'll be hear to make you coffee and be a giant listening ear." I literally held my hands up in surrender and she laughed. That seemed to be enough to calm her nerves and she headed off to commandeer the TV to watch her various documentaries on castles, history, yetis? I try not to be in the room when she's watching them.

I decided to make the most of my mood and this sudden uplift in energy and searched for London running routes and took the Three Parks run through Kensington Gardens, Hyde Park, Green Park and St James' Park. It was difficult weaving in and out of tourists, but the scenery was beautiful. *London is a magical city,* I thought as I stopped to catch my breath. I even called Mum and Dad when I got home to fill them in on my date.

"How did you meet?"

I explained.

"And that doesn't seem odd to you?"

I explained again in more detail.

"Still seems odd. What does she do?"

I explained that as well.

"I think I'll have to meet her."

"No! It's been one date!"

"What happened with Sarah?"

"Oh I don't know."

Did I mention that Mum is very critical? I decided not rise to her probing and continued on with my positive Sunday. I was improving my life this weekend.

I dropped Robert a line as I'd been neglecting him recently and I barely heard from him now, so we arranged for him to come and stay a week on Saturday. Nathan and I would take him drinking and hit a couple of fancy London clubs, I didn't know if Nathan was free, but I would make sure he rearranged his plans for a good ol' boys night out.

**Emily**

**11**

That night I dreamt about him. We were walking towards each other in a crowded room: he was barefoot and in a grey suit and a white shirt. The top few buttons were undone and I could see his chest hair. His hair was greying, a similar colour to his suit.

When I looked at his face there were creases around the eyes. His eyes were piercing though and he spoke to me, through the dream.

"You're dream walking." I said but he didn't hear me, he just kissed me and our energies combined causing sparks and fireworks above us, around us and within us. In that moment my heart exploded, tears ran down my face as I kissed him. I could taste his lips and feel the pressure.

I laughed when he asked me if he was dead.

**James**

**18**

Emily and I arranged to meet at 10am the following Saturday outside my work, unfortunately the waiting made the whole week was utterly unbearable, which in turn made it a real struggle to keep up my good mood.

Work dragged. A wet week meant hours could go by without anyone walking it. I got caught up on the world news (bad); how the economy was doing (worse) and completed a few crosswords (not too bad). I definitely wasn't trying to make sure I had topics of conversation for Saturday. I don't know why one would think that... We would anyone think that...

I spent my days fending off questions from The Girls, but as adorable as it was that Gemma and Alice were happy for me, I couldn't handle the questions. Plus, I was also worried I was going to blurt out my true feelings. Although I hadn't dreamt about her again I was still certain I was in love. This felt like love. Part of me knew this could just be a stupid crush and I couldn't risk anyone confirming my suspicions: I was enjoying my obsession - my addiction - and I wasn't ready to give it up.

In my lunch breaks I went shopping for cool, but casual outfits. Emily had sent me a short message about having planned a day out for us and I should wear "comfortable shoes", which sounded ominous. I felt more than a little out of my comfort zone having no control, I was used to being the group organiser. No really! Whenever I did anything I made sure I had at least a hand in organising it. Believe it or not I am a bit of a control freak.

I was alone most evenings. Nathan was spending the week at Alice's and I was pretty certain that he was still pissed at me, or because he and Alice were getting serious. It had only been three months but they seemed to spend all their time together.

On the plus side, they had stopped giving me the visceral details of their sex life at work and at home and on night's out. Instead, I only had to see them snuggling together on the few occasions Nathan stayed at home.

I didn't mind, I like my own company and it gave me a chance to carry on with my health kick: healthy dinners, cleaning, running, and push-ups. I was starting to look ripped. *If I do say so myself.* I was also planning our lad's weekend, mostly because I had no idea where he would sleep: there were no spare rooms. He was insistent on three things:

1. Booze.

2. Steak.

3. Women.

I found:

1. Multiple bars.

2. A steakhouse

3. A strip club.

I would never admit it to Nathan and Robert, but I really didn't want to visit the strip club, not because I wasn't interested in the women, some of them were phenomenal, but because I'm not interested in the concept. I couldn't see the point in strip clubs. I would rather a woman take her clothes off or dance for me because they wanted to, not because I was paying them.

I've also been told I'm cheap.

I knew once Robert had a few drinks he'd forget about the strip club anyway.

By the time Saturday rolled round my home was clean; my body was a well-oiled machine; my outfit was on point; I'd lost a few pounds and my nerves were shot to pieces. *What if she cancels? What if she's not interested? What if I scared her away?* She'd been very distant, I didn't hear from her for most of the week and I was getting paranoid. *Only the paranoid survive.*

This time she was only 20 minutes late and came jogging up, bag bouncing at her thigh, in a sturdy looking pair of ankle boots and tight fitting jeans and a thick, loose hanging, black wool jumper. She looked like a student. *How old is she?*

"Sorry! Sorry! Sorry! I had a clothing nightmare." I leaned in to politely kiss her cheek in a greeting, pleased that she had at least arrived. Once again, I was casually leaning in a doorway, alone, contemplating the very real possibility that she had stood me up. And once again, my stomach was churning and I was trying to decide whether I could get away with vomiting in a nearby alley. There were only a few people walking through.

The nausea was exacerbated when she cheekily turned her head to meet my lips. I almost pulled my head away in shock, thinking that was my error but her arms wrapped around my body and her tongue, seeking mine, slipped between my lips. She made a happy moan in the process. I melted into her, my legs quivering and threatening to buckle underneath me.

When she pulled away I could feel the warmth of her smile and her eyes searching mine: I stood with my eyes closed for a few more seconds. Savouring the moment. Savouring her kiss. "Come on."

"Hmm?"

"Coffee?"

"Hurble."

"I'll take that as a yes." She linked her fingers in mine - her hands were freezing but she was a lot more animated than our first date. "So we're starting with coffee, then I thought we could go for a walk and I have booked us dinner later."

"Where?"

"Not telling, it's a surprise." The tension returned at this point, I couldn't handle not knowing and not being in control. *Will you stop being a control freak?* She must have sensed my muscles tighten she stopped me in the street to kiss me again. "Do you trust me?"

"Implicitly." I said with my eyes closed, realising it was true. She smiled again.

"You probably shouldn't, you know. We don't know each other that well."

"Then I don't trust you, tell me where we going now."

She punched me lightly on the arm with her free hand. "My, aren't we forceful?" She winked. She winks a lot.

I was tugged me towards a French patisserie where we settled over drinks that she paid for: mine a standard, large, filter coffee, Emily's an extra hot, Matcha green tea latte with almond milk and a shot of vanilla.

"Do you order that to confuse the staff or do you actually like that drink?"

"I like it." She sipped the steaming pool of luminous green. "But the look on their face is always priceless. Anyway, they have to work for their tip."

"You've said that before, don't you believe in tipping?"

"I was joking." She said icily.

I tried to lighten the situation by asking the boring questions about her week and her evenings. Apparently, a bit of an exercise fanatic, every evening was spent down the gym and cooking when she got home.

"I make an amazing carbonara." I bragged, polishing my nails on my lapel.

"It won't be better than mine. Maybe we should cook together next time." She sipped her drink as I waggled my eyebrows at her. "But don't get any ideas boy."

I struggled to keep the conversation going as all I could think was: *Tell her you love her! Tell her you love her! Tell her you love her! Tell her you love her! Tell her you love her!*

*Tell her you love her! Tell her you love her! Tell her you love her!* It's hard to concentrate when you have the verbal equivalent of a steam train looping round your frontal cortex.

"What about you? How are Nathan and Alice?"

"Did we talk about them last week?"

"You don't still think I'm stalking you do you? You said your best friend was sleeping with your co-worker, of course I'm going to remember a story like that."

"Oh no! I don't think you're stalking me, I just couldn't remember what I said about them. They were on the sofa together when I got home that night."

"Awkward?"

"Very. Luckily I only saw Alice's top half. They keep asking about you."

"What are they asking?"

"Everything, they didn't think you existed for a while."

"A while? Why would they think that?" *Oh shit.* Now I would have to explain.

"Well I kind of mentioned the few times we met before and they started to doubt your existence. Seeing as I never had your name, or had evidence."

"That wasn't Alice with you in the bar?"

"No, that was Gemma and I didn't mention you to her, and she hasn't talked about the fact Alice told her about you."

"This is getting a little confusing." She made a little slurping noise. *She's adorable.* "I did make an impression then." She tended not to look at me when she wanted to drive home a point. A silence followed as she finished her swamp-like drink and I finished my pint of coffee.

"Are you sure you enjoyed that?"

"What the drink? Yes, it's delicious, plus Green Tea is good for you."

"It was glowing. It looks nuclear or like pond water. Do I need to get out a Geiger Counter?"

A short tube ride later we were strutting hand in hand round St. James Park where we got in the way of joggers and buggies, whilst I got the third degree about my career prospects by this woman who interviews people and sniffs out liars for a living.

"Are you sure you're not a spy?"

"I couldn't tell you if I was. Do you always insist on questioning me?"

"Yes. It's only half as much as you question me."

"So what do you want out of life?"

"Wow, I wasn't prepared for that. Deep."

"Fuck the small talk, remember? Tell me about you. Where do you see yourself in five years time?"

"I don't know yet. I feel like you're interviewing me."

"Not at all, I just want to get to know you."

"It feels like you already know me pretty well." I was starting to feel uncomfortable again, it was bad enough having someone else take the lead, but Emily could be very intense, almost dominating. I tried to relax again, but I could feel my palms sweating, I let go of her hand and subtly wiped them on my jeans.

"I believe it was Oscar Wilde who said 'I love to talk about nothing. It's the only thing I know anything about.'" *But she hates small talk,* I thought. She had a quiet, sad chuckle to herself.

"Your humour is very dry."

"Come on, you must have some idea." She ignored my comment. *Breathe James, be honest, that's all she wants.* We sat down on a free bench, I kicked back walking two women with buggies walking by: there was a young, blonde boy in dungarees running in between them.

"I moved here because my mum had a baby and there wasn't enough room for all of us. I was in a dead end job in the town I grew up in and, to use an old idiom, I was going nowhere fast. I started to worry I would just exist and drift through life without living it. When I told Nathan I was flat hunting Nathan said we should move in together in London, it was a chance to experience new things." I continued to watch the mothers. "Yes, I'm in another dead end job, but at the moment I don't care, I've visited art galleries, museums, tried new food and met interesting people." I paused to gesture to Emily who was turned away from me watching a man with a German shepherd.

"So where do you see yourself in five years time?" She repeated without looking at me. We sat in silence for a few more minutes: I didn't like this line of questioning.

"Like I said, I don't know. I can't picture where I'll be in five months or five weeks, so at the moment, all I want to do is live in the moment, take each day as it comes and enjoy it."

"Mindful." Her arms were crossed and lips were tight. I grunted a question in response. "Mindfulness, trying be in the moment rather than worrying about the future or the past. That's a good way to be. So is there anywhere in particular you would like to go today?"

"Don't think you're getting off that lightly. Where do you see yourself?"

"With you." With that I was mute. My tongue was suddenly too big for my mouth and I gawped at her, trying to work out how to respond to that.

"I'd like that." Date two and we were both in deep.

The mood lightened once we'd both started to acknowledge our mutual feelings. We chatted for a while, laughing at Nathan and Alice's insistence that I needed to find myself a woman and how quickly he had managed to settle down with her.

She told me about her friends Tamzin and Beccy, both very different people by the sounds of it, but both single. Tamzin was a teacher for primary aged children; fluent in French; loves her job; asexual with no interest in a relationship. Beccy: Estate Agent; a bit older than Emily and in and out of bad relationships.

"I mean it's my opinion - behind closed doors it may be different - but she's a sucker for the 'Bad Boy' type but unfortunately it means she ends up with the worst people sometimes."

"Oh yeah?"

"Yeah she... I've had to pick her up a couple of times from an ex's house. Nothing physical." She answered pre-emptively. "She just got upset."


We walked and talked, until the temperature dropped and our stomachs started grumbling.

Turns out she shares a flat in Chiswick. "It's not much, but I've made it mine. I have a lot of art on the walls, I wanted to paint a mural but I wasn't allowed."

"You paint?"

"Not well but it's about self-expression and art is subjective. I like my work, but I'm not technically skilled. You won't see me in the Louvre any time soon. Unless I was visiting of course."

"Oh of course." *Note to self, I need to take her to Paris.*

"Come on, time for dinner. I wanted to impress you."

We ran together, Emily dragging and pulling me along until we reached the OXO Tower. The view from the restaurant was utterly spectacular. I looked out across the Capital and took in the view of my home and life. It never ceased to amaze me that such beauty could exist in such a busy locale, full of polarising architecture and people. I sat across from my love, the most beautiful woman I've ever seen, eating a delicious meal and looking at this view. Until this point I had never believed that life could be perfect, but right now, right in this moment it was.

Emily looked up, a mouthful of beef stopping her asking the obvious question about what I was thinking. I had stopped eating and had sat there for about five minutes in silent contemplation. In response I took her hand and gazed into her eyes, willing her to know my feelings. And for a moment, I thought she did and I thought I knew hers. *How could we fall so hard and so fast?* In the back of my mind I worried that the brightest stars burn out the fastest, which surely meant we were doomed. I shook my head and went back to my meal, trying not to think about it.

After the meal we walked to the tube together, but this time I didn't push for her to take me home or for her to come back to mine. I gently kissed the top of her forehead and held her in my arms, breathing in her perfume. And for the second time this evening life was perfect. Once again time seemed to slow whilst I was with her and the people walking around us melted into colours, pixels and shapes. I could hear nothing but Emily's breathing and see nothing but the atoms that connect us all.

"Next weekend?" She asked muffled by my chest. Reality came crashing around me and I saw a group of football lads in blue laughing at our public display of affection. I didn't care, I held her for longer.

"I can't, sorry. I promised a Boy's Weekend with Robert. He's coming down from York." I added; my Northern twang accentuated on the word 'York'. Emily giggled mimicked me. "Don't laugh at my accent." I tickled her and she squealed with delight as I leaned in to kiss her again. "One evening afternoon work?"

"I'll struggle with that. How about the weekend after Rob's?"

"That sounds like a plan."

"It certainly does. I think I hate that phrase, it just sounds stupid. Fill words."

"And I know how much you hate fill words and small talk." I interrupted laughing. "It will be our third date…"

"Don't make any assumptions boy." She winked as she walked away. I could still smell her perfume and taste her on my tongue: *I don't think I could get any happier.*

**19**

Work ruined that happiness: work dragged. I was busy, but it was repetitive and unchallenging: I was starting to feel stagnant, which must have been Emily's effect. She insisted on challenging me, plus in the two weeks since we'd started dating, I'd gotten into the habit of living for the weekends, as it meant I saw her. She was never available during the week, but we spoke every day by text.

Repetitive as my life had become I was getting in quite good shape as I spent my evenings running and doing strength exercises in my room. I contemplated joining a gym but it seemed like a waste of money.

Did I mention I've been called cheap?

"Looking good Jim." Susan catcalled as I walked out of the shower with a towel round my waist. I no longer hid my body in shame: my former stockiness was forming into muscle quite nicely.

"Feel free to stop by my room if you want a better look."

"Oh Sir! Someone is getting confident," She pretended to be shocked and fanned herself with the papers in her hands, "but I think your new girlfriend would rip my eyes out if I did, wouldn't you agree?" I knew she was referencing the date with Rachel and I would never admit it, but Susan was right, Emily probably wouldn't be happy.

The biggest problem I had was I was starting to miss Nathan, we still did the Friday night drinks thing, but he was never in for dinner: he was always with Alice. I mean I was happy for him, he seemed more settled and calm now he was no longer chasing tail, but I was feeling a little lonely. I've known him for about 13 years - we met at school.

Robert, Nathan and I were joined at the hip from the moment we met at secondary school. Nathan was surprisingly awkward and nervous when he was younger; Robert was the confident one who kept the bullies away and I've always been a bit socially awkward. Not nerdy, I'm not a computer geek or into fantasy books/movies/games, but I've always blended into the background. As we got older Nathan and Robert would get the girls and I'd always be the friend and confidant. Don't get me wrong, I'm not complaining I'm not one of those prats that think if you're friends with a woman it means you have the right to get inside her, but it would have been nice to be considered sexy.

Then I met Sarah and it all changed. We had our sexual awakening together and I realised I could be sexy. I had the ability to make her feel wonderful and it was great. *I worry I've lost that now, seeing as Sarah and Rachel won't speak to me again. I hope Emily won't run away.*

This weekend the boys were going to hit the town hard. You could tell that was Robert's plan as he came barrelling up to me at King's Cross, cracking me on the back and making me cough. He was certainly glad to see me and I realised quite how much I missed him. I didn't see him enough when I was home last. I thought he seemed more pleased to see Nathan seeing as he picked him up and span him around, but Nathan looking horrendously humiliated and I realised he did it to embarrass him.

Robert was a great mountain of a man: a big lad, bearded and a keen rugby player, he was a software developer for a little organisation in York and his accent was a lot thinker than the both of us put together.

"Pub?"

"Of course." It was 11am - the old Nathan was back on top form.

"Tell me you have a strip club planned for this weekend?"

"Of course!" I could almost taste the hangover already.

It's a well-documented fact that you're supposed to have two litres a day, probably not two litres of beer and definitely not before 1pm

After the pub - for breakfast and pints - we hit a cocktail bar. After the cocktail bar it was a Mexican restaurant for Burritos and Tequila. After the restaurant it was another pub, then another bar. Luckily for me, Robert got plastered quickly and distracted by the amazing pairs of legs around us, and we ended up skipping out on the strip club. It was a lot warmer down south and the women were out without coats. We ended up at a swanky underground club.

We could hear the music from the street: this place played upbeat house music. It was getting quite nippy for an April night and the temperature dropped rapidly after the sun set, but thank goodness it wasn't raining, judging by the clothing and the hair of the other patrons. Nathan's eyes were popping out of his head.

As we entered my eyes adjusted to the lack of light and I tried not to slip down the stairs. Nathan managed to get us on the guest list for as it was apparently **the** place for the celebrities, or at least some of them, to dance and get drunk. I sure as hell didn't recognise anyone, but I'm not hip to popular culture. I mean I just used the word hip!

We squished our way to the bar, sweating bodies pushing up against us, simultaneously thrilling and awkward. *What a strange thought? I've never thought of it that way before.* The girls in ridiculous dresses were dancing on chairs and the tables had half full glasses and bottles with sparklers in.

We found a table to lean against while we had a couple of drinks to top up our Dutch Courage. *Please don't throw up. Please don't throw up.* I was feeling pretty quite tipsy, but it was also the first time in weeks that I felt completely out of place, I thought I was settling into this life, but I sat shifting nervously in my seat, uncomfortable in my clothes. Robert was in his element and Nathan was relying on me to be good.

"For God's sake Jim, you've got keep me away from these women." He said as he rubbernecked a blonde in a black cat suit that left almost nothing to the imagination.

"That's quite a feat actually." I was staring as well. "She looks modestly covered but I'm pretty sure I have an accurate image of her naked."

"YOU'RE NOT HELPING!" Nathan bellowed over the music.

The Boys say I have no rhythm whatsoever, but what I lack in rhythm I make up for in enthusiasm and I joined Robert on the small square of space they called a dance floor. The music pumped through my body and my ears were already ringing, but I felt a strange feeling of euphoria from the adrenaline and alcohol. Although, for some reason my attention was drawn back our table where Cat Suit was giggling and flicking her hair towards Nathan who was lapping up the attention, of course. Then I turned round and Robert was rubbing himself up against a leggy beauty with black curly hair, they were grinding in a vaguely inappropriate fashion and I contemplated telling him to calm down but Nathan was my priority.

I plonked myself next to him and grabbed my drink, which was right in front of Cat suit: he glared at me. I took a big gulp of my drink and said: "Alice."

"Damn it," he mouthed before leaning into the blonde again, who abruptly got up and left looking put out. "I want to hit you right now," he chugged he drink and pointed towards the bar "but thank you, I owe you one. A fresh one? Where's Robert? When do you want to head off?" I pointed towards the dance floor where Robert's tongue was firmly lodged down the girl's throat. "Bloody hell! Is he staying with us?"

"Yeah, I've set up a bed on the floor or Andy said he can crash on the sofa if he wants."

"We might need to give him his stuff back in the morning." And in the perfect example of comic timing, we watched her slap him and storm off with a couple of other people. "Yeah, he's still handsy then." Nathan yelled, laughing. Let's say his hands went... wandering and not all women want to be felt up on a dance floor in front of a couple of hundred of people.

"So what's happening with Emily?" Nathan asked as Robert came over looking simultaneously ashamed and proud, which shouldn't be possible. *I guess tonight is another night of wonders.*

"Yeah, you mentioned her briefly earlier."

"There's nothing to say, we've had a couple of dates."

"And...?" Nathan had greatly improved his interrogation skills since being with Alice.

"And we've kissed, that's it."

"When are you seeing again?"

"Next weekend."

"Third date? You going to seal the deal?"

"I would like to. I mean she's gorgeous, but I don't want to ruin things."

"DO IT! DO IT! DO IT!" They chanted.

I pointed to the bar. "Nathan, you said it's your round, get 'em in and then let's go. I'm exhausted."

We stay for another four and crawled out the club at 3am and I certainly tasted my hangover the next day. You would think I would know my limits by now. "I want to diiiiiiiie." I groaned as I vomited for a third time. "Why can't I keep water down? I want to eaaaaat."

"You're becoming a Southern pansy." Robert laughed chewing noisily on a bacon butty. I could hear every bite and tear and the smell made my empty stomach heave.

In my life there seemed to be a direct correlation between how fun the night was and how bad I felt the next day, and this time I felt like my head was being split in two by a tiny man with a jackhammer and golf spikes on his feet. I was huddled on the bathroom floor letting the tiles cool down my soaring body temperature, trying work out whether I felt better with my eyes open or closed. It didn't seem to make any difference, so I lay watching the light-fitting whirl around and around, before I slammed my head back into the U-bend and prayed to the porcelain God.

"I'll take Rob to King's Cross." Nathan yelled from the other side of the bathroom door. He sounded like he had his mouth full and I could hear him chewing. *Why are my senses heightened? Let this hell end please?* "Drink some water and do you want anything to eat?" I responded with a loud zombie groan between retches.

I finally crawled back into bed when Susan threatened to kick the door down and step over me to shower if I didn't get out. I unlocked the door and - true to her word - she stepped over me to switch on the shower squirting me with the head to get me moving quicker.

I spent the rest of the day switching between unconsciousness, the bathroom floor and watching bad horror DVDs, finally arising from the brink of death to crawl to the fridge at about 8pm. Nathan walked in to seen me shirtless, sockless and leaning in the fridge.

"Hungry?"

"Just about. I can feel myself wasting away." I poked at my stomach to emphasise the point. "I really fancy pizza."

"Look in the freezer." There was a double pepperoni pizza just waiting to be cooked. Nathan was smiling.

"I could kiss you! You know me so well."

I left Nathan a slice and climbed back in bed to eat it. I lay there watching Freddie vs. Jason and looking forward to Monday, as this hangover would end.

Of course I was wrong and I had my first experience of a two-day hangover.

**Emily**

**12**

**(B) I need to speak to you. Xx**

**(Me) What now? I've just got in from the gym. I'm cooking. Xx**

**(B) Yes now. Are you about? Xx**

**(Me) What did I just say? Hold on, I'll phone you. Xx**

When I answered the phone Beccy was making strange gurgling noises. "Beccy?" I was greeted with the sound of a sniff, cough, a gulp and a couple of wheezing noises. "If you don't speak I'm going to call the police, you sound like you're dying."

"He can be such a jerk sometimes."

Hung my head and kept my eyes shut as I spoke. "Is this the guy with the chest and the suit?"

"Yes, John." *How is this woman older than me?* I plugged in my hands-free set and continued cooking. Beccy was... melodramatic might be a little too harsh, but as a self-confessed princess I can't think of anything else. And somehow, even though she had 10 years on me, she had much less life experience. I assume this was the reason that she had a terrible time with the opposite sex.

"He said he's not looking for anything serious." I chopped up some vegetables, stirred the premade pesto in with the pasta and added the last of a pack of ham for protein. I'm not a fan of cooking for one. I like pesto and I like vegetables. And chilli, I stirred in some habanero flakes.

Do you want the background on John? This is an interesting one. They met on Tinder (of course, doesn't everyone these days) and hit it off; same taste in music, movies, similar humour. He seemed to good to be true... So they went on a date, and it went well. So they went on a second date the next day, and that went well. They kissed that evening and had their third date the following weekend, then the fourth, which is when they - *finally* - slept together. She thought by holding out it would make him more interested...

*I now return you to your regularly scheduled programming.*


"And it was by fucking text? What kind of man dumps someone by text?" I thought back to a couple of my exes as I shovelled my green and beige meal into my mouth.

"Well maybe he wanted to avoid..." *This,* is what I mouthed. "...a confrontation." is what I said. "I've done it before. He's not good enough for you." I clicked open my laptop and started watch Preacher repeats with the subtitles on. I mouthed along to Beccy whinging.

"But what's wrong with me? Why can't I keep a man?"

"Why do you feel the need to evaluate your self-worth based on the interests of the opposite sex?"

"I just want a nice guy that tells me I'm pretty."

"There are thousands of those: you're fussy." That was when she started arguing with me. I let her rant and rave, she'd be fine soon, but I was uncomfortable enough speaking on the phone, let alone having to deal with large amounts of emotions being hurled into my ear holes. *This is how I spend my Saturday night? When did I get so boring?* I thought about James and wondered whether it's too early to text for a booty call. Granted, I was doing a Beccy, I was holding out, but my reasons were very different to hers.

*Are they? Remind me again why we're holding out?*

*Some modicum of self-control.*

She was still talking when I switched on my laptop and started watching something with the sound down and subtitles on. To this day I can't tell you what she said, but I must have made the right noises in the right places because she text me telling me I was a good friend.

**James**

**20**

Standing on the tube the rocking motion, usually soothing - like a mother with her child - made my head pound and my stomach churn. I sank to the floor, much to the disgust of the commuters around me, with my head in one hand and the other desperately trying to fish out the bottle of water from my bag. I ended up getting off a stop early and walking the remaining distance.

"You look like hell!" Nathan's brutal honesty was rubbing off on Alice. That or they were a lot more alike in the first place

"Why are two day hangovers a thing?" I groaned still shielding my eyes from the unnaturally bright sunlight through the door and the painful fluorescent strip lighting we sit under.

Gemma placed a hot of coffee and a fresh glass of water in front of me. "You need to stay hydrated. And distracted, most of this will be in your head and you don't want the blues to kick in. How was your Boy's Weekend? I'm guessing it was fun."

"The blues? What? I'm going to get depressed?"

"You may get sad, but you won't be depressed. Depression is medical, and this is self-inflicted, dehydration and exhaustion."

I spent the morning giving them details of between customers, steadily starting to feel better and by lunch I was famished. They burst out laughing when I told them about Robert, and Alice asked me how Nathan behaved, then flushed, looking embarrassed and proud, when I told her he was on his best behaviour. They were good to me and I'd been neglecting their friendship recently. If I was being completely honest with myself I was jealous of Nathan and Alice's relationship. I had doubts initially and I was concerned he was going to hurt her, but they were really happy and she knew how to put him in his place.

I thought Gemma a busybody, but she genuinely did care and just wanted to make sure that I was happy and healthy. I made a mental note to arrange a dinner out: I hadn't met Gemma's fiancé - James - but she talked about him enough. And I'm sure I could convince Emily to meet my friends. How would they react to her? She can be intense. *It will be fine. I'm sure it will be fine.* I would ask later them all later in the week, once I was completely straight and sure that this was a good idea. Plus, it will look like I'm only asking them out of gratitude for nursing me. It wasn't. *Really!*

It was at that point that I realised I worry too much and the blues had well and truly kicked in. I was quiet for the rest of the afternoon and indulged in the melancholy.

That evening, in an attempt to rid myself of the remaining toxins coursing through my system, I went for a 10 mile run, all be it at a much slower pace than I would usually run. My running mantra tonight being: 'I hate this. Why am I doing this? I'm tired. I want a donut. My legs feel funny. Can I go home yet?'

As I gasped for oxygen on my glorious return, practically dragging myself through the hallway, I fixed myself a large green smoothie on my return. The ingredients being various limp looking vegetables and leftover fruit. I'd forgotten to go shopping so dinner was out of the question and this was at least edible. It didn't make me sick.

I crawled into bed after that and I think I fell asleep before my head hit the pillow. The build up of the lack of sleep, the hangover and the run meant I struggled to keep my eyes open as I pulled off my running gear, deciding to go to bed without showering.

I woke up at late the next morning, feeling grotty and groggy. I hadn't had a sex dream for a while, and I missed the passion and lucidity. I even missed the near constant state of arousal that accompanied them. Or was it that I just missed Emily - I was hearing from her less. She was rubbish at responding at the best of times, now it took days, rather than hours to respond to a message and I was getting paranoid. I'd drunkenly messaged her on Saturday afternoon and she responded on Sunday evening. I replied on Sunday and I didn't hear back until Tuesday morning. I wasn't naïve enough to message her multiple times, but bloody hell I wanted to. Between the distance and the hangover that just wasn't shifting I was starting to think this week couldn't get any worse.

And of course I managed to curse myself with that one.

*How cliché?*

**Emily**

**13**

My wrist vibrated. I looked at the screen and saw Beccy's picture flashing up and I stared it, contemplating letting it go to voicemail. Instead I took my watch off and threw it across the room, sinking back into downward facing dog and attempting to find my centre again. And when I failed miserably I slumped in my knees, sulking.

Don't get me wrong, she's a good friend (she says I'm her best: I don't believe in 'best' friends) but this was getting a bit much. She was calling me every night. She interrupted my runs, my yoga, my gym time. All my me time was being given over to her listening to her whine about a man that didn't treat her right in the first place.

I could feel myself retracting in my own head. I could tell I was being sullen and I was no longer fun to be around. I couldn't even bring myself to get in touch with James. Let alone any of the others I kept on standby.

I mean I'm the one that's supposed to be an energy sucking leech and she was taking all of mine. What does that make her?

*A bigger leech.*

*Thank you for your valuable input.*

*You're welcome.* I heard my phone vibrating on the side now I was back in this world.

"Hi Beccy. You alright?" *I'm too fucking nice.*

**James**

**21**

I'd managed to make it through my first four months of employment here without incident. To the best of Deborah's knowledge I kept my head down, I was polite and blended into the furniture. She either didn't know or didn't care about my frequent hangovers and my sullen periods.

The clientele were polite, but cold: they only acknowledged me when necessary and never held eye contact. I didn't mind. They knew that we covered the Reception for the whole building and had no influence on the organisations with it, so they had no reason to be polite to us. We wouldn't influence their clients/employers/etc. That I minded, but never enough to comment. Until Mr. Smith walked in. Yes, that was his name and not an alias.

Mr. Smith smelled of money, it oozed from his pores. With an expensive suit that was the perfect cut for his build, shoes that looked more expensive than his suit and a smart leather briefcase. He had a thick Scottish accent and fiddled with his glasses while he waited. When he pushed up his sleeve to look at the time I saw he wore the latest Apple Watch, it had only been out a week and surpassed all its competitors so much it sold out in minutes.

He was here to see the investors on the third floor. I hadn't signed Mr. Gregory in that morning, so I was quite certain he wasn't in. I didn't want to make an assumption (my English teacher used to say: "Assume and makes and Ass out of U and Me".) as one of The Girls could have checked him in. As usual I called up to let them know he was waiting and to get authorisation to buzz him through. Then Geoff - Security - would check his pass and lets him through the gate.

"Hi, I've got Mr. Smith here to see Mr. Gregory." I smiled at him: he looked away. *Nice.* "Oh. I see."

"Is there a problem?" He glared at me. *Now he looks at me.*

"When will he be back?"

"He better be in. I've travelled for five hours from Edinburgh to be here." The volume increased in his voice while I continued to try and listen to Jacquie - the PA.

"It's just he's travelled from Edinburgh." Pause. "A five hour journey." Pause "Ah, is there really no-one..." Pause. She was getting irritated now with my persistence. "OK. I'll let him know." I hung up the phone while my heart sunk into my stomach, and judging by the scarlet colour his cheeks had turned I could predict what was to come. "I'm sorry…"

"You're not about to tell me I travelled for five hours and he isn't in? That he's forgotten our appointment?"

"Yes sir."

"And that he didn't think to call and let me know?"

"I'm sorry sir, she said that she tried to get hold of you."

"No-one tried to contact me. Let me up there, I want to speak to them."

"I can't do that sir."

"Let me up there now. I need to speak to someone there."

"Please calm down sir." I saw Gemma wince when I said that. I was trying to diffuse the situation, but the hissy fit that ensued was of Titanic proportions.

"You jumped up little shit! You obviously have no idea who I am if you think you are going to stop me going up there to give them a piece of mind. His business partner must be in at least. That office won't be empty. You stuttered your way through a conversation with someone." He leaned on the desk until he was nearly nose-to-nose. I could smell the coffee on his breath. "I earn your salary in a day: I could buy and sell you." *Seriously? Who says that in real life? I thought it was only said in movies.*

"You're right." A ring of darkness surrounded my vision. "I have no idea who you are." I stared into his eyes and saw how shallow his soul was. He was a walking, talking puddle. "But who the hell do you think you're talking to?" *Oh God, tell me I didn't just say that.* "You think you're a big man talking to me like that?" *Oh God, it is. That is definitely my voice.* I was standing up and leaning over the desk staring him down. I could feel my pupils dilating and his confidence and bravado shrivel.

When Mr. Smith launched himself towards me Geoff intervened and escorted him out the door. I watched him leave as Gemma dragged me away from the desk and the gawping, waiting clientele, who were whispering to each other. She sent me to lunch and told me to "Calm the fuck down. I will have to tell Deborah about this you know." I knew she was right and I knew I was in a lot of trouble. Deborah was going to kill me.

I was hauled into her office that afternoon. "This isn't your first job, you're an adult. I shouldn't have to explain to you that that was an inappropriate way to speak to a customer." I stared at my hands in my lap. "I know he was out of order, but you need to be the bigger person. As a gatekeeper you will get the brunt of their anger sometimes." She sighed. I hadn't spoken since I'd entered her office. "Gregory has asked me to put through disciplinary procedures as he has lost a valuable client. Smith is moving his money elsewhere and he had a **lot** of it."

I took a deep to justify my unjustifiable actions, but she held her hand up and continued. "I know, I know. But Smith was at fault as well, so we'll call this a verbal warning and leave it at that. I know you won't behave like that again."

What I liked about Deborah is that she didn't give a damn about me personally, so she didn't ask me about the change in personality. She hadn't even noticed. I was getting sick of people questioning me.

Nathan greeted me like a proud father when I got home, smacking me on the back and handing me a beer. He proclaimed that I deserved it for showing that I had balls. "Well Jim, I never knew you had it in you." Alice had obviously told Nathan about my little outburst before I go home.

Andy grinned at me as he sauntered down stairs, taking off his T-shirt like a soft drinks commercial; waving it around like a football fan and cheering like a loon.

"Did she call you the minute she left?"

"She text me. What happened?"

Andy put the kettle on and started making tea. I chugged my beer and poured myself a large glass of whiskey. I couldn't explain how I had the nerve to act that way, but I could explain why it happened - Mr. Smith's attitude was the trigger. I sat at the table and stared in my whiskey glass, swirling it round, searching for answers. "It was like... It wasn't me. I've never acted like that before." I got up to leave the room. I didn't want to talk about this anymore. *You need to accept you're changing.* The voice in my head didn't feel like my own. It echoed strangely and I let the words run rings between my ears.

Nathan put his hand on my shoulder and pulled me back. "Dude, you've been different recently, do you want to talk?"

"No." I'd finished my whiskey before I got to the top of the stairs. I felt blue again.

That was Wednesday. On Thursday Emily cancelled our date.

**Emily**

**14**

Jim, I'm really sorry but I'm going to have to reschedule Saturday. Beccy's is going through a bad time of it at the moment and she's feeling really low at the moment. I'm worried about her so I said I would spend the weekend with her to try and cheer her up. Can we move it to the following weekend? E x x x

    I tried not to be angry as I sent the message. I failed. It is very hard when my friend's poor life choices were now effecting my life. I felt like shit. I was getting weak from hunger. I wanted James. I wanted to fuck James. I needed to fuck James. *I knew I shouldn't have played hard to get.*

    That night I went to bed with a bottle of red and my new book, when I should have been going to bed with James.

**James**

**22**

The only plus was I received her message after my evening run, so I didn't feel as guilty for taking the whiskey bottle to bed with me and finishing it in anger and upset. I really needed to scale back the drinking, but not tonight. I lay in the dark and let my mind drift, not thinking about anything. At some point I must have fallen asleep, although it certainly didn't feel like it, because the feeling of lightening bolts piercing the back of my eyeballs woke me up on Friday morning. With the familiar feeling of nausea and the taste of dehydration accompanying it. *I really need to drinks less.*

As I took stock of how I was feeling I became aware that I was still in last night's running gear, with feeling of damp Lycra sticking to me, and the smell of body odour, I wrinkled my nose in disgust. I stared at the rainbow-style artex that patterned the ceiling and there was a long crack running along the coving. I stared at this crack for about half an hour, wondering when it was originally formed; what did it mean; was there subsidence and why the hell was I so fascinated with it. *I can't keep this up. I tried so hard to be the old me and I buckled. I'm just a different James now.* I reached for my phone:

**Yes of course. Same time and place. See you then. J x**

I stared at the crack for a few more minutes contemplating getting up, but my alarm hadn't gone off yet so it was still early. Mum would be up with Grace though... I started typing again.

**Mum, you'd better set up the spare bed; I'll be home tonight. Love you xxx**

I got a response almost immediately.

**(Mum) Oh that's great news! What's happened with Emily then? Xx**

**(Me) Nothing. I'll see you tonight. Xx**

**(Mum) Ah ok. I'll get Dad to get you that whiskey you like. You'll be back late? Do you mind picking something up and I'll make meatballs tomorrow night? Xx**

She knows me too well. When it gets too much for me all I want it my mum and dad to make it better; I want to be big brother and spoil the kids, plus I had a baby sister I'd only met once that needed fussing and cuddling. My phone went off while I was in the shower.

**Yes of course. How about lunch next week? I'm off on Wednesday, or we could catch up in the evening? E x x x**

*She's never free during the week; she must know I'm pissed.* I realised now is my opportunity to play hard to get: she was chasing me now. On the other hand, I'm not that manipulative. Although, I didn't want to miss my run...

**(Me) Running on Wednesday night? X**

**(Emily) Come to my gym! You'll love it. Xxx**

*Three kisses?*

**(Me) I'd rather not thanks. Meatheads in Spandex make me uncomfortable. Swimming? Xxx**

**(Emily) It's not that sort of gym and I'm really not a fan of swimming. We haven't known each other long enough for you to see me without make up. Hope you're well. Xxx**

I ended up deciding to leave it for the weekend: maybe she was just trying to be nice when she offered to see me during the week. I don't know. I was more interested in going home as the homesickness was beginning to kick in.

I packed my bags and took my stuff with me to work and when 5.30pm came I ran straight to King's Cross, skipping the usual Friday night piss up. I was so excited to get back that I didn't even mind that I stood for most of the journey, or the fact a ticket at the station on the day of travel was exorbitantly expensive. Seriously though, I thought it was supposed to be cheaper now it's been renationalised.

This time I wasn't greeted at the station, but it was 9.30pm and raining. I stopped off at the chippy for some proper fish and chips: I wasn't going to have a limp pre-packaged train sandwich when I could the best fish and chips in Yorkshire. I started eating on the walk back, starving as the York air gave me an appetite. I now understood why people walked around London in filter masks. The constant pollution effected my appetite. And it gave me black snot.

Mum squeezed me as I walked in through the door, squishing my chips against my jacket. "Come here you!"

"Mum! Grease!" I tried to move away, but I she gripped me like a constrictor. I just managed to wriggle the chips out of our cinch.

I heard Dad's laughter coming from the other room. "So what happened?"

"Can I at least sit down and get a drink first?" Dad thrust a whiskey into my hand and they both pushed me onto the sofa, spilling some of the whiskey and the remainder of my chips onto my lap. I stared at the marks and made a mental note to find a good dry cleaner. "OK, I get it." I sank into the cushions, kicking off my shoes and letting the weight lift from my shoulders. "Where are the kids?"

"Matthew and Olivia are at sleepovers. Though I'm pretty sure Matthew is at a party, he was wearing a lot of aftershave when he left the house and I've noticed a bottle of vodka has gone missing. Grace is asleep in our room and the bed is set up in your room/her nursery."

Taking a sip of the whiskey (better quality than the dreck I had been buying) I told them how odd I'd been feeling. Mum looked unimpressed when I told her about my outburst at work and when I'd finished venting Dad stated matter-of-factly: "Midlife crisis."

"I'm 25."

"A sub life crisis then. The natural changes you go through as you grow up can be a lot to try and handle. And you've had a lot of changes in a short space of time - new job, new house, new city, new girlfriend and new sister. All these changes can make you feel weird. It's normal."

I smiled, looking at the TV to hide the wetness that was forming in my eyes. Luckily Dad wasn't looking at me, but I felt Mum's burning gaze. *Uh oh.* I blinked away the few tears that had formed. "So Emily." Mum's interrogation was about to begin, which was an excellent distraction from the emotions that were threatening to overwhelm me. "How did you meet?" I told her about falling at her feet at the train station and their collective laughter was so loud it woke Grace. They had a video monitor and she looked adorable in her crib. Mum went to soothe her while Dad and I sat chatting, mostly about news and world events.

"When are you seeing her again?" Dad didn't usually ask questions, that's Mum's area of expertise.

"Next weekend, I'm planning on going for a few drinks. I had planned to take her on the London Eye but..." I paused, unsure of how to finish. "I don't know. I was thinking of something more casual. We've had two romantic dinners and I feel like we need to find a pub and veg there for an afternoon." *Especially after she ditched me this weekend.*

"Good idea." Mum walked back into the room. "You like her then?"

"Yeah I suppose." She stared at me and I knew I had to continue. Mum stares a lot. "OK, she challenges me; confuses the hell out of me; when we're together she makes me happy and when we're apart I miss her. We were supposed to be out this weekend, but she had to see her friend who is miserable."

"Which is why you're here. You're worried she's going to cancel on you completely and you're already in deep." I finished my whiskey in silence. I hated it when people held a mirror up to my feelings. "When are you seeing her again?"

"Next weekend." Dad answered for me.

"Just be careful. I don't want you getting hurt."

## 23

On the journey back to London I contemplated packing it all in and moving back to York. I knew I could crash at Robert's while I found a place, but I shook it off as homesickness. Although, every time I go home I leave feeling more human, more myself, so why wouldn't I doubt my little adventure? My head was clear, the near constant ache in my chest was gone and my temper had relaxed. The further away from Emily I was the less I felt like I was changing. But I missed her so much, and when I was with her I felt whole, like she was making me into someone I was always meant to be.

Although Matthew had plans, I still managed to get him for long enough to catch up. He confided in me that had a girlfriend and he'd started smoking, I told him how much I disapproved of the smoking, but he was growing up and he needed to make his own mistakes. *Yes I am a hypocrite.*

I went shopping with Olivia, who talked me into buying her make up (Mum was going to kill me) and told me about her latest crush - some brown haired boy called Patrick with an Irish accent. He was 12.

Even Grace was already holding her head up by herself. They were all getting so big it scared me, forcing me to accept I was growing up, but I was old enough now that the excitement of getting older was fading. I thought I wasn't ready to take on responsibilities, but I was wrong. Change isn't a bad thing and I had to stop fighting it.

This whole weekend reminded me of my own mortality, which may seem like a negative but was actually very soothing. I felt calm. At peace.

When I walked through the door I wasn't quite greeted with quite the same warm reaction I got from Mum. I, on the other hand, greeted the quiet house with an obnoxious yell from the doorway. "Honey I'm home!" Silence. I heard the TV on and I could sense Nathan's mood from the hallway. It felt thick like I was wading through mud as I entered the front room. He was sat in front of the TV with a stony look on his face. "Alright?"

"Not really."

I put my bag down and sat next to him. "What happened?"

"How was York?"

"Good. Family's good. The kids are good. It's all good. What happened?"

"Alice told me she loves me."

"That's good! How did she say it?"

"With her mouth. Stop saying good."

"It is good... Sorry... You're happy aren't you?" I started to feel like I'd passed my bad luck virus on.

"I didn't say it back. It's really soon and I don't think I do love her. I think I could love her, but I don't think I do."

"Well, it's better to not say it than lie to her, surely?" He looked at me piteously. The same look he gave me whenever I discussed women. *Patronising sod.*

When I returned to work on Monday I was starting to think that - *heaven help me* - Nathan was right, it would have been nicer to lie. She looked like hell. Her face was completely bare of make up, which revealed freckles and a clear complexion and her hair was scraped back from her face. I couldn't work out why she wore make up in the first place, she looked lovely, but you could tell she wasn't making the effort she usually did. Her mood washed over me like a black cloud and again I felt like I was wading through mud. I could feel her embarrassment and rejection.

"You look lovely without make up." *Did I really just greet her with that?* She took a moment to work out whether I was being sarcastic or not. She smiled and bowed her head in thanks, then proceeded to avoid me for most of the day, which was understandable, she didn't want me listening as she poured her heart out to Gemma. They kept disappearing to the bathroom when Alice bubbled over and started to cry. I was grateful for that: the further away she was, the better I felt.


I didn't hear from Emily until Friday and that was only to confirm the time and place for Saturday. I probably would have been more concerned except I had Nathan to worry about. Alice still wasn't talking to him and as he was home every evening I had to forfeit some of my runs to play Agony Uncle and listen him to whine about Alice, over and over and **over** again. He does love her but he's scared: I wished I could just sit them and tell them how they felt, rather than watching them run from it.

Saturday was the highpoint of my week. I met Emily at Euston and she met me with a passionate kiss, which took me off guard and I froze, eyes wide open, as she wrapped her arms around me. *I guess she really missed me.* "I did miss you." She said in agreement to my thoughts.

We went on a pub-crawl around Camden, which was, of course, a much better idea than the London Eye. We finally completely relaxed in each other's company and it turns out Emily is a funny drunk: flirty, giggly and loud, with a wicked glint in her eyes. We swapped stupid stories and she wet herself laughing (*not literally*) when I told her about my run in with Mr. Smith. We were sat next to each other on a sofa and she slapped me on the thigh and left her hand there, caressing my leg through my jeans. "You sound like your changing."

"How would you know? We haven't know each other that long."

"You seem different. More confident."

"I feel more comfortable around you." I thought about Nathan and Alice, *I should tell her.* I put my hand on hers steeling myself for what was to come next. "Emily…"

**Emily**

**15**

By Saturday I was climbing the walls my mind was full of all the nasty things I wanted to do to James. The hunger made my skin itch and my senses peak. I could smell pheromones in the air. The unseasonably warm air made everyone sweat a little more and I was really starting to enjoy my tube rides. *Ride. Gods I want to ride James.*

When I saw him I couldn't control myself, I threw my arms around my neck and kissed him. I felt him tense in surprise and tasted his shock. *I guess she missed me*, ran through my head. "I did miss you."

The first drink went right to my head. *I knew I shouldn't have ordered Gin.* I felt my inhibitions lower and I couldn't help but run my fingers over his thighs: he looked stocky and felt strong. He was still quite young mentally, but physically he was all man. He was maturing rapidly though, this was apparent when he told me about his fight with Mr. Smith.

"So why did you snap like that? You haven't done it before?"

"I haven't had someone speak like that to me before. And…"

"And…?"

"Well, I don't know. I've just been a bit… tense recently." His blush was obvious even in the reduced light.

"You sound like your changing." I picked up my glass, swirling the wine and trying to guide him towards what he is. It's hard to tell someone they're a vampire without them freaking out and calling you crazy (I learnt that the hard way with the ex.)

I stretched out my energy and I could feel the tension, his mind was racing and I drunk in his sexual energy. He was open to suggestion, especially if it lead to him being inside me.

What a thought! I almost couldn't take it. I started to giggle, loudly and slightly hysterically. Then he touched my hand, looking at me with love in his eyes.

*No, no, no, no, no!* I pulled back, spiritually, emotionally and physically: suddenly sober and wishing I wasn't. I downed my drink and refilled quickly. *I need to be drunk.*

*Hurry up! You need to tell him what he is, what you are.* I turned my head and stared at my reflection in the window and started talking without thinking.

**James**

**24**

She pulled away and shifted nervously suddenly sober and cold. "James, stop." She downed her drink and refilled her wine from the bottle on the table. "I need to be honest with you." She inhaled deeply.

"Oh?" I straightened preparing myself for the worst. *I'm just a friend.* I tried not to let the pain I was feeling show on my face. *Fuck. I'm OK, I'm OK.*

"Look at me, I really like you…" My heart flipped. "…and it scares me. I don't want to… I don't want to hurt you." She refilled my glass. "I want us to have some fun, but I'm not worth falling for."

"That's ridiculous. You're intelligent, funny and stunningly beautiful."

"I'm dangerous."

"What is joy without sorrow? What is health without illness? You have to experience each if you're going to appreciate the other."

She stared at me. "Mark Twain. That was a Mark Twain quote right?"

"I have no idea. I thought I was being creative."

"You're not listening to me." She swirled her wine around her glass and looked around at the rest of the distracted crowd, she seemed to be looking to see if anyone was listening or in hearing distance. She looked at me and her eyes seemed darker. "You're right, I'm not like anyone you've ever met."

"Emily, stop this. I…" *Don't say it.* "I care about you, why are you fighting this?"

"Why aren't you listening to me?" She looked exasperated and hurt.

I put her wine on the table and took her face in both her hands. "You make the world stop when I'm with you." I kissed her and it was unlike anything I had ever experienced. I could hear the insects coming to life outside, I could see the stars from behind my eyelids and I could feel a chilling breeze. It was like we were outside. My breath caught in my throat and my head swam, senses burning with the smell of her skin and perfume, the products in her hair. My hands moved down her shoulders and into the small of her back and as I pulled her in closer she tried to pull away.

I kissed her harder and she finally melted into me, resting one hand on my heart, the other on my hip and I noticed her grip was tight and unmoving. My chest burned and I could feel my pulse slowing. The stars span. I opened my eyes and they were still there. Emily's eyes were closed and she moaned and leaned into me. I felt dizzy. *Oh God I'm going to faint.*

**Emily**

**16**

When he kissed me my barriers shattered, the hunger took over and our worlds connected. My teeth ached, I wanted to bite him, rip his clothes off. My fingers dug into his back and pulled him tight into me, drinking every part of him in. I could feel him weakening, I could feel his barriers breaking, but he wasn't feeding from me. It was too much. I tried to push my energy into him, but I couldn't. I was so hungry.

**James**

**25**

She stopped suddenly and pulled back sharply. Her head whipped around to check no one was paying attention to us, but it was like we were invisible. Although, we must have made a scene with that public display of affection.

"I'm sorry." She looked ashamed and tried to go back to her wine, but I was too quick for her. *I'm never too quick for anybody!*

"I'm not. Come with me." We almost knocked over the bottle and our glasses as we sprinted out the bar. We barely made it out the door before I pulled her roughly into me and started kissing her again as we walked out the door. Security just glared at us, I knew they wanted to say something. She pulled me along the street and we ended up at a deserted part of the lock. She pushed me against a wall and her tongue slipped through my lips, her hands exploring my body and running her nails along my back underneath my shirt.

The unabated dizziness merged with the incoming blackness as I fought to pin her arms behind her back. She lashed out and slapped my face, hard, which only shockingly enhanced my passion. I ground my hips hard into hers and kissed, sucked and bit her neck.

"I should stop." She panted.

"Why?"

"Because you'll make me lose control."

I pulled her hair, yanking back her neck. Her mouth made a little O. "That's a good thing."

**Emily**

**17**

My head is spinning and my legs turned to jelly. *I need him. I need him. I need him. I need him. I need him. I need him. I need him. I need him. I need him. I need him. I need to fuck him.*

Get control.

"It's not." I've melted into his body and my eyes were shut. I could feel him probing me, the need was getting too much.

Then he snapped and the real James showed himself.

James

26

"It really is. Give yourself to me." A distant part of me wondered why I said that, but the brain I kept in my boxers didn't care and didn't question.

She span us round so I was pinning her against the cold and clammy wall. She hiked up her skirt, hand on my heart again: her eyes looked black in the shadows. "Do you want me?" Heat spread throughout my body and my chest and crotch burned. I ran my fingertips along her thighs - teasing myself as much as her - and sought out her knickers, which were soaking, she was practically running down her thighs. I couldn't take it and leaned in to kiss her again. "Do you want me?" I nodded. "Tell me you want me."

"I want you."

"Do you need me?"

"Stop…" The need was too great I needed to be inside her.

"Do you need me?" I could feel barriers breaking down. I was a drowning man and she was oxygen.

"I need you."

"How much?"

"For the God's sake woman I love you!" I fell into her.

We dissolved into one and I could smell, taste, touch, but no longer see. My fingers pushed deep into her and she bucked and moaned into me, seeking out my jeans and slipping her hand inside the zip. Her touch was soothing and maddening; we fought for gratification; the hunger and need getting too much when…

The sound of distant laughter and conversation started growing louder. We pulled apart and tidied ourselves up like teenagers behind the bike sheds. I was so frustrated it made me angry, but Emily giggled as we walked nonchalantly back to the tube station. The dizziness was almost too much and I fought to keep upright and there was a nagging pain in my chest. "Yours or mine?" No matter how I felt, I needed to be with her. I needed her.

"Neither." I didn't hide the frustration flashing across my face, followed by blatant disappointment. "Next Saturday? At mine. I'll cook." She winked and walked away before I could protest or say goodbye. And I was left standing alone in a brightly lit tube station, my eyes burning from the light and body weak but burning with unsatisfied lust, chest tight, and clothes, damp, creased and covered in algae, or lichen, or whatever that slimy, green stuff is that grows under tunnels.

**Emily**

**18**

*Why the hell did you walk away?*

    *I don't know.*

    *You don't know!?* I was screaming at myself. I wanted him then and there but part of me wanted to wait. What if I broke him? What if I hurt him like the others? What if he hurt me? What if I fell in love?

    *You are in love.*

    *Exactly! So what if he hurt me?* I sat on the tube home feeling unsatisfied and a little sad, torn between not trying to move to fast and every cell of my being screaming at me to move faster. Part of me hoped that if I dragged it out then maybe it wouldn't be over as fast. Instant gratification is satisfying, but I know me, it's all about the chase.

    *What if it's just the chase for both of us?* Should I follow my gut or my head? My head, which is influenced by the idiotic world around me? Or my gut, which is influenced by my loins?

I finished off a bottle of Merlot when I got home and fixed myself a gin. I shouldn't drink my feelings, but I couldn't think about James anymore. And masturbation made me think about him more.

**James**


27


Sunday I woke up feeling immensely unsatisfied, but pretty amazing, all things considered. Then the memory of telling her I loved her slammed into me like a truck, and the quickly following aftershock was dread.

When realisation hit I sat bolt upright in bed, with my pulled into knees in my chest and my head in my hands. I sank back down groaning and went over every possible excuse I could give for telling her that: the copious amounts of alcohol, the passion, the London smog/air? *Oh God this is so stupid. How is this possible?*

The frustration was more maddening than the embarrassment and the feeling of being utterly exposed: nothing was satisfying me, no matter how many times I tried. In the end I gave up and went for a run. I attempted to run away from my problems, and to distract my body and hands. *Idle hands... I'm going to go blind if I'm not careful.* I contemplated texting her, but what would I say? I decided to wait for her to message me and if she brought it up I would tell her the truth and if she didn't mention it, I wouldn't. I mean perhaps she didn't hear me... Denial is just a river in Egypt.

I found my temper worsening and the ache in my chest, which I had attributed to my emotions, had become a rasping cough that I couldn't clear. I was in pain but the world was bright and beautiful: I felt high, my head light. Though as the day progressed my eyes felt like there were on fire and I felt a fever building. I went to sleep early trying to shake it but by Monday morning I was a mess.

I awoke with a migraine. I assumed it was a hangover because the lightening bolts behind the eyeballs had returned, then I remembered I hadn't drank since Saturday night. Plus, my body was alternating between feverish sweating and freezing and trembling.

I lay with my forearm shielding my eyes from the daylight that creeped in through the gap in the curtains and I called Deborah. There was no way I was going in today. I left a message on her voicemail, text Gemma and went back to sleep. I lost most of the day through unconsciousness. During the short periods I was awake I read, I finally finished Dune and started on a few paranormal fiction books Emily had leant me.

Wednesday came and I just wasn't shaking this, so Mum threatened to come down and look after me. When I started coughing up blood I almost took up on her offer. Luckily I have

Nathan and he insisted on taking me to a doctor. Alice came along too. *Obviously*. I didn't know why, but I was too weak to ask and she did help me downstairs, so I was grateful for her being there.

The pain and burning sensations all over my body seemed to be exaggerated by the doctor's hard plastic chair; strip lights that burned my retinas and his pen tapping, which reverberated in my eardrums. He checked my ears, heart rate, the usual and made unhappy grunting noises as he did. "Have you been swimming in cold water?"

"No."

"Have you done anything physically taxing?"

"I've taken up running."

"Hmmm… I supposed that could do it, but it's highly unlikely."

"Flu?"

"No."

"Have you had a cold?"

"No."

"Have you been ill at all?"

I shook my head. "I've felt a bit out of sorts recently, but I thought it was just life. You know."

"You seem to have a mild case of pneumonia. Don't look so concerned, it is easily treatable." He started writing out a prescription and before I could question him further, I burst into hacking coughs. He handed me two slips of paper as I reeled and rubbed my chest. I decided not to go into more detail about the mood swings, the pain kept my mouth shut. "Take these antibiotics, get plenty of bed rest and try to avoid going outside until you're better. You've been signed off work for the next week and come and see me again next Thursday if you're not better."

Bambi's first steps came to mind as I stood to leave, my thighs quivered and my knees threatened to buckle under my weight. "When you do start running again, wrap up warm." Concern creased the wrinkles in his face further as his pen tapping followed me out of the surgery.

This obviously meant I was going to have to cancel my date with Emily. Between choking coughs I ranted about this to Nathan and Alice on the way home, we took a taxi to avoid the nasty looks from the other commuters. No one likes sharing a tube with someone who is obviously sick because the automatic assumption is that the person is contagious. They exchanged concerned glances when I slammed my fist against the taxi's leather seats, which brought forth another coughing fit and a glare from the driver.

"Damn it!"

"How did you get ill?" It was Alice's turn to start the questioning. I shrugged and repeated what I said to the doctor. She left it at that, which was completely out of character.

I genuinely didn't know how I got ill, it happened so quickly. I was healthy on Saturday and ill on Sunday. I didn't care anyway, I needed to focus on getting better so I could see Emily again.

I text her on the way back and I hoped she wouldn't be mad, that would be quite selfish if she got angry because I got ill. Unless she was mad that I waited until Thursday to contact her. That would be understandable.


I slept the whole of Friday and only woke to take a call from Mum in the evening. She still offered to come down to nurse me, but I assured her I had my own nurses here. Alice and Nathan were still flitting about after me. I saw that I finally had a message from Emily


**Get well soon. X**


It is hard to interpret a message that was only three words long, but it didn't stop me spending Saturday morning trying. I fell straight asleep after reading the message so I didn't get a chance to run it round my head last night.

I stared at my phone and then berated myself for being a poor excuse for a man for not calling her. This went on for a few hours. Being cooped up and feverish had made me feel quite sorry for myself.

I decided to spend the rest of the day curled up in bed watching my favourite zombie movies and whilst completing crosswords on my phone. Distractions. Plus, the antibiotics had started to kick in so I was feeling better, but I wasn't quite of sound mind to do anything too taxing.

**Emily**

**19**

*I fed too deeply. Oh my God I drained his energy and made him vulnerable to viruses.*

*Or he's rundown.*

*Stop kidding yourself.* I paced the bedroom in silence, listening to the sound of my bare feet on the carpet. I needed to think about this properly. Why did he get ill? Because he wasn't feeding on me properly and retaining the energy I was giving, so rather than it being symbiotic, I was leeching. I grabbed my phone off the bed and Googled the leaky bucket story.

"A normal human is like a bucket that has water in it. This water represents energy. When the bucket loses water or it spills out... it can be replaced with more water, and generally stays the same... The Psychic vampire however is like a leaky bucket, with holes in the sides of the bucket...constantly losing water, or energy. The rate, at which one loses the water out of the bucket, depends on how "leaky" the psivamp is. Thus determining how often some psivamps need to feed."

Because he can't retain energy yet I caused him harm, which means I need to give him some to tie him over. An energy transfusion. I ran out the house, grabbing my coat and bag on the way.

**James**

**28**

There was a knock at my bedroom door, assuming it was Nathan or Alice checking in on me I croaked for them to come in. They really had been my personal nurses fetching me food, drinks and damp towels whenever my temperature soared. I owed them for being so kind to me. What I wasn't expecting was a massive bunch of flowers to walk in, and behind it was a nervous looking Emily behind them.

"Shit!" I jumped in shock and quickly started gathering up the snot and phlegm covered tissues I'd left strewn over the bed. *What was she doing here?*

"I also brought chocolate, lemon and honey." She started as if we were mid-way through a conversation. "If you can drink add a drop of whiskey it will help." She still hadn't made eye contact even as she found space on my dresser to put the flowers, which were already in a vase. I recognised it from the kitchen. *How long has she been here?*

The cloudiness in my head was starting to lift just from her being here. "The antibiotics I'm on say I can't drink. I mean the instructions, they don't talk to me, that would be..." Quite obviously it wasn't lifting quick enough. "What are you doing here?"

"I was worried." She fussed with the flowers. *Do I look that bad?* "You look surprisingly well."

"Did I say that out loud?"

"Say what?"

"Never mind. I mean how do you know where I live? I don't remember telling you."

She perched on the edge of the bed and looked at me, for some reason her eyes were wet. "I'm really sorry. I'm sorry I hurt you." I tried to interject, but she wasn't looking at me and wouldn't let me talk. "I... I didn't know... I should have controlled myself. I was so worried I was going to hurt you and I have..."

Maybe it was the illness, but she wasn't making any sense, did she mean she hurt me emotionally or gave me pneumonia. I thought about asking if pneumonia was contagious, but I didn't want to look stupid. She carried on talking, but I couldn't make out what she was saying and she looked like she was going to cry.

"Emily, please stop." I leaned in to hold her and tried to suppress the cough that was forming. "I'm fine. It's basically bad flu. I'll have a couple of weeks off work in bed and I'll be right as rain. It's nothing you've done. You didn't give me pneumonia, it's not contagious." I hoped I was right.

"You seem OK in yourself."

And in a perfect example of comic timing the pressure in my chest swelled and I had a coughing fit. "I am. Don't let the cough fool you I'm the picture of health. Men's Health are round tomorrow for a photo shoot. Now make yourself useful and go get us some popcorn from the kitchen: you can watch Dawn of the Dead with me."

"Original or remake?"

"Does it make a difference?"

She looked at me quizzically. I knew she was trying to work out how ill I was, so I tapped her on the arm and pointed to the door. "Remake. Make sure you return with plenty of snacks."

## 29

*What. A. Night.* She left in the morning.

When Emily got back upstairs she pulled off her boots and jacket and curled up on the bed with me. Her socks had teddy bears on. I pulled a face at her about them, but she ignored me and shoved a handful of popcorn into her mouth. We watched the movie in silence apart from the crunching of us eating.

When the movie ended she moved to leave, but I dumped the empty popcorn bowl on her head and yanked her towards me. She squealed and thrashed about.

"What the hell?"

"You're not leaving."

"You're ill."

"I've never felt better, now put Diary of the Dead on, you'll love it. Are you hungry?" She muttered something about being a servant and having seen the movie. We settled back down and ordered pizza and by the time the food arrived Emily had relaxed and I felt completely well again. My temperature had levelled out and even my coughing had stopped. I made a joke about her being medicinal to me and she offered to give me a massage.

She put on a third movie and ran downstairs to steal Andy's olive oil from the kitchen so she could baste me. I would have complained but I became a puddle the moment she started running her fingers over my skin.

Whilst she was loosening the knots under my shoulder blades she talked about Beccy who seemed to be better, her Mum was improving and she was dating again. She briefly mentioned Tamzin, but I have no idea what she said because the pain of my muscles popping and releasing made me deaf to my surroundings. The wave of pleasure that flooded was worth it though.

"Are you listening to me?"

"No."

"Well, at least you're honest." She tapped my side and I rolled onto my back. She straddled me and started rubbing my chest, saying something about it helping my cough by loosening the tightness. The tightness I was more concerned with was the ever increasing one in my boxers. There was nothing but her skin-tight jeans, my jogging bottoms and a pair of thin, fitted boxers between us. It sounds like a lot but when her crotch was pressing into mine it felt like nothing. I tried to focus on something - anything - that would distract me from my increasing arousal. I even contemplated feigning illness and asking her to stop, but I was drawn to Emily's eyes, which were boring into me intently. She leaned down and kissed me softly, rearranging herself so she was pressing herself harder into my obvious erection. I reached up and ran my fingers through her hair.

The lights - or my brain - flickered.

I wrapped my arms round her and pulled her closer into me, feeling the last of her apprehension melt away. I knew she needed me, but she tried to gather herself and pull back.

"Don't. I'm fine, please stop worrying." I whispered. She saw something when she looked at me because a huge grin spread across her face. She held my face in her hands as she kissed me, giggling to herself.

That night we made love for the first time. We didn't have sex: we actually made love. It was slow and intense and lacked the anger of my previous encounters. I felt like our souls connected.

She told me she loved me.

My fingertips left trails of blue light along her skin and hers left red along mine. At one point I could have seen my soul in her eyes. She was right, we were so alike and her heart was mine.

There must have been a power surge or a rolling blackout at some point because I saw the lights flicker and my laptop blue screened of death.

I told her I loved her as we came together and fell asleep almost instantly.

She left before I woke up, but she left a note on the side.

**You look adorable when you sleep, didn't want to wake you. Text me later. E xxxx**

I always cherished that note.

I lay in bed staring at the same crack in the ceiling, replaying last night over in my mind and contemplating the state of my physical and mental health. I felt healthy and last night was clear as a bell: no blackouts.

I decided not to push my luck and spent the next few days in a daytime TV and old movie blur. A talk show set in space with robot zombies and superheroes arguing over who was the father of their child. I managed to check over my laptop (I had no idea what I was doing) and it seemed to be OK - a little slow. I wouldn't know what I was looking for anyway.

**Emily**

**20**

*What. A. Night.* When I ran out the door with my bag and my coat I hadn't consciously decided to sleep with him. Part of me (a huge part, neck down) had wanted to, but I didn't know what state he would be in when I arrived. Little did I know that he would be a lot better than I thought he would be, still very ill so I decided to spend some time with him without trying to fuck him.

We have a lot in common, he's very funny and I could tell I was really falling for him. However, I could still sense he was lacking large amounts of energy so I offered to give him a massage. For me it's the quickest way to exchange energy without having to actively think about it.

I ran my hands over his shoulder blades, tracing his spine and feeling every spot, mole and hair on his back and shoulders. He was going to be quite hairy one day. The olive oil made his skin glisten and I found myself being hypnotised in the rhythmic tracing of his skin. I drew patterns, pressing down and manipulating his flesh. I talked about Beccy who's mum was now ill - she didn't have any luck at the moment. I tried to educate her on the benefits of a positive mental attitude - *irony!* - but she wasn't having any of it.

James was just grunting at me at this point and I realised he wasn't listening, so I watched the delicate lights of energy I was creating. They warmed us both and his levels increased - he made a happy grunt and I could feel his arousal between my thighs. I couldn't help myself I rolled him over so I was pressing onto him. I didn't want to wait any longer, but I didn't want to hurt him.

We made love that night. I've never made love before and it is terrifying. It makes you feel exposed and emotional in every sense of the words. I left before he woke up, leaving a written lie to hide the fact I wouldn't see him again.

**James**

**30**

By Wednesday I was bored to tears, but I was hoping that my IQ must have increased by a few points.

Emily seemed a little distant. We messaged almost constantly in the evenings, and she even responded faster than usual. I tried to arrange another date, but she refused to plan anything until I was completely better and back at work. I tried to call her, but she hadn't picked up. I attributed it to paranoia or cabin fever, after all, last weekend was spectacular and why would she be avoiding me?

But when I got a garbled message about family troubles and being in touch when she could, I started to worry. *What if I had hurt her? Like I hurt Sarah? And Rachel?* I didn't push it; I was learning that if I pushed, she ran. She said she loved me. *She must be scared of her own feelings.*

She needed time and I needed a distraction, so I pulled on my running clothes and hit the streets. The rest had done some good because broke my personal best, hurtling through the streets and round the parks, racing past other runners and earning some approving glances. Or I could have imagined those. I'm happy to pretend they were real approving glances.

*I must remember to sign up for a race.*

When I returned I had the second best shower of my life and as I wiped condensation from the mirror, my reflection made my breath catch in my throat. It was the first day I felt better but it felt like the first time in my life I was truly awake. Other than when I was with Emily. My eyes looked brighter, although it could be because my senses were sharper from the haze I had been in for the past fortnight.

*I need a haircut.*

I hadn't shaved for a few days and contemplated growing a beard. Plus I noticed an inevitable weight loss from the fever fits. I was shocked with what I saw, but I guess I was a lot sicker than I thought I was, now I was finally better.

Andy complimented me about how good I looked as I went to the kitchen to cook dinner. "You should get pneumonia more often." He slapped me on the behind as he walked into the living room with two glasses of champagne: I didn't see whom the second one was for.

Thursday came and I finally returned to work. I've never been so pleased to go to work and speak to people. It was great having Gemma (as well as Alice) fussing round me. I could get used to having handmaiden.

I had a return to work meeting with Deborah before I got started. When I explained what happened she showed more concern than I had seen before.

"If you don't feel well, feel free to go home. Don't rush back to work if you're ill." She was a brilliant boss. Though there was no point, my first day back flew by and then it was nearly the weekend. *I could get used to two-day workweeks.* I was looking forward to this weekend and seeing Emily again, after last weekend I could barely imagine what we would get up to this weekend. I text Emily that evening.

**So I'm all better and back at work, how about this weekend I cook for you? Xxx**

About 30 seconds later my phone went off: I was concerned she never responds this quick. I usually have to wait a minimum of an hour.

**I have plans this weekend. X**

*Blunt.* I had spend entirely too long trying to interpret her four word messages and - as per usual - I used my nightly run to work out how to respond. Listening to my internal debate rather than music. In the end I decided to try and call her, we obviously needed to talk. She didn't pick up. She never picks up. I text her again, but she responded a few days later with a garbled text message about still having family problems and she would be in touch when she could.

**31**

Without Emily I realised quite how boring my life had become. Six months into a new city and I'd managed to work myself into my same old rut. Or was it that I had grown as a person and realised how easy it is to just drift through life. Just exist.

*Not again.*

If it wasn't for my new addiction to running (to clear my head) and strength training (to get rid of my pent up tension and anger) I would have snapped. Every morning I got up and put on my mask and barely 45 minutes into the day I could feel the mask slipping.

*I believe I can see the future / 'Cause I repeat the same routine*
*I think I used to have a purpose  / Then again, that might have been a dream.*

Monday to Friday blurred into one grey, bland mass.

My alarm goes off at 7am when I shower; clean my teeth, dress (always after because if not I **will** spill toothpaste on my shirt) and breakfast - cereal, toast or a smoothie, depending on what I can be bothered to prepare. I then ride the tube to work with all the other zombies in business suits, crammed onto the tubes like sardines in a can: the smell of shampoo, shower gel and skin infiltrating my nostrils and remaining with me for the rest of the day.

Occasionally I'll be pressed up against someone I find attractive, the smell of their perfume making me dizzy. On a good day we'll exchange a shy smile and if I'm really lucky the more brazen ones will press their bodies backwards into me and we'd have a secret moment. It was almost as if I could feel their longing: taste their need.

From 9am the doors open at work and then it's answering the phones and checking people in until 1pm. On one particular Wednesday I checked in Mr Turner, Miss Nicholas, Mr Black, Malika, Sarah, Umar, Salvartorio and Jessica.

1 to 2 is lunch when I would usually pick up some new clothes if needed, but mostly I would eat my lunch (a healthy homemade sandwich or salad), complete some crosswords, or read the news or a book.

From 2 to 5.30 it was more of the same from the morning. Answering phones; completing admin work; updating the records of the organisations within the building and the staff they held; photocopying; shredding, etc. On the same Wednesday I checked in Alex, Isabella, Mrs Spencer-Wilson, Mr Taylor, Ms Khan and Mr Carlton.

Then I travel home, the smells of the other commuters more potent after a days work. When I got home it was a quick snack before a minimum of an hour of running, shadow boxing, sit ups and press ups, including variations, e.g. one handed, press and clap, burpees, etc.

From between 7.30pm to 10pm I cooked and ate dinner, sometimes with Nathan, Susan and even sometimes with Andy, although he preferred to keep out of our way. He'd had live-in landlords who'd helicoptered over him and he didn't intend to be one of those.

10pm until bed I had a glass (or three) of whiskey, did some more reading or watched or played something on my laptop. (*Note to self: get a games console*).

About 11pm it was bed, where I lay there desperately trying to will myself to sleep.

My life was so boring I could have screamed and some days I did scream. It's very cathartic although I wouldn't recommend doing it in a public park. You may have a local police officer approach you...

All my out of work activities were to distract myself from thinking about or contacting Emily, even resulting to leaving my phone at home so I wasn't constantly checking it for a response. I failed miserably. She was all I could think about.

When I eventually heard from Emily it was for her to tell me that the problem with her family was more serious than I thought. She wouldn't tell what was happening so I assumed it was bad or she was lying to me. I believed the latter. I was even tempted to get Robert down for a night on the pull to get someone to distract me. Best way to get over someone is get under someone else after all. *Hell's bells, I sound like the old Nathan. But are we monogamous?*

One week later there was actually a break in the routine. On Friday Alice was on holiday - she'd gone to the Lake District with Nathan and Gemma called in sick, so it was just me to stem the crowds. Deborah had tried to get a temp in (apparently), but there was no one available (apparently).

The phone rang a total of five times - with direct lines to the companies inside there was no real reason for anyone to call us. Geoff wasn't much of a talker so I sat in silence most of the day, trying not to cry from boredom. I failed at that was well. I punched a wall on a bathroom break.

I noticed that Alice and Nathan seemed to be much better. Their happiness was a stark contrast to my mood and it made me bitter. She was round a lot, so I had resorted to sleeping with earplugs in and leaving the room they were in. They were constantly holding hands and exchanging soppy glances when they thought no one was looking. *Jealous? Me?*

**Emily**

**21**

There were two shocking things that happened to me in my time away from James: 1. In a prime example of black comic timing, the excuse I used about family problems came true when Dad threw my Step Mum out. 2. I realised absence does make the heart grow fonder and I truly missed him.

*So now it's time to eat crow and go crawling back to him.* I'm not good with apologies and I need to explain why I got scared. And what he is. I still hadn't mentioned that. *Crap.*

**James**

**32**

It was a grand total week before I heard from her and nearly a month before I saw her again. By this point I had already drafted up the message to tell her to forget it. *She's playing me for a fool.* She must have sensed it because she asked me to meet her on a weekday evenings and at the same Starbucks from our second date, which I read as her trying to make an effort to be romantic.

I was getting sick of these games though: she was emotionally distant, but still she managed to rope me in. She tells me she loves me then disappears for weeks on end. *I'm old for these games: a five year old would be too old for these games.*

I should have told her to fuck off. I didn't of course. I'm a fool in love.

She greeted me with a hug that went for ages, with her arms wrapped tight around my chest. She squeezed and whispered softly in my ear: "I missed you so much."

"I missed you too. How's your family?"

"Better." She paused. "I don't want seem distant or rude, but I don't want to talk about it. It's been a hell of a few weeks." I ordered her Matcha green tea thing and I had a caramel latte (I was getting a bit of a sweet tooth, which isn't a good thing on top of the taste for whiskey I have developed.) before we snuggled together in a sofa in the corner. Her legs lay on mine and the was constant skin-to-skin contact: every time I moved my hand her fingers would move to another part of my body. I caught her staring at me more than once.

"You OK?"

"Yeah." She talked about work, whilst chewing on her lower lip. I couldn't work out whether it was nerves or... She squeezed my leg and kissed me. She nipped at my lip and the shot of pain turned the surrounding noise into static. I pulled away to sip of my drink and arrange my thoughts.

"Are you seeing someone else? I just want to know what is happening between us. You haven't been about for the past month and I know you said it's your family, but then you're distant and..." I took another sip and stared at the melting whipped cream. *Don't say cold.* "And you can be cold." *Shit.* "I want to be there for you."

There was long silence as she thought about how to respond. She ran her finger along the green foam and sucked on it, which turned my legs custard, and when she smiled it was genuine and it made me feel warm and happy. "I do love you, you know that right? You may have picked up that I'm not good on the phone, or by text. I'm just quite difficult to get hold of." Silence: there was no polite way of responding. "I wanted to talk to you but…" She paused. "It's hard. I don't…" Another pause: this conversation was obviously very difficult. "I don't open up to people."

We finished our drinks and I went and got the refills. I could tell she was trying to work out how to word… whatever she was going to say next. My mind spun with the worst possible scenarios. I took deep breaths and I tried to lower my pulse: my hands were sweating so much I almost dropped the cups as I sat back down.

"My dad split up with my step-mum. This has happened before, they row, but usually they get back to together but this time she packed her stuff a moved out. I've been home the last few weekends playing mediator."

"Did it work?"

"Yeah, she moved home. I got a chance to stay with Mum as well." Emily stared over my shoulder, at my hair, anywhere but my eyes. "I couldn't get much time off work, so every weekend I spent in Nottingham and every evening I spent trying to keep on top of my life here: cleaning, chores, etc."

We kissed and we talked, until the baristas shooed us out the door. It was a nice evening and I walked to the tube station feeling elated and light-headed. "I'm sorry I didn't trust you." I couldn't look at her, *how could I have doubted her?*

Emily's head swivelled to look and me and she was smiling again. "I'm sorry I pushed you away. I want you to know me."

*Let me in.* I felt the barriers breaking again and again, when we kissed we became one.

## Emily

## 22

I was shocked when I saw him. His face looked pallid, pale and like he was perspiring. He looked sick, but he moved like he was in full health. *Nerves?* Striding like a man on a mission with an expression of exasperation and irritation when he looked at me. I recognised the symptoms, his immune system was weak, in anyone else I would suggest rest but...

I felt his heart chakra reach out to mine and I breathed out in relief, it is automatic for him. Now it's just explaining...

"I missed you too. How's your family?"

"Better." *I'm not talking about this.* "I don't want seem distant or rude, but I don't want to talk about it. It's been a hell of a few weeks."

He seemed offended but I'm fine as long as I don't talk about it, or think about it. I hate Freud, but sometimes I wonder if he has a point. I'm not great with people and my family isn't great at being a family. Now all I need to is fall for someone like my dad.

I looked at James spooning up the whipped cream from his drink with his finger. *Nah.*

Pulling my bag closer to me as some sort of subconscious shield I prepared to launch into it. I had the Codex in my bag. Two women laughed loudly from the table within spitting distance of us and I kicked myself for not choosing somewhere quieter, but I didn't trust myself. He sucked his fingers clean and shiver ran through me. He was so childlike and carefree at times, was I really going to ruin that? But he may just think I'm crazy. Is that better?

"Are you seeing someone else?" I choked on my drink. It scolded the back of my throat and my eyes started watering. I could have guessed that he would think that but... "...you can be cold." *Well, he is perceptive.*

*Shut up and let me think, how am I supposed to explain?*

*Tell him the truth.*

So I did. "I do love you..."

I just spoke without thinking and when I realised I was still talking I had told him everything about my family. I didn't tell anyone about my family. I didn't talk to anyone, but when he kissed me... I don't have the words.

When we were kicked out of the coffee shop I knew I should just give him the Codex and leave, but I didn't want to so mysterious. Not mysterious… evasive. I didn't want to be evasive. I like being mysterious.

When he kissed me goodbye I relaxed, I let slip all my barriers and I felt my head lightening. My heart chakra burned as it connected with his and I felt our souls combine. My eyes were burned through closed lids and I felt like I had swallowed a star. My entire being was on fire.

**James**

**33**

I fainted when I got home. I walked in and collapsed with the front door still open. All I could remember was my head spinning and that oh so fucking familiar blackness clouding my thoughts and vision. I just had time to think: *I'm dizzy,* before my head collided with carpet.

I woke up on the living room floor at 3am and went to work five hours later.

When my alarm went off at 7am I felt fine so I decided to go in. There was no way that was pneumonia related - I assumed it wasn't pneumonia related - and I couldn't risk taking more time off work. The day went without a hitch so I decided I wouldn't bother going to get checked out either. Although I did go dizzy on my lunch break, the blackness only encroached and receded, but I assumed my blood sugar dropped and I just needed to eat. And it returned in the bathroom of the bar we went to after work: I almost blacked out at the urinal, but I assumed that was the booze.

Of course it was. I was fine. *I am fine.*

Susan filled me in when I got home. She was sat in living room and she called out to me as I walked in. I put my hand on the sideboard to steady myself. *You're OK. You're OK.*

"You OK?"

*No.* "Yeah, what happened?"

"Everyone else was out last night, which is why you were on the floor. Sorry I couldn't get you onto the sofa, but you were a dead weight." My head started to spin. "I don't know how long you were there but I was cooking and I realised it was freezing, walked out of the kitchen and I saw an unconscious heap on the floor with the door wide open." I couldn't look at her; I was focusing on a point in the distance, trying to subtly stop myself swaying. "You've lost a hell of a lot of weight by the way. I copped a feel of your muscles as I was dragging you to the living room."

"I didn't wake up when you moved me?" Her compliment didn't register. How is that possible? I must have been dead to the world.

I didn't stay to hear her answer, I went straight upstairs to book a doctor's appointment for the morning, where I had a once over and was given the all clear. I was offered another week off work, but as I was out the office more times when I was in it I decided to work through it. I really didn't want to lose this job. Anyway, it was nothing and all I needed was rest.

I didn't even believe my lies.


**34**


I'm not going to bore you with details of my boring weekend and my even more boring week at work. My life was boring me so the last thing you want to do is bore you about it.

I arranged to meet Emily the following weekend and she was **finally** inviting me round to hers to cook. She wouldn't be doing much cooking... There will be a lot of eating though. *Oh come on! That's so crass.* I despair of my internal monologue sometimes.

When we were together the sexual attraction was palpable, but when we were apart it felt like she didn't miss me nearly as much as I miss her. She could go days without replying and often did and when she did reply it was blunt to the point of rude.


During a quiet spot on a wet Wednesday afternoon - does everyone cancel their meetings when it rains or just our clientele? - I arranged with Gemma and Alice for us all to go out for dinner. One big, happy group date. We decided on a week on Saturday and we would go to this "quaint, little Italian" Gemma and James regularly frequent. Alice said Nathan was definitely free and I said would double check with Emily. I was so excited to introduce her properly to my friends and to get their approval that I text her on my coffee break.


**Are you free a week on Saturday? I've arranged a meal with Nathan, Alice, Gemma and her fiancé James and I would love you to come. N XX**


She responded quicker than usual, only six hours later.


**Sounds great. Let me know a time and a place. E xx**


I slept well that night and woke up happy after dreaming about Emily and I swimming and making love in a crystal, clear sea. It didn't last long.


I'd booked the Friday off to recover in my own time and even though I wasn't working I woke up in an unexplainable bad mood. I decided to run off my bad mood, so I took the tube to Alexandra Palace and I ran around the grounds a few times. I even packed a little lunch in my new running bag and to spend the day alone and outside.

As I ran my mind drifted and I meditated on my surroundings and fruitlessly tried to work out why I was in such a bad mood. It was as I passed the nine mile mark I felt the blackness closing in on me. This was getting ridiculous. My lungs were burning and my legs were aching, but I was used to that feeling: it was the overpowering sensation of suffocation that spread from my chest to the rest of my body. It was like my pores were blocked and my whole body was being starved of oxygen. The music grew louder and my feet pounded the concrete in time with my increasing heartbeat. I couldn't seem to stop moving.

*Hungry.* The pain was getting worse and my vision was beginning to blur.

*Hungry.* I could see Emily's face in front of my eyes and a low rumble escaped through my gritted teeth. I must have looked like a madman. I sped up, chasing nothing.

Then my feet left the ground and I was falling. Thank God for small miracles, I don't remember the contact with the floor: it must have hurt. When I woke up my arms and legs were bleeding. I checked myself for broken bones: none, and for all my possessions: nothing stolen. I had four missed calls from Nathan and the time said it was 7pm, I'd been gone for six hours, but I had no idea how long I'd been unconscious.

I got some strange looks on the journey back, especially from the police officers I passed. I was covered in blood and wearing muddy running gear. I looked dodgy.

Things only got better when I got home and Nathan was waiting for me like a pissed off mother and proceeded to go nuts at me; he went home when he couldn't get hold of me.

"What the hell happened to you? You look like you've been in a fight." He got me a glass of water and sat me down in the kitchen, looking concerned. As much as I appreciated the care I felt uncomfortable. Smothered. Mothered. I explained what happened, only because he threatened to call the police saying I was attacked.

"What did the doctor say?" Nathan's eyes were full of concern. I told him I was fine. "I don't believe you. I want to take you to A & E now. It's not normal to keep blacking out like that."

"Look it's probably nothing. Stress. I'm fine and I don't want anymore time off work."

We agreed to disagree. Nathan was insistent about me going back to the doctors, so I decided I would lie and tell him I went. The blackouts are nothing. The body does strange things when stressed.

*I'll be fine.*


Emily didn't think so.

**Emily**

**23**

*Oh my Gods... I'm going to kill him. How is this even possible? How isn't he naturally feeding? I'm draining his life force and he has no way to replenish unless I actively push energy into him. This shouldn't be possible. We're supposed to be emotional leeches. For Christ sake I suck emotions, not blood. How could this happen? There has to be another explanation.*

I was sat at my laptop typing when a sudden chill ran down my spine. About half an hour after I'd closed the window and put on a jumper my phone rang. I'd assumed that the cold caused the chill, but when my phone rung I knew that something was wrong. I hate it when my phone rings, it means someone wants to speak to me. Why was James calling? He knows not to call.

It was about six in the morning when I woke up fully clothed and with the lamp still on. I had a crick in my neck from sleeping sat up on my bed. It felt like someone was gripping the back of my neck and a headache was forming. I had pages of notes; websites bookmarked and books Post-Ited with illegible handwriting. So what do we know?

1. If a vampire doesn't feed it can cause damage. Health complications that are usually easily fought with ease are quickly exacerbated. There are even cases of heart problems becoming.

2. When I've been with him he gets ill. Conclusion: My feeding is draining his energy.

3. He's ill for a while. Conclusion: He's not replenishing said energy.

And the cause of this?

Option 1: His awakening. Some awakenings manifest in the most extreme way. Mine was subtle, doesn't mean his is.

Option 2: He doesn't know how to feed.

Option 3: Me. I'm completely wrong and he's not a vampire and I'm damaging him.

*Could I just be damaging him like the others? Oh God. What if I'm wrong? I really like him but what if he's not strong enough to be with me?*

*Don't start.*

*What if I'm crazy?*

*Don't start.*

*I'm not starting. You know that the unknowing stir up drama to feed; the knowing are more careful, but the unwilling?*

*I don't know, which is why I've been awake half the night.*

The tears dripped from my chin; my head was spinning; I couldn't breathe. *Oh Gods. Oh Gods. I'm killing him. I'm slowing killing him.*

**James**

**34**

Although I could give her credit for actually picking up the phone I was pissed off by the tense conversation and that she was distancing herself when I needed her. If I was contagious I would understand, but it wasn't. She sounded scared for me when I said I collapsed, but I assured her that I would be fine for our date tomorrow evening.

Can you guess what happened next kids? She cancelled.

I was a little bit annoyed. Just a tiny bit. And I didn't want the rest of that bottle of scotch anyway. And the new scotch stain on my bedroom looks like a wonderful example of a Jackson Pollack painting. And the smashed glass makes walking around my room a fun game.

I was tiptoeing around trying to pick up the largest shards of glass when I heard the sound of footsteps thundering up the stairs; Nathan's hushed, urgent whispers; then footsteps treating back into ground floor.

I slipped out of my room and sat on the roof terrace for a few hours. The wind was still and the night was pleasant, but it didn't take long for goose pimples to appear all over my legs. The night soothed my nerves, but couldn't settle this burning ball of anger in my chest. That or I had heartburn. All I could think about was Emily cancelling and how I should find myself another woman, one who cared about me enough to stick around.

It didn't take long for the cold to get too much and I crept back to my bedroom, where I stayed for the majority of the weekend, only venturing out to eat and pee. The ball of anger in my chest hadn't subsided so I was scared of being around people.

# Emily

## 24

I eventually calmed down enough to work out a plan. I hoped that this wouldn't be the most difficult conversation I'd ever had, but I doubted myself. I had played out a dozen different scenarios in my head on my commute, in front of the mirror while doing my teeth and on the treadmill at the gym with only a few strange looks when I realised I was mouthing along to the conversation.

I've always had a bad habit of "getting lost in my own head", as my mother would call it. It's hereditary. I would go to a therapist but... well, imagine telling them I'm a vampire that feeds on the energy of others to survive, plus I have a tendency to over think things. Delusions, hallucinations, high sex drive... Yeah, I don't need that.

I pulled a copy of my Bible - the Psychic Vampire Codex - off my bookshelf and shoved it in my bag, along with a couple of other gifts.

**James**

**35**

Credit where credit is due, Emily did reschedule and we met on Thursday evening for Chinese. A proper date on a weeknight and everything! She even arrived with a jar of Manuka honey, a lump of ginger and a lemon, which apparently is a miracle cure.

She seemed overly concerned for my health and I caught her studying me when she thought I wasn't looking.

"Why do you keep staring at me?" I spluttered between mouthfuls of meat and noodles. Driven by hunger I attempted to my inhale food: my increased appetite was a lot to get used to, I never seemed to be full.

"You seem…" She paused, pausing to think midsentence, as per usual. Some people think before they speak, Emily thinks while she speaks or she doesn't think at all. "…better with chopsticks? Oh hell, I'm just going to say it, you seem very different to the boy I met."

I let the statement hang there as I took time chewing and swallowing. *Boy?* "Yeah I know and I can't say it's a bad thing."

"No of course." She laughed nervously and in an amazing example of turning a conversation 180 degrees she blurted out: "What's your view on the supernatural?" She eyed me intently as she elegantly handled the chopsticks.

"Ghosts and stuff, or the TV programme? Because I've never seen the latter and I don't believe in werewolves and Wookies."

She snorted at my atrocious attempt at humour, staring at her bowl. I wondered why she stared at her food whenever she was intently thinking. Perhaps she was seeking a vision like a crystal ball. Or perhaps she was wondering how to continue.

"I mean 'ghosts and stuff.'" She was getting good at mimicking my accent. "Fuck it." She said to her chow mein. "What…" She filled her lungs completely. "What if I told you vampires are real?"

"I'd say you've been watching too much TV. Vampires are the latest fad isn't it? It was witchcraft not that long ago. Or is zombies?"

"No, not the Dracula 'live forever and transform into bats' kind. No, I mean, what if I told you some people don't need just food and water to survive? Some need blood or life energy. Chi?"

"There are a lot of crazy people in the world. Don't tell me you believe in vampires?" There was a cold feeling of realisation creeping over my body. I tried to focus on the taste of my food but I had to ask, the pressure was building in my temples. "Do you think you're a...?" I trailed off.

"No!" A little too fast and an octave too high. "No. I'm not saying I'm a vampire. I'm saying some people need certain energies to survive, energies provided through emotions."

I stared at her incredulously. I couldn't believe I was having this conversation, what had happened to my life? The tension built and was finally broke when I broke into snorting laughter. The diners surround us looked at me in disgust as I choked on my food. *Death by noodle.* Embarrassment flashed across her face, before her posture and tone changed. And she started laughing as well. "Of course not, it was something I was reading about. I wanted to make sure you didn't believe in such rubbish. What about aliens?"

We discussed the supernatural for a while. I'm not an utter sceptic, only a little bit of a sceptic, but I was thoroughly unconvinced by the whole conversation. I tried to assess Emily's views but came up blank. She fought both sides eloquently and I certainly didn't want to believe that the woman I had fallen in love with had such a massive personality flaw as to believe she was a vampire. She had backtracked pretty fast, but I had a nagging doubt.

**Emily**

**25**

Note to self: for future reference a public place is not the best place to have these conversations. And if I had four wheels I'd be a car. At least two tables of couples heard and sniggered. I'm not usually one to give a damn but when you're baring your soul... *He didn't believe you?*

*What do you think?* When I brought up subjects that tested his belief system, it wasn't concern that I felt emanating from him: it was doubt to the point of being almost fearful. It is human nature to protect your beliefs and to fight whoever questions them. Which is why you're not allowed to discuss politics and religion at work.

"I'm saying some people need certain energies to survive..." It was when he started laughing I decided not to give him the Codex. Although thinking back on it I probably should have. On the other hand we haven't known each other that long and it probably would of killed our chances of a future.

But then what sort of future if we can't be honest?

Or if I constantly make him sick?

My head was spinning, the meal hadn't gone as well as I'd hoped, so I poured a large glass of wine and mentally wrote out my options while drinking my pain away. I had no idea how to convince him what he was; my presence literally makes him sick; I couldn't teach him how to get better; I can't control myself...

*When you're out of options, sometimes the only choice is to run.*

**James**

**37**

The day of the big group date day arrived and I had arranged to meet Emily at Tower Hill tube station: she said she would let me know when she got on the other end so I wasn't waiting too long. I didn't hear from her but I thought nothing of it and I didn't expect anything less. I went to wait for her anyway, standing in the doorway trying to look casual. It was when I had been waiting half an hour and I called Nathan to let him know I would be late. At this point I was worrying. Her phone was off and she wasn't responding to any messages.

Another half an hour went by and I made the firm decision to give her 15 more minutes, which gave me time to work out the most subtle way of leaving without making it obvious to the staff and commuters that I had been stood up. Because that is exactly what happened. It's not that I hoped that anything was wrong, but there had better be a damn good reason.

As I stood in the doorway pretending that I wasn't cold and upset, I stared at the fluorescent lighting contemplating not going to the meal at all. I couldn't handle the questions about where my so-called girlfriend was or their pity that she had ditched me. However, you can't not show up to your own event and I organised this. Plus I needed the distraction and the support of my friends.

The restaurant décor was a little dated, but a white haired waiter with glasses and a Mario moustache greeted me eagerly. I'd called Nathan on the way and let him know what had happened, at least then he could warn them and there wouldn't be a barrage of difficult questions. The only good thing to come out of this was that any nerves I had about introducing Emily or meeting James were thrown out the window, by an overwhelming urge to punch something made of glass - a window or a door.

*Deep breath and put your best face on. It's Showtime!* Internally I did jazz hands and walked over to the table. "I'm so sorry I'm late." There were the remains of two dishes of oil and balsamic vinegar and a few crumbs on two wooden serving boards. My stomach woke up then.

"No it's fine." Gemma was already pouring me a glass of wine and she gestured towards a man sat next to her with gunslinger facial hair and a ring in his ear. *He looks like a postmodern pirate.* "This is James." He stood up and shook my hand. James was a mechanic and he was… a really nice guy… very… interesting? He had a tendency to make jokes only he laughed at and quote books and movies that only he and Gemma had seen. *He would have got on with Emily.* He chatted away completely oblivious to (or purposely ignoring) the tension that I courteously brought in with me.

I finished the first glass of wine in two gulps. *Don't drink your emotions. Don't drink your emotions.* The waiter with the Mario moustache recommended the Cabonara and damn, it rivalled mine. It was so good I actually forgot about Emily as I ate it.

I don't remember much about what we talked about. I tried to focus on the conversation and not check my phone, but it was hard. What I do remember was for the first time ever, seeing Nathan blush. I didn't think he had blood vessels in his cheeks.

"So when are you moving in together?" Gemma blurted out as she finished her third glass of wine, and I had a feeling she had been pre-drinking.

Nathan choked on his pasta and Alice shot him a withering look. "We hadn't discussed it yet." He managed to stammer out.

"Not that I haven't tried." Alice muttered: this was a planned attack and to avoid any more questions Nathan threw me under the proverbial bus.

"So did you hear from Emily? I won't repeat the four letter word I muttered under my breath hurled at him.

"Thanks Nathan. No, I haven't heard from her yet." I drummed my fingers on the stem of my wine glass. *Don't drink your emotions. Breathe.* "She's disappeared before but she's never stood me up like this. Anyway, have you started house hunting or would you move into each other?" Revenge is sweet and Nathan isn't as bright as he thinks he is. Nathan changed the subject pretty quickly after that and we spent a while discussing James and Gemma's wedding plans as Gemma visibly tensed up. A lot of planning, arranging, re-arranging and expense in planning a wedding: who knew?

In the end it was a fun evening because I suppressed the anger into a wad in my stomach; I stayed relatively sober and us lad's decided we were going to have a lad's night out. Aren't I a great host?

Two weeks later I still hadn't heard from her. I didn't know her home address and I sure as hell wasn't going to look like a madman and go to her work, but I was getting desperate. She didn't respond to emails, IM, texts. Hell, I'd send a carrier pigeon if it got a response.

My mood had reached an all time low. I missed her and I was miserable, but I faked it at work and when I got home I tried to stay out of most people's ways. Which was easy enough as Andy was seeing someone so he was out most evenings and Susan was doing extra shifts to save up for a mortgage.

I sat on the chair in the corner of the living room. The TV was on, but I didn't know what was playing. I had my leg swung over one arm and I had a bottle of rum in one hand and a glass in the other. In my mind's eye I hoped I looked like a scene from a black and white movie. All brooding and handsome. I hoped wear melancholy well. I know I don't.

I heard Alice's voice as she entered the house and saw Nathan jump when he switched on the light. Apparently, I'd been sat in the dark.

"James! You're home. Why are you sat in the dark?" I emptied the glass and refilled it in silence. "What are you staring at?" I became aware of how tense my forehead and mouth were and I was scowling at nothing: I forced my facial muscles to relax.

"Sorry." I drained my glass and glanced at my watch before refilling my glass. *How long have I been sat here?* I saw Nathan make eyes at Alice who kissed him and left the room. A few moments later the front door went again.

Nathan mimicked the voice in my head. "How long have you been sat here?" He yelled as he got another glass from the kitchen and took my bottle from me, switching off the TV in the process. Apparently, I had been watching a costume drama of some sort. A man in a starchy suit was arguing with another man in a top hat and a starchy suit. Actually, it could have been a wedding show.

"I don't know."

"Talk to me." I smirked: he'd put on a terrible, untraceable accent. "Talk to me." He repeated sounding vaguely like a car salesman.

"Looking back I think it was obvious what was going to happen. Those two weeks after she told me she loved me..." Nathan choked on his drink and I realised that I hadn't told him that. "Her distance, coldness, she was downright rude at times and yet at the time I was blinded by the thought you couldn't do this to someone you love."

"You couldn't have predicted this."

I stared at my rum: my glass was running low again. *I shouldn't be dwelling on this.* "But then she was so lovely when we met for dinner."

"Perhaps she got scared. Have you heard from her?"

I gave him a condescending look. *I really should get over her.* "Of course not and spare me the pleasantries. She was trying to mess with my emotions. She was trying to make me love her and it fucking worked." I chugged the remaining mouthfuls. "I feel like a fool. Fucking vampire." My choice of words resonated in my head. "I wonder what she did during that month she didn't speak to me. Because I bet she sure as hell wasn't with her family!"

"You're better off without her."

"I am!" I really was, but it didn't feel like it. I wanted the conversation to end I couldn't handle him being nice to be anymore and talking about her felt like salt and lemon juice in an open wound.

*"Waiting is painful. Forgetting is painful. But not knowing which to do is the worse kind of suffering."*

**38**

Nathan lay on his back staring at the sky whilst Alice and Gemma sat chatting. I was playing catch with a rugby ball Robert had brought down with him and Jo and James were bonding over art deco architecture and steam punk fashion. Every time they fell about laughing or their conversation reached an excited pitch I saw Gemma cast a nervous look in his direction. It was less than a year until their wedding and her wedding jitters were palpable.

I caught Jo looking over at me in adoration more than once and I revelled in her attention. Robert pelted the ball at my head and I just caught it before it smacked me in the eye.

"Cat-like reflexes? That's a new one. I'm proud." He wiped a no-existent tear away as I hurled to ball low, aiming for his nether regions.

"Yeah I'm not quite the klutz you once knew and loved." Robert dipped down quick and managed to save his future children.

Jo came over and explained that she had some shopping to do but she would be ready for our date tonight and gave me a long kiss before she walked off blushing. *Man, I hate to see her go but I love to watch her leave. No, wait, I mean...*

"Things are going well." Robert formed it into a statement, rather than a question and interrupted my internal confusing. I just shrugged and sat down next to Nathan, who's light snoring indicated he dozed off in the unseasonal summer sun.

Britain's summers are mostly rain, so we were making the most of it by killing the day in the park. There was dance music coming for a group not to far of us, and London was packed with shoppers and day-trippers. The energy was electric and it was almost enough to distract me from Emily.

Almost.

Nearly six weeks and she hadn't been in contact. I had given up waiting after my conversation with Nathan and I drifted through life, grieving for the love that I almost had. She was never truly mine.

During the day I had managed to keep myself directed enough that I could easily go all day without thinking about her, but at night... The emotions came flooding back at night. In the early days I cried myself to sleep more than once, then I was so angry I couldn't sleep. How could she do this? How could she mess with my emotions? What kind of person was she? What kind of...? My mind regularly fell back to our last conversation. I did do a little research on vampirism before dismissing it as ridiculous. *She definitely sucked the life out of me though.*

Gave up trying to speak to her. She definitely wasn't going answer and she made her feelings abundantly clear by humiliating me in front of my friends.

Enough wallowing in the past: I met Jo a couple of weeks ago. We met in a club on a Saturday night. *How retro? We didn't even meet on the Internet.* We were both queuing at the bar and I was being served before her, so I offered to pay for her and we got talking.

She took me back to hers that night.

She looked similar to Alice, in the same way as they both had blonde hair. *So not similar in the slightest then? No.* She always had a full face of make up and had massive... eyes. And breasts, but genuinely massive eyes. I wasn't just drawn to her looks (although it was a massive pull), we had similar taste in music and movies and she was a lovely lass. She was everything Emily wasn't: shy, open, honest and warm. Without wanting to blow my own trumpet, she was utterly smitten. I saw her almost everyday and she got on well with my friends.

However... However, she was a welcome distraction; a scratch for an itch; a time killer. That's it. And I knew what a monstrous thing that was and I what a heartless, hypocrite I was being, but I couldn't seem to break it off.

Every time we have sex I would leave and debate the best (and easiest) way to call it off, but then a day or so later when my head fogged over; the ache in my chest returned and something inevitably pissed me off I would end up calling her. She made me feel better and that's enough for the early stages of a relationship. *Right?*

I assumed a similar position to Nathan and lay on the grass staring at the clouds. I found my mind wandered to our first date. I knew Jo had strong feelings for me, not love - *surely, not love* - but she had text me the minute I got home from hers after that first night. We arranged a second (technically first) date.

I dunked the bread in the oil and balsamic vinegar and tried not to dribble it on my shirt. She watched me as I sucked my fingers clean with a clear look of lust and wanting in her eyes. It was the first time I had been aware of someone blatantly finding me attractive, usually I couldn't pick up on it and doubted it if I did.

"So come on, shall we get the boring date stuff out the way? Favourite colour, book and movie?" In an attempt of gross out humour I flicked the end of her nose with my oily fingers. She squealed in apparent delight.

"Do that again and I'll pour my drink on you." I raised my eyebrows in a challenge and she giggled and reapplied her face powder, pulling a strand of blonde hair from her lipstick. She had the hugest lips and I wondered whether or not she'd had work done.

"I'm a bit of a stereotype, I love pink and the movie The Time Traveller's Wife. Book... well I don't read for fun much. To be honest, my coursework takes up so much time and I just like to relax and go clubbing when I can. Like most students, Cilla, I like socialising." Jo is in her final year at university studying computer programming. Computer Science she calls it but it involves programming computers and I'm not too proud to admit that she might as well be speaking French when she goes into detail about her projects. Static is more coherent to me.

She had an adorable way of slurping her spaghetti. *She truly is beautiful, but she's not Emily.*

The conversation flowed organically and there weren't any long silences or difficult questions. We even chatted about the latest dancing and singing related reality TV show, not that I'd seen it but it's amazing how easy it is to blag those things with: "Oh yea him! What's his name?" Look away and click fingers a few times and she inevitability gave me the answer. I knew I should be being honest about my likes, but this was more fun and I was trying to ignore the fact that I was completely bored. Don't get me wrong, Jo wasn't boring, she just wasn't what I wanted. Who I wanted.

I stared out the window whilst Jo 'powdered her nose' and found myself looking for Emily. I knew I didn't want to see her but I felt like poking at that wound: picking the scab.

I noticed a woman with short, black hair and red lips eyeing me over her dates shoulder. She looked away a few times, but her eyes always returned to me. I turned and raised my glass and she smiled coquettishly, causing her date to look over his shoulder and whom she was smiling at, but Jo was back and I returned my attention to her.

*I could get used to this.* I felt wanted. Gazing at her I suddenly realised she had been talking for a few minutes and I had no idea what she had been saying.

"You haven't been listening to me, have you?" Jo frowned at me but there was a glint in her eyes, so I knew she was teasing me.

"Not in the slightest, why do you cover your mouth when you laugh?"

She started and flushed. "I might have something stuck in my teeth." I took her hand, and let go again as our desserts had arrived.

Like the classy adults we are we made out on the tube on the way back to her two bedroom flat. With her flatmate out and two bottles of wine between us, Jo felt relaxed enough to truly cut lose, so she screamed so much the neighbours banged on the ceiling. The feeling of her skin on mine...

I was shocked out of my daydream by a rugby ball smacking me square in the face.

"Think fast douche bag!" Robert's laughing boomed throughout the park and I saw people turning to see what the commotion was.

"Go fetch." I shouted as I hurled it past him, laughing as Robert cursed and went sprinting after it. I settled back into my reverie.

I ran my lips and tongue across her soft and delicately perfumed skin, lightly nipping at her flesh with my teeth. She squealed with delight every time I bit down a little too rough. Some lazily written R&B music played in the background, segmented by an overly enthusiastic DJ and ad breaks for something or other. I slowly started to phase it out as I became more engrossed in Jo's body, so different from Emily's. *Stop that! Stay with her.*

I teased and tickled her with my fingers, making her gasp and moan, bucking against me and shuddering with pleasure. I hadn't even begun and she had melted in my hands. The haze had started to overtake and I was learning to enjoy the sensation of losing control and giving into my baser instincts. I growled and pounced on her roughly, pinning her down and watching the trails of pink and purple light over her skin.

"Please..." Jo begged breathily, thrusting her hips into mine to indicate what she wanted. I gave it to her. I felt us connect at a deeper level, like I had tendrils protruding and exploring from my body and connecting onto her, like a seedling, or a tic.

I pulled her on top of me, throwing her around like a rag doll and I watched her bounce away, thrusting myself into her. The lights flood at a spot on her chest between her breasts and looped over her head, she panted and whimpered as she shuddered, her eyes rolling into the back of her head.

For a moment I thought I saw Emily, flicking her sweat drenched, dark hair off her face; running her nails down my chest until she drew blood and the smell of her filling my lungs until it drove me to insanity.

I pulled myself back to reality before Jo realised something was wrong, regaining my rhythm and throwing her onto her front.

Her cries and our combined moans of pleasure rang throughout the night and we finally collapsed into a deep sleep just before dawn. As I dozed off I watched the patterns of pink and purple that I had branded onto her twinkling in the grey light. Like branding or a gang tattoo, I had made a mark to indicate that she was mine.

The pleasurable tingle that ran through my crotch pulled me back reality pretty sharpish and I sat up and to distract myself. I really didn't want to be a 25-year-old man with a public erection, like a 14-year-old boy. Jo certainly had that affect on me.

"Come on, let's go get food. I want to go to that all you can eat barbeque place." I could hear Robert's stomach rumbling.

"It's hard to believe you're not a local." James called out to Robert as he clapped his hand into mine and hauled me up. Luck must have been on my side - I managed to calm myself down quick enough for no one to notice my predicament.

"You southern pansies aren't a patch on me."

I exchanged glances with James. "All three of us are from York."

"Yeah, but you've turned into a pansy." I contemplated cracking him on the back of the skull for his insolence, but I thought better of it: a few pints down his neck and he'd humiliate himself later. After all, revenge is best served cold.

I chatted to James about his future stag do, which had rumours of heading to Amsterdam so I was gunning for an invite. It wasn't for another year so I had plenty of time to bond. "So... the red light district or the legal weed?" Gemma gave me a sideways glance. *If looks could kill...*

"Neither, the clubs are supposed to be good, the desserts better and the city is stunning." James lowered his voice to add, "Strip clubs and cafes can get expensive so you better start saving." We high-fived to the suspicious glares of Gemma and James promptly jogged over and wrapped his arms round her.

**39**

I knocked back my forth straight shot of Tequila and wobbled into the bar, holding myself outstretched with head bowed to steady my spinning head. I felt like Regan: The Exorcist, not the American president. The chant of "SHOTS! SHOTS! SHOTS! SHOTS!" reverberated in my head and I knew I would regret this in the morning - I regretted every Sunday morning when Saturday night was spent with Robert - but I was having fun now.

Did you know that stomach acid is bright orange? I was going to find that out tomorrow as I tried to remember the side effects of alcohol poisoning.

We had intended to go home and get ready, but we got distracted by conversation and drinking. We were in the fifth pub of the day when I sacked off that idea and arranged to meet Jo at the restaurant. When she arrived in a little red dress - which flowed out at the bottom, skimming the edge of her butt - I knew I should have changed from shorts.

"I love your skater dress. You look so hot!" Alice squealed and bounded over to her to feel the fabric and grope her waist. "Your breasts look huge!" We all turned to stare at Jo's impressive rack and she turned the same shade as her dress.

"I'm so sorry! Alice gets a little loud when she's been drinking and we've been drinking since you left us." I interjected.

"Don't try to change the subject. Look at that chest!" Gemma dragged Alice away giggling.

A couple of bars later and Nathan had to literally carry Alice back to hers. She was still conscious, but her eyes were heavy and she protested constantly as Nathan bundled her into the back of a taxi. James, Gemma, Robert, Jo and I hit a club.

We were drinking and dancing until the early hours of the morning, Jo grinding up against me and whispering what she was going to do to me when we got back to hers. We spent the weekends at hers because Susan wouldn't be too pleased with being woken up in the middle of the night - again - and Jo's housemates didn't seem to care.

As we danced the club lights cascaded over her body, changing her skin from blue to red to green and yellow. I thought about the lights that I drew over her body as we had sex. The brighter the lights on her body, the louder she moaned and I was getting good at controlling the patterns. I was pretty sure she couldn't see them as she hadn't commented on them.

I probably should have been worried about what they were and what I was seeing, but I wasn't. I had made the assumption that it was a hallucination or something caused by the dopamine being realised at the time. Like ecstasy. The brain is a wonderful piece of technology and I had no idea how it worked with no interest in finding out. *Ignorance is bliss.*

We sat back down sweating and giggling together. Through my drunken haze I watched her joking with Robert, realising I could see some sort of a future with Jo, but it was early days so I wouldn't tell her. I felt happy, but... We had a lot in common, she was smart, funny and gorgeous: a life without drama or manic highs and lows, a nice, comfortable... rut. The nagging lump in my chest wasn't just the nausea from the booze, it was that I could feel the rut forming again. I shook it off for the time being. *I'm too drunk for this and I'm back in York next weekend, I'll think about it then.*

The following weekend was the longest time Jo and I had spent apart since we met and I realised I was going to miss her as I boarded the train home. However, with Mum's birthday I had to go back and, I couldn't wait to see Grace who was becoming quite the little person just by the many pictures and video calls I had with her (Mum talking for her and holding her up).

She giggled pleasantly as I cooed over her, only a few months old and already sitting up by herself and rolling all over the floor.

"She's getting so big." Mum's voice cracked and she stared at the light fixture.

"Would you have another one?" I picked Grace up and threw her up in the air and caught her.

"NO!" Dad bellowed from the kitchen and Mum fell about laughing. "She's feeling hormonal and emotional, don't ask questions like that." He continued. I held my breath and the rude and incredibly brazen statement of the fact, but Mum just nodded in agreement.

"He's right. I've been a little crazy recently."

Her eyes looked wet so I changed the subject. "Have you started weaning her yet?"

"No, not yet. Anyway, enough about us, you said last week you're getting bored at work?"

I picked up Grace and tickled her nose, who looked fascinated with a spot just above my head. I waved a hand over my crown thinking my hair was sticking up. It wasn't. "Yeah, it's just... I'm bored. It's so boring. Only seven months since I moved and already every day is merging into one.

Don't get me wrong, I am competent; I offer excellent customer service and I score highly in every meeting and review, but there is no challenge and no advancement opportunities. I mean look at Gemma, she's not even officially my team leader and she's been there forever."

"Have you started job hunting?" Dad walked into the room as I jiggled Grace on my knee, getting no reaction; she was still staring just above me.

"OK I fold, is she OK?" I turned round to see what she was staring at, but she looked at me apparently unimpressed at my lack of understanding. *I'm sure Patrick Stewart narrates your internal monologue*, I thought to Grace.

"Yeah, she's just doing baby stuff." He stood in the doorway looking at Grace with love in her eyes.

"I wonder what she is thinking about. Anyway, I've been looking, but I haven't applied for any, I don't know what I want to do."

"You used to want to be a doctor."

"I can't handle the studying, although I have been looking into distance courses. I was thinking PA, so I think I'll stay a little bit longer and apply with one of the companies in the building."

"Men can't be Personal Assistants."

Mum viciously hurled the remote at Dad's head, which he caught and looked a combination of angry and smug. This made him look like he had indigestion. "Why on Earth not? I'm not having that sexist talk around Grace. This isn't the Dark Ages."

"I meant James can't... James shouldn't just aim for PA, he should aim for CEO."

"Nice save Dad." I handed Grace back to Mum and went to catch up with Olivia and Matthew, who were arguing in the kitchen as they cooked Mum's birthday dinner. I wanted to take them out, but they had planned out a three course meal, so I settled on getting Mum a spa weekend for two, which I would present at dinner.

"HOW DID YOU FORGET THE GARLIC BREAD?" Olivia was screeching at Matthew: she had inherited Mum's pipes. Matthew swore under his breath and hissed something about olives and meat.

"Whoa, whoa. Calm down. I'll go the shop before I have to break you two up and don't you swear at your sister. What do you need?"

I got given a surprisingly long list ("Are you sure you need chocolate and sweets, or are you just making me buy them for you?") and no money ("I'm paying, aren't I?") and was pushed out of the door.

I walked through the streets reminiscing about my childhood. I used to buy alcohol from this shop from I was underage. Well, we got Robert to buy it for us as he looked like a fully-grown adult since he turned 15. I walked past the spot we ran and hid when the police chased us for underage drinking. *Crime doesn't pay kids.*

The apprehension grew and I could feel my palms sweating. Wracking my brains for why I was so nervous I realised I was half expecting to bump into Rachel. My life had recently become a comedy of errors recently and Sod's Law kept biting me on the arse. And sure enough… I didn't see her. I sighed with relief and cursed under my breath, just in time to get a dirty look for a passing parent with a small child in an army uniform and a tiara. *See? Sod's Law.*

I picked up a French stick and some frozen garlic bread and I was staring at - drooling over - the confectionary when a flash of dark hair out of the corner of my eye made my stomach flip. I turned and saw a form agonising over the biscuits. I must have been staring for a while because when she stood up she looked me square in the face and said: "Can I help you?"

"No. I was just admiring the sweets." *Did I really just say that?* I noticed an aura of light surrounding her, I rubbed my eyes and it went away. *The light.* She giggled and picked up a packet of sweets and added it to her basket. I couldn't help but noticed it was full of snacks.

She giggled again. "I have a sweet tooth."

"Me too." I wiggled my eyebrows at her, even I was embarrassed by my cheesiness, but she seemed to enjoy it. The glow around her returned a pink colour and it disappeared again when I blinked. *I need to get my eyes tested.* We chatted for a little while longer and I left with bread, garlic bread, two packets of sweets, two large bars of chocolate, a bottle of champagne and her number. *I'm on fire!*

And I wasn't the only one it smelt like the kitchen was on fire when I got back. They'd managed to burn the toast for the starters and they were hissing each other angrily when I walked it. It looked like two cats fighting in the street, circling each other and seeing who moves first. They cheered up when I emptied the bag on the table.

The meal was lovely, considering we were all expecting to get food poisoning from the homemade chicken liver pate. Turns out, Matthew is quite the chef and Olivia makes and excellent overseer. But my mind kept wandering back to the girl in the shop. I've never been particularly confident around women, in fact I've never been a confident man, but over the last few months I've started to feel good. Better than good.

As if she had read my thoughts Olivia said: "You seem different. What's wrong with you?" I fell about laughing in response and changed the subject.

It wasn't until I was alone in my sofa bed that I had a chance to think about the glow surrounding the girl in the shop and whether it's connected to the lights I've seen when I'm Jo. The dopamine theory is out of the window because I was completely sober and obviously not having sex in the shop. They were certainly coming more often and part of me was sure they weren't a trick of the light, no matter how much I wanted them to be.

I'd been ignoring them, half expecting and half hoping they to go away, but seeing them in daylight like this had changed my mind. I used this convenient insomnia as a chance to do some research. I searched for aura.

- **A distinctive and pervasive quality or character; air; atmosphere.**
- **A subtly pervasive quality or atmosphere seen as emanating from a person, place, or thing.**
- **Pathology. a sensation.**

*That's not what I'm looking for.*

**The aura is the electromagnetic field that surrounds every organism and object.**

*This sounds more like it.* I found a piece on auras and fell asleep reading about the science of electromagnetic fields; the spirituality of chi and how we are all connected. It sounded a little farfetched, but I was almost sure I could see a haze around my fingers when I tried a couple of exercises. I may have fell asleep during these as I woke up with my arm across my face.

## 40

I returned home on Sunday tired because pullout sofas aren't comfy. I spent most of the journey dozing off and waking up when the train jolted and my head crashed against the window. This happened four or five times and I had a red welt on my forehead.

I was rubbing my head in irritation as I hauled my bag off the train and my yawning was rudely interrupted by a familiar *tap-tap-tap*. My stomach sank to my knees as I frantically looked around for the source. I shuddered as a bead of sweat ran the entire length of my back and I saw a shock of dark brown hair and the most perfect hourglass wiggling its way out of the station.

Angry tuts walked past me and I felt someone crash into my shoulder: I had been stood in the flow of the crowd staring at Emily(?) leaving the station. I was torn between chasing after her and letting her walk away. I couldn't work out how she knew I was here. *No, not this again. She was obviously getting off a train, or - more likely - it wasn't her.*

"James!" A hand waved in my peripheral vision. I turned my head very slightly to see, but my eyes wouldn't obey and didn't move from the spot I saw Emily. *I should text her.*

"James!" The voice was louder, unsure, and two hands waved frantically. More people were staring so I finally - and begrudgingly - acknowledged Jo, who was thrilled to see me. She looked paler than I remembered. "What were you staring at?" Her concern was palpable.

"I could have sworn I saw…" I paused and looked at her, "an ex. I thought she'd left the city. So odd. Miss me?" I quickly changed the subject when I saw the concern creep into her eyes. I pulled myself together. "Hold on, what are you doing here? Did we arrange to meet?"

"No you said what time your train was getting in and I wanted to see you. I thought we could grab dinner if you're hungry, but…" She studied my face. "I'm guessing you're tired."

*What's wrong with my face?* "I'm shattered, do you mind if we do Wednesday? I need a couple of days to catch up on cleaning and running. I'm getting a little chunky." I patted my belly and she giggled, attempting to mask her obvious disappointment. We arrange dinner on Thursday - Jo was seeing her family on Wednesday, so I spent Sunday and Monday evening doing chores and chatting to Nathan. Completely boring.

Until Tuesday. Tuesday was very much one of *those* days. It was worse than one of *those* days: it is only a slight exaggeration to say my computer exploded.

It started off normal. My alarm went off at 7am when I showered, cleaned my teeth, dressed and had breakfast - cereal. Then the sardine can that the Transport for London calls a tube to work with all the other zombies in business suits. This time I was pressed up against a blonde women in a trouser suit who smiled seductively and bluetoothed her contact details to me before she left. *Surely this doesn't happen in real life?* I felt frustrated and tense when I got to work.

Usually the doors opened at 9am and then it's answering the phones and checking people in until 1pm, but today our computers couldn't connect to the network, but this wasn't a massive problem and we had to open the doors.

Luckily it wasn't busy.

Unluckily the phone lines went down at 10.30am. No incoming or outgoing calls and then 10 people walked in at once. I suggested closing up but the companies inside don't take 'but we can't contact you' as an excuse. So it was all notepads for telephone notes and sending some unlucky fool across the lobby, up the lift and across multiple other lobbies to deliver them. Guess who that fool was? Guess who was the only one wearing comfortable shoes?

With Gemma and Alice in inappropriate footwear for running found a five story office building, I was the schmuck that was up and down the stairs and lifts.

I was sweaty and livid by lunchtime and we were assured everything would be up and running by 2pm, so I didn't take a lunch break and inhaled a sandwich on my way to relay a message to the Property Developers on the top floor.

Then we were promised the systems would be back up and running tomorrow morning.

"I'm exhausted. I can't do this much longer!" I slammed my hands into my desk in frustration and my screen flickered and a white line appeared through the middle, before the whole computer blue screened and died with an electronic screech.

*I hate computers.*


That evening I ate dinner with my laptop open, desperately scouring the Internet for jobs. In my frustration due to a terrible day at work I applied for two PA roles, one Administration at an Insurance company and two Sales roles. *I'm not a salesman but it's worth a punt.*

I had a replacement computer the next day and the systems were up by lunchtime.

My week didn't improve, although I did feel better when I met up with Jo. We met straight from work and found a pub with booths to cosy up in. She looked ill and got progressively worse throughout the evening.

We chatted about our days and cooed over photos and videos of Grace. Jo stared into her glass like a crystal ball, swirling her wine. A few droplets splashed over the glass onto the table.

"I do that." She looked up confused and I nodded towards the glass. "When I'm nervous I play with my drink. What's wrong?"

Moving her fingers away from her glass she shook her head. "I'm not nervous, I just haven't been feeling too great - exhausted and a little irritable. Sorry for being such rubbish company."

"You're not rubbish company."

"Can we go back to yours?" Jo barked the question and it stunned me silent for a moment, before I nodded and led her out the door. She wasn't being particularly affectionate. *I wonder what she wants.* A small part of me subconsciously hoped she was going to break up with me, but as she clung to me arm as we walked down the street I knew she was hooked. Literally.

"Can I have my arm back please? My bank card is in my pocket." I wiggled free and walked into the tube station.

The journey back to mine was silent, Jo looking like she was going to doze off with the rhythmic rocking motion of the tube. I made her a cup of coffee while she sat on my bed. "She wanted to come back here." I whispered to Andy who was cooking his dinner. He just raised an eyebrow. "No, not like that, I think she wants to talk."

He put a hand on my shoulder. "You worry too much."

We both sat on the edge of my bed sipping at the steaming drink. "Can we talk?" Jo blurted out. Her speech patterns were odd and her voice wasn't as lilting as usual.

*Here we go.* "What's up?" I muffled my words with my mug and refused to make eye contact.

"Are you OK? You've seemed distant but..."

"I'm fine." I said warmly, trying to remove the edge from the words.

She sighed. "I know. I know it's all in my head it's just..." She seemed really nervous, I could see beads of sweat on her forehead. "It's just I really like you..." My heart stopped.

The world stopped. This was worse than I thought. *Please don't say it.* She can't... She surely can't... Not seeing as I've been so apathetic, so unsure... There is no way... "I think I..." I realised I hadn't been breathing. I took a swig of my drink and relaxed my posture, trying to seem nonchalant as I silently chanted. *Don't say it. Don't say it. Don't say it.*

Jo looked at me eyes watery and confused. I could hear the cogs turning and a weight sank onto her shoulders, she visibly sagged as she whispered, "I just really like you."

The weight lifted off mine, but I couldn't escape the pang of guilt. I could see our dynamic: I was distant so she chased me. She was just entertainment for me. This isn't right.

"Look Jo," I took her hands in mine and I could feel my fingers warming up as I caressed her palms. I felt the ache in my chest building, the guilt becoming a pressure behind my eyes. *Not guilt.* The voice in my head apparently disagreed with me. "I like you too." She smiled sadly. "I mean it." I kissed her. "Let's not move too fast. We have fun together right?" She nodded and the smile brightened.

It occurred to me that I hadn't seen her aura. "I'm hungry." I growled as I kissed her. She looked shocked and laughed nervously.

"We've just eaten."

"Not what I meant." I climbed on top over her and washed her sadness away in a wave of kisses. She is lovely, sexy, funny, smart and smitten: I wanted to make her feel that way.

**Emily**

**26**

I didn't realise how much I missed him until I saw him. He was walking out of work and running his hands through his hair. He looked tired and dishevelled, like one who had a stressful day at work, rather than one who's life is being drained from that drop by drop.

He looked older, maturing: a fine wine or a good cheese. Although telling someone they're a good cheese usually results in a slap.

I will admit it was my own fault: I decided to poke that wound so I went to his work and waited. I had the best of intentions. I had intended to talk to him. Instead I just watched him walk out and rub his neck with those big hands. I watched him pull a face when he was out the door with his work colleagues watching his back. I watched him walk up to another woman and...

Oh.

**James**

**41**

That night I saw Emily. The universe is against me or, more likely, my subconscious hates me. As Jo was on top of me I saw Emily's face, Jo's body became hers and I came thinking of her. That's when I knew I needed to end it. No matter how hard I tried I couldn't escape the fact I was in love with someone else.

She left in the morning, late for work but happy but that evening she cancelled our weekend because she went home sick from work. A really bad flu: migraines, sickness: the works.

I didn't deny the relief I felt for getting a few more days to work out my emotions. I was lying in the bed staring at the ceiling to trying to work out what to do when my phone went again. I'd offered to take round supplies and I reached across expecting it to be Jo and - *can you guess what happened next kiddies?* - notification said: Emily.

**Hi, how are you? Xx**

**Emily**

**27**

After seeing him kissing some blonde, busty, leggy thing I decided I really needed a drink, so I followed them to the bar. I grabbed a table near the window where I could see them and they definitely couldn't see me. The booth they were in obscured James, but I had a good look at the woman he was with. Blonde, pasty skin, looks tired, big eyes, blonde, really pretty, blonde. *Eurgh, blonde.* She's gorgeous.

I was on my second large glass of red when they left. Together. Arm in arm. *Blonde. Eurgh.*

I decided to get a little drunk, not steaming, just nicely pished so I had an excuse to text him: I don't care what anyone says drunk texting is always an excuse. It took an hour and another large glass before I came up the perfect message.

**James**

**42**

That was it. Four words. Two kisses.

I lay my phone face down on the bed and went downstairs, trembling as I walked. My mind was blank and I was in a peaceful Zen state as I walked into the kitchen and poured myself a large glass of whiskey. Then took a swig from the bottle. Shock. I was in a peaceful state of shock.

"Hello stranger." Nathan walked in and his eyes switched from the bottle, to me, to the glass, to my face. "Uh oh, what's happened? Jo hasn't dumped you has she? I heard you the other night and she sounded *really* into you."

"Emily just text."

"Delete it."

"What?"

"Delete it, I mean it, you don't need her in your life. I mean what did she say to make you like this again?" He gestured towards the bottle.

"'Hi, how are you?' With two kisses."

"That's it?"

"Yes."

"Delete it."

I knew he was right and I agreed with him. Why was I even considering responding? *I'm in a relationship with a wonderful woman who is smitten with me. Who I was planning on dumping 10 minutes ago...*

**Emily**

**28**

By the time I went to sleep I was certain I wasn't going to get a response. Feeling a small amount of regret, a large amount of rejection and massive chunk of insecurity, I deleted his number and put him out of my mind.

I guess I'll never get the chance to explain and he will continue to hurt the ones he cares about. Well fuck him, that isn't my problem.

**James**

**43**

I text back the next day. I decided to go with a chatty, friendly response, even though I wanted to know where the hell she's been for the past two months. She responded to every one of my replies almost instantly, and they started stilted but became warmer and more in-depth. She had been promoted and was now the Head of HR.

There was an increasingly guilt that developed as a lump in my throat and an ache in my chest. This was contradictory to the joy and elation I felt for speaking to Emily again. I knew I shouldn't have been but how could I not? This woman was exciting.

I went to look after Jo, not just because I felt guilty, but that was the main reason. Jo looked dreadful. I took her round some orange juice, tea bags, healthy ready meals and a couple of pots of noodles so we could have dinner together. She looked really pale, but she was pleased to see me so I made us hot drinks and we snuggled down together to eat.

She fell asleep on my lap. My phone went off in my pocket and the vibrations made Jo stir and sleepily ask: "Who's that?" I pulled it out my pocket, but I knew who it was.

"Just Mum. Go back to sleep." I kissed the top of her forehead.

**Can we meet for coffee? I'd like to talk to you and I know that I owe you an explanation. E xx**

**I have a girlfriend. I don't think that's a good idea.**

**Please? Not a date. I don't want to interfere with your relationship, but I want to explain and it would be better in person, don't you think? E xx**

Jo made an adorable little snuffling noise and I snuggled further down with her under the duvet. I fell asleep thinking about Emily and when I woke up with Jo in my arms, I was still thinking about Emily. Not that was any different to any other day. I responded whilst I cooked Jo breakfast.

**OK. Coffee. After work on Thursday? X**

## 44

The wait until Thursday was unbearable. Jo was still bedridden and had her housemates and her parents looking after her. Her dad went round in the evenings and cooked, but she was happy to keep me away in case she was contagious.

I applied for a couple more jobs and went for a couple more runs but I wasn't up to much. The nerves killed my appetite for most of that week and I had to invest in a heavy-duty antiperspirant, which did not live up to the tagline of 'Suitable for stressful situations'. It was barely suitable for relaxing by the sea.

I was so nervous. My hands quivered and my back ran with sweat. I could feel a bead threatening to split my face in two, so I quickly rubbed it away as I walked. I tried to slow my pace because I knew pit stains marks were rapidly growing, which is why I wore black, heavy fabric shirt.

I was torn. I wanted to see her, I needed closure but I thought I might hate her. I couldn't think of Emily as a heartless bitch who toyed with my emotions, not if we were supposed to talk. I managed to suppress my feelings enough to text her politely. I'm sure I can do it in person.

She was there first. I saw her through the window, she was staring into a mug and she seemed to be concentrating. Her brow was furrowed and her hair pulled back off her face. I stood at a safe distance and watched for a few minutes before going in. She looked stunning: a loose fitting, black vest and a black cardigan thrown over the back of the chair.

She looked warm. Tense.

I could feel her eyes boring into me as I walked in and ordered a drink. She waggled her fingers in greeting and then returned to drumming them rhythmically on the table. I smiled knowingly at the barista as her eyes flitted between us.

When I sat down we made fleeting eye contact and she looked away rubbing her neck. I realised I've never seen her nervous.

**Emily**

**29**

I sat staring into my mug, wishing I had been better at divination, although even without the power to read the future I still could sense how it would go. It would be tense; there was the slight possibility he was going to walk out and the strong probability that he wasn't going to believe me. *He's going to think I'm nuts.* But so what if he does, this isn't about my feelings, I wasn't seeing him because I wanted to see him. This was for the greater good. *And denial is just a river in Egypt.*

*Very witty. Go away.* I needed to let him know the reason why I left (I was making him ill) and reason I returned (he is making his new girlfriend ill). Easy. Straightforward. Nothing to worry about.

My leg shook nervously and my bowels felt like they had liquefied. Yeah, nothing to worry about. I meant we're officially in the future, pretty much everything is touch screen, there are over 75 accepted and normalised genders and yet the talk of the supernatural still makes people nervous.

He was late. This was a power game, he's an idiot if he thinks I'm naïve enough not to notice it. Or maybe I'm early and paranoid. Probably the latter.

God my head is spinning. Calm down. Breath. Why didn't I take some Valerian Root or calming tablets or something. I'm going to be sick.

I had felt prepared, even talking through different scenarios to my reflection whilst getting ready for work, but now I'm here my head has gone blank. My only option is to wing it. *Or run.*

*Not again.*

As long as I don't forget the two reasons I was there why I left (I was making him ill) and why I returned (he is making his new girlfriend ill). Just remember th...

Then he walked in and I forgot what I was thinking about. He looked stunning, even in his work uniform with the questionable quality of fabric. I was staring. He could tell I was staring. I waved at him and turned back to my drink as he walked over. *Damn, should have got another one.*

*I might actually be sick.* "How have you been?" My voice noticeably cracked.

**James**

**45**

"How have you been?" There was a quiver in her voice and her fingers still drummed - irritatingly - on the table.

I let the question hang there as I took a sip of my scolding drink. I burnt my tongue. *That was stupid.* "There is no need to be nervous."

Her expression didn't change. "I'm not."

"You are."

"You seem different."

"Oh how I have missed your questioning."

"That wasn't a question."

"Fine. How have you been?"

"I... I've been better." She drained her mug and got up to get another one. Leaving me feeling tense and bemused.

"Can I just...? OK, breathe. Can I just explain and then you can decide whether you want to walk out that door?"

"Well," I took another scolding sip. "I'm not leaving until I finish my coffee."

**Emily**

**30**

Forget a knife you could only cut the tension with an axe. It was stifling, suffocating and I was concentrating on remembering to breath so much I forgot what why I wanted to see him. All my eloquently crafted monologues went out of the window as I took a deep breath…

"Being around you is hard to do in more ways than one. No wait, that doesn't sound right. I mean you know you got quite ill? Well that was because of me. Wait, that's not a good place to start. I mean I want to be around you. No, hold on, I'm not trying to get you back. I just… Oh God, how do I explain this."

He stared at me bewildered, jaw slightly slack with one eyebrow raised. I'd been talking too fast for him to understand.

"OK, so…"

## James

## 46

"...it's not just that I love you." She blurted out and I choked on my coffee in response. When my coughing fit died down she continued. "It's not just that I love you: it's that we can't be together. When we were together you got very ill and I can't keep hurting you like that. I'm bad for you." I tried to interject but she was just carried on talking, she had obviously rehearsed this. "I thought it would be easier if I wasn't near you, after all, you got better. You look great. I'm sorry I hurt you, but..." She paused.

My coffee was cooling. It was light brown and the bubbles on top occasionally popped. I focused on my coffee so I didn't have to listen to the demented ramblings of a woman I thought I loved. How wrong can a guy be? I took a large mouthful and made eye contact, her eyes were wide and watery and she opened her mouth to continue speaking.

*I don't want to hear this.* "I have a girlfriend." She tried to interject, but I held my hand up. "I came to see you because I wanted closure. I cared about you and thank you for being honest, but I don't want to talk about this any further. The door has closed, but perhaps we can be friends." My cup clattered on the table as I finished it. "So what's it's like as Head of HR?"

I didn't want to talk about my feelings and I didn't want to listen to hers. What I caught of her babbling was that she blamed herself for me getting the flu (*creepy*) and I was having horrible flashbacks to the vampire conversation.

I could tell she was disappointed and her shoulders visibly sank, there was something else she wanted to say, but instead she said: "You should get a new job: you're better than your current role."

"How would you know?"

"I know. I know you."

"Do you now?"

"Don't play games. Anyway, tell me about your new girlfriend." I didn't want to, but I did in an attempt to dissipate the tension, I couldn't keep arguing with her. Emily wasn't seeing anyone, or if she was she certainly wasn't telling me. I felt like she was being deliberately evasive, but I always felt like that talking to her.

I told her about Jo and she was fascinated by the fact she was currently struck down by flu, asking about her symptoms; how long she had been ill; whether it was similar to my illness until I snapped: "Why? Why are you so fascinated by this? Did you give me something?" The doctor had tested me but not for everything.

The offence was written all over her face. She coloured a deep red and slammed her half-empty cup on the table. "What are you accusing me of giving…?"

"You wanted to meet up and you said you made me sick." I interrupted.

There was silence as she breathed loudly and deeply. "Yes. So we were talking before about the supernatural."

*No!* "No. No I am not talking to you about that."

"James you have to listen to me, this is all connected. Don't you see that Jo is just as ill as you were."

"No. I'm not doing this. I am happy to try and be friends, but on the proviso you never discuss religion or vampires or werewolves or whatever."

"I would like us to be friends, so fine."

"We have a deal then."

We even shook on it.


I was walking on air when I left. I felt like the part of me that was missing was back in my life. I didn't realise how much I missed her until we started talking again: the ache in my chest became a happy glow and I could almost forget the fact she is completely batty.

However, I couldn't escape the background noise, the nagging sensation of guilt. I knew that I couldn't just be a friend to Emily. I wanted her, I needed her, but she is a fruit loop and there is Jo…

Jo was still ill. I spent most of the Bank Holiday weekend nursing her, but she didn't seem to be getting any better. The racking cough seemed to be getting worse and she still looked pale. *Bless her.*

She didn't want me to stay but I insisted.

Her dad didn't want me to stay, but I insisted.

Her housemates didn't want me to stay and I started to think that no one wanted me there. Anyone would think they didn't trust me. There were subtleties that gave it away, like glaring at me constantly and insisting that I leave.

We watched movies, I cooked and I fell asleep each night with Jo in my arms. *Bliss.*

I text Emily on the way to the home on Monday to see how her weekend was.

**47**

I was dreading work. I couldn't hack working there anymore. I was sure it wasn't the place, I loved working with Gemma and Alice, even Geoff (on the rare occasions he spoke to us, or anybody), and Deborah (when she spoke to us, or was in), but the days meshed together and I was bored to tears. When no one was in the office I had been known to spin round in my chair until dizzy. Or someone walked up to the door.

I got caught when I span off my chair. *I hate my job so much.*

Wishing for the weekend was a daily occurrence and it affected my mood. I wasn't worth speaking to until 3pm on Monday and I didn't cheer up until Wednesday afternoon.

Speaking of Wednesday, that afternoon I had a voicemail from the insurance company I applied for inviting me in for interview. I listened to the voicemail on an extended bathroom break. I spent most of my toilet breaks sat on the closed seat contemplating my life and what I was doing with it.

I danced uncaringly around the men's toilets and in the lift on the way down, forgetting there were security cameras that recorded everything. When I remembered I stuck my tongue out at the camera and twerked in glee. Well, twerking is a bit of an overstatement, although it does make me laugh when I remember that I'm a grown up: a respectable member of society.

I text Emily the good news on the walk to the tube station after work. Usually I would be afraid to come across as a stalker, but I couldn't contain myself. I called Jo after who sounded a lot better. She always sounded better when I wasn't around. Emily had text back when I got off the tube at the other end.

**I know you'll ace it. Did you want some interview tips? E xxx**

Three kisses. She seemed to be getting a little over friendly so I didn't respond until after my run. There is a game with text messages: a subtle etiquette. Three kisses means she's into me, two is ambivalent and one is a friend. Sarah used to send me about 10 but she was in love. Nathan has been known to send me about five when drunk. I always ended up trying to translate Nathan's messages, but they usually consisted of:

**I really love you, you know. I know I never say it but you're great. Xxxxx** *(Editor's note: I corrected the spelling and grammar to make it understandable.)*

I text back thanking her for the offer, but I was OK with my own research. Then she started questioning me about Jo's illness again: asking about the symptoms; whether she went to the doctors; was I sure that it wasn't like when I got ill?

**Cough, fever, chills, sweats, sneezing. It's flu. No she didn't go the doctors. It's flu. She's not blacking out so it's not like mine. She has flu. Please leave it.**

I didn't ask why she wanted to know. I don't want to know and she would just lie to me anyway or be ridiculously evasive. She had an infuriating way of answering a question with a question when she didn't want to answer.

**Emily**

**31**

After our awkward and argumentative coffee date I realised the only way I'm going to get to educate him is on the sly. At least if he's in my life I've got more chance of helping him. I mean, just because he flat out refused to listen to me then it doesn't mean he'll always be so closed-minded. Right?

Perhaps I could introduce him to some books or movies. Or maybe he'll learn naturally. Or perhaps he'll drain energy from me and not his girlfriend. Although if his girlfriend keeps getting ill she will leave him.

*Or die.*

*Well, no one has died.*

*No, but people have committed suicide.*

*In extreme cases only.*

OK, so I don't have a plan, but I do have James as a friend. For now. Maybe we could make it work. All I have to do is make him realise I'm so much better than Jo. Eurgh, what a boring name. Jo. She's no challenge. But first, I need him to be friends with me and he has that interview for a job he's too good for.

## James

## 48

The interview was Friday afternoon. I entered a glass fronted building similar to my own but surrounded by the original Victorian brickwork: a wonder of modern architecture, moulding the old and new. Which was a short summary of London. I couldn't help but notice it wasn't as nice as my building.

The Insurance office was on the first floor and was greeted by a sour faced receptionist/security guard who just grunted and pointed to the stairs when I went to sign in. He was talking on a mobile phone. *If I acted like that I would have been fired a long time ago.*

Another sour-faced receptionist who shooed me to some seats where I sat waiting. I had arrived 10 minutes early, feigning a doctor's appointment to get out of work, and yet I waited for a further 20 minutes. *I'm glad I didn't book this in my lunch break!*

A man in a brown suit, beige shirt and brown tie met me. I tried not to look at the mirage that was his hairline. He led me through an open plan office into brown meeting room with another beige man in glasses and a grey suit. There were no windows, it was dark and pokey and we sat at a round table, so close I could feel the heat from their legs. It's amazing how nervous you get when you think that someone might touch your leg.

It was the standard questions:

What can you bring to this company?
*A bit of Goddamn personality.* I'm enthusiastic, driven... *blah, blah, blah.*

Where do you see yourself in five years?
*Doing your wife.* I'm looking for a company I can progress within. Although I have only been with my employer a short time I have already assessed there isn't any progression unless I moved to one of the companies with the building, rather the facilities management organisation themselves.

What is your biggest strength?
*Come on! Look at me. I'm awesome.* Excellent customer service; a smile for every customer and excellent organisational skills.

What's your biggest weakness?

*I'm just too brilliant.* I'm a perfectionist to the point of anal.

And so on and so on.

It wasn't a difficult interview but I left feeling I hadn't made the grade and I was very pleased about that. They were all the Bs: boring, balding, bland and beige.

I called Jo on the way home to see if she was free. I'd finally made my decision: I was going to break up with her, as long as she was better. She answered her front door looking healthier than she had done in the past fortnight. In fact, she answered the door wearing nothing but a pair or black stilettos and holding a bottle of champagne.

"I wanted to thank you for being my nurse." She said huskily as she led me into her bedroom. Her pale skin looked luminescent in the light and her hair cascaded over her small but pert breasts.

She tapped the bottom of my jaw as a signal that I was gawping at her. Mentally I was spinning round in circles. I couldn't deny my feelings for Emily so I had to end it with Jo. On the other hand, I made her happy, she made me happy, who was getting hurt?

The popping of the champagne corked pulled me from my reverie. "So how was the interview?" She poured us a glass each.

"Beige." She looked at me: I realised I hadn't fully understood the question and I had been staring at her nipples. She giggled and pretended to be embarrassed. "They were boring, it was boring; can we please stop talking?"

The next morning I skipped in through my front door still wearing my work clothes from the night before. Because Nathan had utterly no way of keeping his mouth shut with Alice I hadn't told him about my interview. I didn't want Gemma knowing that I was job hunting because she'd tell Deborah. She was a lovely woman outside of work but an utter creep inside.

I attempted to run up the stairs before anyone saw me. So of course Susan was sat in the kitchen reading the paper. "Wee ooo wee ooo! Walk of shame alert! Someone had a good night. What happened? I take it you didn't shower before coming home." She wrinkled her nose and grinned at me, waiting for an explanation.

I lifted my collar and sniffed my skin. I could still smell Jo on me. I bet I smelt of sex that whole tube ride home. I felt myself heating up as sat at the table opposite her.

"Aren't you working today?" She shook her head, still waiting for my story. "I stayed at Jo's." She still stared at me, knowing there was more to it than that. I sighed loudly and put my chin on the table. "I had intended to break up with her." Sue spluttered in response. "I know, I know. I've been worried that my feelings for her weren't as strong as her feelings for me and I've been scared of leading her on."

"What happened then?"

"She answered the door naked apart from a pair of heels."

The first slap Sue gave me rang out through the house as Andy came down the stairs. He walked into me rubbing my face and Susan angrily yelling at me for being shallow, selfish and toying with Jo's emotions.

"LET ME FINISH!" I yelled over her. "And then I realised that I was being stupid. Jo is a wonderful woman who cares about me and I do care about her. Bloody hell. I'm not that type of man."

My face hurt.

Susan sat back down looking sheepish and huffy. "I was going to say how cold that would have been if you had been playing with her like that."

"You did. Just before you slapped me the second time." I rubbed my face again.

"So you didn't get dumped or do the dumping?" Andy asked.

"No." We responded in unison.

"So what's the problem?"

"There isn't one." Jo.

"So why did you slap him?"

"Crossed wires." Jo got up and put the kettle on, waving my favourite mug at me in an offering of peace.

I sat reading my messages and catching up on the news as I sipped my tea and contemplated a shower. I knew I smelt but I was enjoying wallowing in my own (and Jo's) filth. I noticed I had two missed Facebook messages and two missed text messages. All of which were from Emily. She asked me who the interview went; what I was up to; links to a couple of articles regarding interview tips and a news story I may find interesting.

I stared at my phone in disbelief: she's never this clingy. I text back.

**Hi, sorry I went to Jo's straight from the interview last night and just got home. Yeah the interview went well but I don't particularly want the job. Thanks for the links. Did you have a good night? What are you up to today? x**

I thought that sounded suitably friendly. I wanted to ask what she was playing at but I thought that might be too harsh.

That afternoon I went for a 20 mile run. Nothing felt real: it was utterly beautiful but that could have been the runner's high. The adrenaline pumped round my body and the sun's rays beat down on my skin. Nathan had invited me out with him and James, but I felt like a bath and bed. Jo took a lot out of me last night.

As my lungs burned I contemplated giving up and getting a taxi home, but I fought through it and distracted myself from the pain in my legs by thinking about Emily.

*What is she up to?*

*She loves you, she said so herself and she wants to get you back.*

*It's never that simple with her.*

*How would you know?*

*You've known her for months.*

*I feel like I've known her for lifetimes.*

*You're over thinking again. Just roll with it.*

*That's easy for you to say.*

I argued with myself all the way home.

**Emily**

**32**

There was trash on the TV but I wasn't watching. My roommate was sat with me completely engrossed in the story. "You realise this isn't real right?"

"It's reality TV and these people are pretty trashy so I'm pretty certain it's real."

"This can't be real."

"It is."

"They're having sex on screen!"

The mindless conversation, combined with the bottle of bubbles we were sharing was a welcome distraction from the background noise in my head. I'd tried meditation, I've tried visualisation and going to the gym but I couldn't escape the nagging feeling in my stomach and chest.

"So…?" She'd turned down the volume and was staring at me intently, whilst pouring the wine. Quite a talent.

"Why the hell hasn't he text me back?"

"James, right? James with the girlfriend? James who you ditched when you got scared of your emotions?" My excuse when she caught me crying into my cooking. I was hardly going to tell her the truth, most people can't handle the truth.

I took a sip from my glass in response and the conversation ended there.


I didn't want to go home after work, so I found a corner of a bar and sulked. I knew I would get more questions about my feelings that I couldn't explain. I didn't want to talk. I truly thought I had met a kindred spirit, I thought I could help him.

But I realised I didn't want to help him. If he's not willing to realise who I am to him and how much he loves me… What's the point?

Second glass of Shiraz.

I'm the best thing that's ever happened to him, I helped him awaken. Sure I made him ill but without me he's just another boring, normal person. Yes, I would like to be friends, but that's not possible.

Third glass.

People watching and reading auras. Not thinking. Just being. It's peaceful. He's going to have to figure it out like I did, make the mistakes I did. Hurt people like I did. It might be selfish but it's for my sanity.

**James**

**49**

Emily didn't respond for two days and when she finally did I threw my phone at the wall. Luckily my phone didn't break but the plaster in the wall chipped away. *Shit!*

**I can't do this. I'm sorry but I can't have you in my life. I wish you all the best for the future. Emily.**

I tried to call her and she didn't pick up so I left her a message. I tried to keep my voice steady and my tone calm but it cracked. I couldn't hide my hurt and anger. I was shaking. To steady my hand I squeezed my phone so hard the screen cracked. *Double shit! How is that even possible?*

"OK, fine. If you don't want me in your life I won't be, but you can do this to my face. After the games you've pulled you owe me this."

I got a text message response almost instantly.

**I owe you nothing.**

My second voicemail message wasn't nearly as calm but I managed to keep my hands loose enough that I didn't make my screen worse.

"I'm sick of your games. I feel like you've toyed with my emotions." *I'm not a ball of yarn.* "Meet me for a drink in a neutral location. I want... I would like an explanation." I corrected myself.

I paced the bedroom floor, wanting to go get a drink but refusing to hit the bottle every time she pissed me off. I was not having her being a negative effect on a life I was improving: she is not going to start that downward spiral.

Five minutes later she hadn't responded so I called her again. It rang until I got her voicemail, so her phone was still on at least and she wasn't cutting me off. "I will come into your work if I have to. Don't doubt me on that."

**OK. Next Saturday. 6pm. The hotel bar. You know which one.**

It was hardly a neutral location. I knew this was a power play but I didn't care, I wasn't going to let myself keep going back to her. *She's obviously a crazy bitch.* I snapped and threw my phone at the wall again, not looking at where it landed and went to have a long shower to calm down.

When I fished my phone out from behind the dresser I had a message from Jo about what a good time she has with me and how pleased she is to have me in her life. She also asked if I wanted to go shopping with her this weekend.

I thought about not responding. I knew I should, it would be the right thing to do, but I was in the mood to be a dick. So I responded, but I said no. I never want to go shopping. *All those crowds... shudder.*


That week was unbearable. Like most weeks. Like every fucking week. It was boring and I was surprisingly disappointed when I got the email saying that I wasn't successful for the position. Part of me was hoping I was going to get the opportunity to decline them.

I met Jo after work on Tuesday. She came round mine and left 45 minutes later, slamming the door behind her. It was our first fight and it had been a big one. I knew I was only taking out my frustrations and my anger towards Emily at Jo. You lash out to the people closest to you after all, but she didn't deserve it.

She was giving me standard sympathies at not getting the job, but I was shrugging them off. I didn't want to speak to her, in fact I didn't even want her there and I was determined to cause a fight to get her to go. Although, I wasn't conscious of this at the time (does that make it better?): I realised what I'd done lying in bed that night contemplating my actions and replaying the evening.

"You don't seem like yourself." She was trying to cuddle up to me on the sofa in the living room.

I sat up and glanced in the mirror. "I look like myself."

"You know what I mean."

"I don't."

"What's wrong?"

I rolled my eyes. "Nothing."

"It seems like it."

"Maybe it's all the questioning. Can we watch this in silence?" I wasn't sure what was on.

Jo sat up and glared at me: I had been behaving like this since she arrived. Her voice was raised when she next spoke.  "If you're going to be like that…" She floundered, running her hands through her hair and staring angrily at the ceiling. When she continued her voice was calmer, colder and almost disconnected. "I think you need to cool off. I'm not seeing you this weekend. I'll call you Monday."

Then she left.


**50**


I daydreamed about surprising her with a dozen red roses and whisking her off a beautiful restaurant. She would be so enamoured with my charming repertoire and dashing good looks she would swoon into my arms. I would kiss her in the elevator on the way to a hotel room and would tumble on the bed to fuck like rabbits all night.

1

Saturday came and so did a sickening sense of déjà vu. James felt like a completely different person: he was a boy last time he walked into that hotel bar. Not quite fresh faced, but very naïve and now he felt scarred. He had learnt some tough lessons about love and falling in love with beautiful and crazy. A prime example of why you shouldn't fuck crazy.

He shook his head to rid himself of those thoughts.

*I don't want to think of her as beautiful, I don't want to think of her at all. She's a crazy bitch who toyed with my emotions.*

He was hurting.

Emily arrived first again. Her almost black eyes were drilling into him as he walked through the door, penetrating his soul. The defensiveness radiated from them both and the couple at the next table clocked the tension and watched with great interest, speculating on the upcoming conversation.

"Definitely exes." The blonde wondered.

"Well they've definitely had sex." The brunette agreed.

*Great, we have an audience.* Emily thought, watching the two men out of her periphery. She drummed her fingers rhythmically to distract herself from the fact she was shaking. When she made eye contact with James she inadvertently looked away and rubbed her neck, then cursed under her breath when she realised what she'd done. Her body language oozed nerves, but inside she was livid for having to have this conversation.

There were two drinks on the table, a glass of red wine with lipstick marks around the rim in front of Emily and a cool looking pint of generic larger opposite. Emily slid it over to the seat opposite before James sat down. That was as much as a greeting as she was willing to give. James stared at it wondering once again: *What am I doing here? Why did I want this?* A couple of seconds passed before he sat down and took a sip.

She broke the silence first. "How have you been?" That quiver in her voice returning with a vengeance and her fingers still drumming on her leg. She continued before he had a chance to response. "You wanted to talk. You're right I do owe you an explanation."

James didn't look up. He stared at his glass and the hypnotic race that was taken place with two droplets of condensation. He named them Bob and Dave. Dave was winning.

Emily watched James watching the condensation. He wasn't listening to her. "James? Please can we talk then?"

The question hung there for a beat more. James was getting good with playing power games: he was making her suffer. "Sure. Why?"

"Why? Because you wanted to talk. You're the one that demanded I meet you or you were going to show up at my work." Her voice was shrill. She coughed, trying to lower the volume and the pitch.

James took a swig of his drink before responding. "OK, why do you insist on dropping in and out of my life? Why do you insist on making me fall in love with you, only to disappear again? Do you know you're doing it? Do you realise what you're doing to me?"

"Oh."

Then came silence and two more tables noticed the awkwardness between them. The punctuated silences were reminiscent of their first date.

"Oh." She repeated. "Well... You didn't believe me when I said I hurt you. I need to explain. Oh Gods, how to explain?" She added to herself. They finally made eye contact and Emily's eyes were wet, much to her disdain.

"Actually I do believe you, I know you hurt me." Emily looked stunned. "You broke my heart." James could have cried but instead her direct all anger at Emily. Emily reeled, feeling this as a blast of heat. "Actually, before we start, you owe me complete honesty. Promise?"

Emily nodded.

James took a swig of his drink. Bob had finally won the race. "Why here?"

"I didn't want to go home after seeing you. Facing the roommate. She asks questions. Plus I thought it would be sweet."

James stared at her drink in hand, not blinking and breath shallow. "Complete honesty you said."

"Plus I thought if I brought you back to the place where we first connected... Maybe..." She took a gulp of her wine. "Power move. I want you to want me, like I want you. You have Jo. You don't want me anymore." *Christ what am I saying?*

"Thought so. You're the one that left both times. Why are you punishing me for you leaving?"

Emily was squeezing the glass so hard she thought it might break. "Because I didn't want to leave. I told you I was hurting you. I was making you sick. I love you, I don't want to hurt you."

The tears were threatening to spill over. "Why have you booked a room?"

"I told you, I don't want to face questions after seeing you. I thought I would be a state. She's... judgemental at times." That was only partially true: Emily was willing something to happen tonight.

The embarrassment of admitting her emotions was etched into her face, which was cast downwards, free hand wringing the back of her neck. She was exposed and struggling. And James was enjoying every moment. There is a satisfaction when you realise that someone you've been pining for is in the same situation as you. She wanted him and it was a huge ego boost. And although he didn't find her pain satisfying, he also didn't feel any need to relieve her of it.

He took a gulp of his drink and coughed - the bubbles burned the back of his throat - spilling a few drops onto his leg. *Smooth move Ex-Lax.*

Emily giggled, original confidence suddenly washing over her like a beam of sunlight and pulling her out of her self-destructive introspection. Taking a deep breath to clear her head she focused on James and how he was feeling. *Get it together girl, you're better than him.*

"It's not polite to gloat. You're enjoying seeing me like this. You're the one that wanted to meet. I'm trying to be civil." There was a cool disdain in her voice.

"You're delusional. I'm not enjoying this." James lied.

"I'm not delusional, although I may be a little bit sensitive." *Deep breath.* "Are you ready to listen? You want the truth?" *You can't handle the truth.*

"Fine." James finished his drink in one large mouthful. "Although I'm guessing I'm going to need another. Same again?" And he went to the bar without listening to Emily's answer.

## 2

James sat down with a thud. The bar was filling up now and Emily hoped to increasing volume would drown out the rest of their conversation. After all, there were already a couple of tables watching the awkward situation unfold like a terrible piece of reality TV. *Surely they have better things to talk about.*

She fingered the handle of her bag that contained the Codex; a fictional story, which was surprisingly accurate and a handwritten list of websites for him to research.

"OK, shoot. Why did you keep disappearing?"

"OK... Right... I'll start by saying I'm sorry I hurt you, not just emotionally but physically as well." James started, but Emily held her hand up and continued talking. "Let me speak and then I'll answer any questions." There was a commanding confidence in her that James hadn't seen before, she was determined to finish. "I'm the reason you were ill and you're the reason Jo got ill. We're not like all of these people." She gestured around the bar. "Yes we're human, but we're also more than that. We spoke before about the supernatural and..."

James snapped. "No." He didn't want this kernel of realisation to be real. His research was flashing through his head again and he remembered the colours around his fingers and across the skin of his lovers. He blinked and saw purple and black around Emily. He shook his head. "Not this again."

"Let me FINISH!" Emily yelled. She hadn't intended to yell but the frustration was building. There was an ache in her chest and tears pricked her eyes. James gestured for her to carry on but there were a lot of people watching now. "Can we go to my room? There are a lot of people watching and I don't want to make a scene."

"That's a first."

"I swear to the Gods James I am going to walk out of here and you can forget your explanation."

"Fine, fine." James made a fluid arm movement in the direction of the lifts. "Ladies first."

*I knew this wasn't going to work in a public place.* They thought in unison.

"One moment." Emily got up and wandered to the bar, her body visibly relaxing as she sauntered over and leaned over the bar to talk to the barman. He glanced over before nodding at Emily and handing over two glasses and a bottle while she pulled out a credit card.

"We might as well get a little drunk, this conversation would be easier if we were both relaxed." She gestured towards the stairs. "And I relax after a drink."

"I know."

"Don't start."

"Lift."

"I would prefer the stairs."

"Why?"

Emily didn't answer. Their little power play was being watch by a couple stood by the reception desk. They watched a man of indeterminate age ("He's definitely not over 30 though.") glare at a woman in a slinky black dress that made her look older than her face betrayed ("25." "No, 21." "Actually she could be nearly 30. When have you seen a 21 carrying a champagne bottle like that?) After a few awkward seconds of silence between them they watched them get into the lift together, faces like thunder. ("No chance that's what it looks like." "Of course it is! I wonder what they were arguing about though.")

## 3

The tension in the lift was palpable and it became incredibly clear why Emily didn't want to be trapped in a small box together. They would never know it but their hearts were beating in sync. Sickeningly fast.

Somehow being in such close quarters amplified the sexual tension between them. Emily was silently willing James to kiss her, while James was desperate trying to keep some modicum of self-control...

Which he failed at miserably. He span round, pinning her to the wall of the rising box and pressing her wrists flat so she couldn't move. The glasses tinkled together and the bottle clunked against the wall. Emily winced and listened for the sound of breaking glass, but the pain in her wrists made her tingle and a moan of pleasure escaped her lips.

"Kiss me." She pleaded and hated herself for begging.

James glared at her, eyes flashing and growling. "Why do you make me like this? I wasn't like this before you."

His words were like an ice bucket and she kicked out, wriggling free and livid. "I don't make you do anything." She looked at the glasses. "Guess these aren't crystal then."

The lift doors parted to a couple dressed in expensive looking casual wear in matching colours, with eyes that betrayed their judgement. They nodded as the two couples passed each other.

Emily stormed on ahead, already unwrapping the champagne bottle as she walked through the hotel room door. James stood in the open doorway repulsed and enthralled as she opened the bottle without spilling a drop, poured a glass, downed it, burped quietly and poured out two glasses in a matter of seconds. James took the outstretched glass and perched himself on the table. The view from the window was stunning, the lights twinkling under the night's sky. The sun was just setting in the very distance and it cast rays of orange that merged without the purple and black. The room was well furnished with beautiful artwork on the wall; a basket of fruit and water behind on the desk behind him - this room was expensive.

"So what is so private that we can't talk downstairs?" James sipped his drink, wondering whether this was really champagne or just sparkling wine. In answer Emily handed him a book, turned to the window and closed her eyes. James could see that the back of her neck was red from scratching and pulling it.

*Focus.* "I tried to explain before..." *Breathe in... 2... 3... 4... Hold... 2... 3... 4... 5... 6... 7... Breathe out... 2... 3... 4... 5... 6... 7... 8...* "...and I know it sounds crazy..."

"The Psychic Vampire Codex?" James read the back of the book while drinking faster.

Emily caught his emotional shift. There was no naivety this time, just disbelief and denial. He tasted delicious and she froze, stomach filled with butterflies and eyes pricked with tears for some reason. Now was time for the self-control she so obviously lacked.

She was pulled from her reverie the sound of the book landing on the bed.

"You're full of shit. Is this a joke?"

"No."

"You're a vampire."

Emily cocked her head. "Of sorts. You are too."

"I don't understand why you're such a drama queen."

"And I don't understand why you keep fighting this. I know you believe this, I know you're doubting your own doubts. There is an internal struggle going on and I know strange things have happened to you that you don't understand."

The purple and black light around Emily flashed in front of James' eyes again and he pictured the lights on Jo's body and the things they did to her.

*Jo.* "You're crazy. I'm leaving. Keep your book." Emily's eyes still faced the skyline and the room was cast in shadow, the streetlights making the tiniest illumination. James got off the desk and made to move towards the door. "How do you know what I'm feeling?"

"I read emotions and you radiate yours. You have a sensitivity towards them too. We're both fire, together we destroy everything we touch."

James didn't move. "Why did you keep leaving?"

"We're both fire." Emily repeated.

"Why did you keep returning?"

"We're both fire. Fire is drawn to fire and you know how I feel, so don't make me repeat myself. Again" She added.

They both stood like statues, neither of them knowing what the right move would be. Emily desperately wanted to hold James, kiss him and smell his skin hers: James was torn between leaving and staying. If he stayed it would question his entire belief system and there is the chance he would stay the night.

*What about Jo? Jo.*

"Jo. She's been ill recently. You mean that could be me?"

"You fed from her, drained her of her energy, made her weak and because she was weak she was susceptible to bugs she could usually fight off. Just like a newborn baby and why you shouldn't be around them if you have a cold or a cold sore." She turned round now and her eyes appeared wet in the light. "And yes, the same from you. For some reason I can't control myself around you."

"So how do I stop?"

"You can't."

"So I'm going to keep hurting people?"

"Learning to feed without focusing on one person, but it would mean you have to believe me. And you don't." A self-satisfied smile crept across Emily's face as she walked to refill her drink. She felt the warm glow of alcohol and the confidence it brought with it. James became aware of the bristling in the air between - like sparks - as she came near him. His mind was pulled away from Jo and down to a much lower, darker place.

"So we're monsters." A statement, rather than a question.

"We're all monsters here, vampire is the term tagged because leech sounds so much worse. It's more like a vitamin or iron deficiency, your body pulls energy from where it can to replenish what it needs. No Dracula and no transforming into bats. Surprisingly boring."

"And what about manipulating energy." James decided to show his hand.

"Well, that involved quite a lot of training." Emily waggled the bottle in front of her face and refilled James' glass. "Or..."

"Or I could be a natural."

"Correct. And you are."

The sexual tension increased as the barriers between them fell. Soon they were laughing and giggling and, crazy as it was, James was beginning to believe her.

"I should go."

"I know." She was staring into her glass. 'And thank you for listening, I know it's hard to believe but... Thank you." Emily's eyes were cast downward and the tone of her voice betrayed her final goodbye. James walked towards the door knowing he was never going to see her again. It had been brutal and passionate, but this chapter of his life was closing forever.

**4**

Unless he turned round now. If he turned around now he would stay the night and God knows what their future would be.

If he turned around now there would be a good possibility he would cheat on Jo. *Excuse me? OK.* If he turned around now there would be a guarantee that he would cheat on Jo.

Someone walked by the hotel room door: there was the sound of footsteps and a pair of black shoes went by as James stared at nothing. James could feel the crossroads and as he battled out the two sides in his head he was unaware he was just stood, stock-still, holding the door handle. He could feel the pull of the bond between them, like an elastic band. Did he snap it or let it ping back and hurt them both?

Emily watched him, trying to decide whether to say anything. She took a deep breath in, but he was suddenly on her, door slamming, her glass fell to the floor and finally broke as he pushed her against the window. The glass strained slightly and the thought of them falling crashed through both their minds. He pinned both hands above her hand with his left and his right circled her waist pulling her into him. She made a soft whimper, wriggled against him and slapped him, hard.

He fell back in shock and confusion, although the slap had heightened his arousal and he was panting. He tried to ask 'Why?' but he just mouthed the word.

"We were going to talk. We talked. You were going to leave. Then leave. I told you, we're not good together. I don't want to hurt you again." She turned away from him again, it was getting really difficult to look at him.

Something tickled James' face and he touched his fingers to it. Red. Blood dripped down his face.

*She must have caught me with her nails.* "Liar. You wanted this, so why are you fighting it?" James eyes were dark and his knuckles white with tension

"I can't control myself around you."

"Me neither." He faced Emily and tucked her hair back behind her ears: she flinched, her eyes glassy. James was aware of the smell of her skin and the sensitivity of his fingertips, he could see the lights on her skin now and he started to manipulate them.

Emily's pupils dilated and the word 'Please' formed on her lips and "I can't" escaped them.

James kissed her.

Emily pushed him away. "I won't hurt you." She yelled, but James just backed her up against the wall and kissed her again - a snarl escaped her lips. When he pulled away her make up was smudged and her hair was a mess, cascading over her shoulders. She resembled the gothic images of fallen angels you see in shops that smell strongly of incense and sell smoking paraphernalia.

"You want me." James growled again, his voice unrecognisable to his ears.

"I do." Emily's voice cracked on the second word.

"You need me."

"I need you to leave."

The begging made his legs weak and butterflies fought and fluttered in his lower intestine. "Stop fighting." Her hunger was burning him: he could taste it melding with his. "You don't really want me to leave."

Emily bit her lip and it took all his strength not to buckle under the meaning from the subconscious gesture. There was an ache in his solar plexus as he pulled her closer again. She moved her head closer leaning in to kiss him.

"This is crazy." James said to himself as his lips met hers. His mind felt fuzzy and his vision seemed hazy.

She pulled back. "Yes, it is." Emily was suddenly cold. "You should go and process this." She tried to move further away but James placed his hand on her throat, pressing her back into the wall again so she could barely breathe.

"I didn't say I didn't like it." He threw her on the bed and a happy giggle escaped her lips. She was nervous of this new creature: this wasn't the James she knew. Emily took a deep breath and let herself go as she kissed him. Their happy growls and moans were drowned out in the sound of tearing fabric.

**James**

**51**

I remembered every moment of that night, although thinking back it is hard to believe that it had actually happened. Although I have the scars - emotional and literal - to prove it, it didn't feel like me that it happened to. Could I have confused it with a dream? It felt like one of my blackouts but I remember everything. At least I think I do.

We dived at each other and snarling, biting at skin and tearing our clothing as we couldn't pull it off fast enough. I reached up and thread my fingers into her hair, massaging her scalp before pulling her hair so hard her neck bent backwards, detaching her from my lips. She hissed and her eyes went wide, but I felt her body heat up and her hips pressed into mine.

As she clawed my shirt off I managed to - literally - rip her black dress from her to reveal her toned but soft looking body and skin. Her eyes met mine and I dropped to my knees and buried my face into her, letting my tongue explore every inch and focusing on one area that made her buck and moan. She pulled my hair and pushed me further into her.

Growling (and I mean growling, I have no idea how or why I made those sounds but they seemed to escape from my throat) I launched her further onto the bed and she squealed with delight as her head collided with the headboard: she should have been seeing stars but she raked her nails across my chest and moved me so I was on my back. Her tongue sucking and teasing the top of me, so I forced her head down, slamming the full length of me down her throat. I felt her gag and I heard her cough, but I ached for release.

"Oh God." I moaned and forced her onto me aching. *Please don't stop.* I tried not to beg. Thankfully, unlike Rachel, Emily brought me to completion and my moans - verging on screams - of pleasure warranted the people in the neighbouring room to bang on the wall. It occurred to me later that these walls should have been thick enough - or sound proofed enough - to block out the sounds. Or perhaps I was that loud...

I fell back, my head spinning as I tried to catch my breath and I lay enjoying the pleasurable feeling coursing though me. I heard her mutter something.

"What did you say?" I craned my head up to face her.

"I said we're not done." She had a wicked look in her eyes and she climbed on top of me whilst I was still hard. Her gyrating and pulsating wound me up again and I rolled her over so I could pin her down, her thighs gripping my ribs - I vaguely remember feeling them pop, but I was distracted by her moans of pleasure mingled with pain as I bit into her neck, tasting blood.

We wrestled, fought and fucked for hours. It felt like I had been drugged: we were part of the night and I could taste the sky and smell the stars. It was indescribable, or it would be might be my memory of that night fading. I mean I felt like I was part her, I could see our souls merging. We truly were one, connected through our utter euphoria.

So of course she left. Oh please, you didn't think this had a happy ending, we were going to run off and get married? She didn't leave whilst I was sleeping at least but that seemed to make things worse. If she had just gone I could have hated her and told myself she was using me, but no, she insisted on waiting so she could explain. And I wish that part of me didn't agree with her.

I woke to find her sat on the edge of the bed, fully dressed with a red bag by the door. She was watching me.

"You're leaving." I said sleepily as I tried to sit up and fell back down gasping at the pain in my chest and head. I felt like I had been hit by a train. The euphoria from that night blocked out the pain of physical damage she had done to me. At the time I had enjoyed it, but now I realised she was right, she had lost control and really hurt me.

"Your ribs are broken." That familiar coldness returned, it was something recognisable and grounding. Although the distain she tried to mask her eyes with was washed away by the wetness, which she failed to hide. So she avoided eye contact. Out the corner of my eyes I saw a stain and I turned to see blood streak on the sheet, raising my hand to my head as I remembered the blood.

*How hard did she hit me?* I had flashbacks of her on top of me and slapping me.

"You're bleeding. Face and back. You should probably see a doctor about the ribs and concussion."

She got up and I pushed myself upright again, wincing. "You're not leaving."

"I can't hurt you again."

"You won't."

She laughed and it was hollow. "How can you say that? You can't lie to yourself. I told you I would do this." She was crying but there was no sound, the tears just streamed down her cheeks. I tried to argue with her but I just started coughing.

*How...? What...?* My thoughts were fractured and I couldn't focus. I was still half asleep.

"I want you to be happy, but that's obviously not with me. I'll contact Nathan to let him know how ill you are. He was good to you before." I was certain she didn't have his number and I tried to ask how, but I was ravaged with wracking coughs. Luckily, the coughing distracted me from how incredibly creepy that was.

*Or was it sweet? Nope, definitely creepy.*

There was a cold smile on her lips as I saw the mask slip smoothly onto her features. I looked at the time and it was barely 7am, but the sun was already cascading through the curtains. I wanted to get out of bed to stop her, but my muscles felt weak. It was like I had run 16 marathons and now nothing worked. I managed to choke out: "You're not leaving." but it didn't make any difference. "I love you."

"I love you too, but you won't hear from me again." She said as she walked out the door, I crawled back into bed and lay there pondering on the strange turn my life taken. Had she really walked out of my life? Was she going to be back in two months time? She had said I would never hear from her again before. Was she a mythical creature of a mad woman? Was I something out of a fairy story or was I losing my mind?

*What has my life become?*

**52**

*"To live is the rarest thing in the world. Most people exist, that is all."*

**53**

When I awoke again the clock was just changing from 9:03 to 9:04. Feeling better I sat up in bed and looked around at the aftermath. The bed was damp with sweat and sex, and stained with light patches of blood. The broken champagne glass was on the floor and there were two empty champagne bottles on the desk.

*Two?*

Somehow we broke the mirror: I had vague recollection of fucking her on the desk and her opening another bottle at some point in the night. Other than the remnants of our sex there was nothing left of her: I'd hoped she would have left a note, a moment. Nope, nothing.

I left without showering. Her scent was still on my skin and I wanted to hold onto it as long as possible. Plus I really couldn't be bothered and I wanted to get out before the cleaners came in. My T-shirt had basically been torn in two so I threw it in the bin and left after washing the blood and sex from my face. I could taste her on my chin.

Guests were staring as I stumbled out the hotel, although I could be paranoid. I think everyone gets self-conscious when they're making the walk of shame. I left without bothering to see if she checked out, I didn't want have to answer any questions about the damage, or get lumbered with the bill. I'm sure she would have settled up.

I saw people whispering but I shot them a look that made them shut up sharpish. *Not paranoid, I must really look a state.* When I was washing my face I noticed my eyes were swollen and red and I had a long cut down my face. As I walked to the tube I wished I had taken a shower. My hair was greasy and limp; I must have smelt and my back was dripping with sweat and possibly congealed with blood. I was struggling not to cough and the ache in my chest was worse.

I desperately hoped that it wasn't over but part of me knew she was gone. I need to get home and lock myself away. *I hope Emily hasn't contacted Nathan.* My chest ached annoyingly. Even thinking her name was difficult.

## 54

I don't remember much of the following few days or even weeks. I felt hungover when I got home so I went straight to bed and I stayed there in my darkened room until my alarm went off at 7am on Monday. I crawled to the shower where I washed off the stink that was stuck to my skin. I felt completely disgusting by this point and it was really cathartic to wash Emily off my skin and out of my head. The latter didn't work.

Skipping breakfast I shambled along with the other zombies in business suits, the smell of shampoo, shower gel and skin infiltrating my nostrils, but also reminded me that I was part of this world. I was already trying to forget the awkward topics of conversation from the weekend. And I was trying my damnedest to ignore the glow most people had around them. I couldn't flirt with anyone today: I could barely handle being around people. However, I did make and maintain eye contact, which is a step in the right direction.

I approached the door to my work and as it's glass I could see Gemma and Alice looking at me through the door, but I didn't care. I took a deep and prepared my Game Face. It felt natural to slip this on and I could feel my muscles relaxing as my stomach knotted into a tighter ball. They were looking at me with odd looks on their faces but didn't pursue it when I walked in faking an overly good mood.

"Good morning my beautiful ladies. Good weekend?" They were just pleased to talk about themselves.

It was a quiet Monday but I was still sleep walking through it so I couldn't recall whom I checked in or how may calls I made. 1 to 2 was lunch and I spent it with my head in my arms, staring at nothing and chewing on a sandwich I ran out to pick up. I was finally hungry.

From 2 to 5.30 it was more of the same from this morning. Answering phones; completing admin work; updating the records of the organisations within the building and the staff they held and staff; photocopying.

From 5.30 to 6 I travelled home again, the smells of the other commuters more potent after a hard days work. When I got home I forwent the usual exercise to spend the evening with Nathan. He walked in while I was cooking and I only noticed when he tapped me on the shoulder.

"I said: 'are you alright mate?'"

"Huh?"

"Are you doing that on purpose? This is the third time I've asked, you alright?" He went to the fridge and waggled a bottle of beer at me. I looked at it as I continued to stir the sauce and realised I really didn't want a drink.

"I'm OK. How was work?"

"Same old, had a fight with my boss over pay again. I got a message from Emily."

The smell of my cooking suddenly made me very nauseous. "Oh yeah?" I waggled a plate at him and he nodded, sitting down at the table.

"Yeah cheers, I'm starving. Yeah, she said you two had a fight, you didn't look well and could I look after you. You two OK? How'd she get my number?"

"No idea mate, she's fucking weird. Yeah I'm OK, she wanted to talk, we ended up fighting and now it's properly over."

"And you're OK? You have a nasty looking mark on your face."

I dished up and sat down and I answered with a mouthful of food. "Emily slapped me. The bitch has nails. Had a fight with Jo as well, it hasn't been a great weekend."

"What about Jo?"

"I'm going to text her and apologise and take her for dinner."

We ate in silence for a while. Nathan broke the silence. "So you fucked her? Emily I mean." I blew my poker face by choking on my pasta. "You gonna tell Jo?"

"No." I hadn't decided until then but I realised I wasn't going to tell her. "No, it was a stupid mistake. I don't want to hurt her. No one will achieve anything by me admitting it." Nathan nodded at me to signalled to show appreciation of my cooking, but he didn't comment on my decision.

10pm until bed I was drinking water and texting Jo (*I never did get that games console*), I apologised and we sat chatting and I tried to arrange to take her for dinner at the weekend. She still didn't want to see me though. *Fuck, I've really blown it.*

About 11pm it was bed, where I lay there desperately trying to will myself to sleep.


The next Wednesday I went to the evening session at the doctor's after I went incredibly dizzy and threw up at work. This was then topped off by narrowly missing being hit by a taxi at King's Cross. I didn't even see it coming and she turned the air blue as she swerved out of the way.

Doctors aren't supposed to judge, but this one judged me the minute I walked in. I was freshly shaved and covered up the scratch with some of Nathan's concealer, and yet I still managed to look like a state. My eyes looked glassy and dead and the bags had gone purple.

*Don't you look a state? You look like a fish.*

*This could all be in my head you know. You are paranoid.*

"How can I help?" The doctor asked, I would have thought it would have been obvious but I suppose they couldn't make assumptions. I started coughing when I tried to explain my symptoms and when I unbuttoned my shirt so he could listen to my chest he caught sight of the purple bruising around my ribs. "Can I take a look?"

It had spread, parts were black and it was difficult to breathe. "I was in a fight at the weekend." It wasn't a complete lie.

"Explains the cut to your face." *Damn.* "Are there any other injuries?"

"Just sore all over and constantly tired."

"You're going to need rest and painkillers. You've ripped the muscles in your ribs. And it feels like there are a couple of hairline fractures. They're not a danger to your lungs so all I can do is give you something for the pain."

"That's fine."

"No heavy lifting."

"That's fine."

"Ice pack."

"OK

"Breathing exercises – 10 slow, deep breaths every hour, letting your lungs inflate fully each time."

"Fine."

"Are you in some sort of trouble?"

"I've never known a doctor to care so much."

"Not all doctors are as amazing as me." He smiled at me and I tried to smile back but my facial muscles refused to respond. Now I was aware of the extent of my injuries I could feel them in a lot more detail. Like a child who doesn't cry until he sees he is bleeding. He started writing out a prescription. "I'm giving you a seven tablets, but it is very strong painkiller, so only take it when the pain gets too much. Until then, follow my instructions and take ibuprofen and paracetamol. And keep out of trouble." He added as I got up to leave. "Come back to see me if it gets any worse."

So of course I didn't.


Jo surprised me after work on Friday. We were just leaving and I was forcing myself to go along for Friday evening drinks. *Must stay sociable. Must stay sociable.*

"Hi. Can we go grab a drink? Or do you have plans?" Jo smiled at Alice and Gemma who pushed me towards Jo and then walked off waving and giggling like naughty schoolgirls. *Now that's a thought…* "How are you doing? Your face looks bad."

"Oh thanks!" I gingerly touched the scab on my face. It was starting to itch already.

"I was glassed in a pub." I lied.

"Oh my!" She stopped walking went to push my hair off my face. "What happened?"

I shied away from her. "Long story. I mouthed off at the wrong person and…" I gestured towards my face. I was hoping that she would pick up that it wasn't nearly deep enough to be a glassing, but she didn't mention it. What you don't know, don't hurt you.

We made small talk until we reached a bar where I ordered a Pepsi. She eyed me as I we sat down. "I've cut down on drinking." I answered. "It's not good for me." I subconsciously touched my head. "Look, I'm sorry for how I acted, I haven't been feeling right and I know that's no excuse, but I do care about you."

Jo took my hand and leaned across the table to kiss me. "I care about you. I understand you had a bad break up, but as long as I'm not just a rebound."

"No of course not!" It wasn't a total lie.

We started slowly: Jo was tentative in my presence in the beginning. I could tell she was careful not to get too attached for fear of getting hurt again. I must have hurt her a lot more than I realised.

Over the next couple of weeks I settled quite comfortably into the rut that had become my life. Part of me wanted to fight it, but it was overpowered by the fact I didn't have the energy to fight it anymore. My life was comfortable, that's more than most people could hope for.

Nathan and Alice were preoccupied with getting a place together. I heard them talking about it and trying to work out what they could afford. We were all settling down. Growing up. Getting boring.

*"Time passes. Even when it seems impossible. Even when each tick of the second hand aches like the pulse of blood behind a bruise. It passes unevenly, in strange lurches and dragging lulls, but pass it does. Even for me."*

## 55

It was a Saturday when I got up early and went running. I went on a 30 mile run and felt like I could conquer the world. As I ran I saw the energy that connected us all running through the trees, the plants, grass, through the parents with buggies, casual walkers and the other runners. I felt the moods they were in and I drank it all in. Jo was no longer getting sick and I was feeling better than ever. Life was finally starting to go my way.

*JINX.*

I came home to find a dozen red roses on the kitchen table. They were in a vase with a card next to them so I assumed they were from Susan, who met someone on a dating website and he was doing his damnedest to impress her. There were always empty bottles of champagne and half eaten boxes of chocolates in the house. I tossed a couple in my mouth before staring in the fridge, hoping something nice would magically appear as I had forgotten to go shopping again.

It didn't. So I closed the fridge and finished on the top tray and picked up the card. My blood ran cold: the envelope hard my name on it, but there was no card. I didn't need a fucking card.

I managed to stop myself throwing the vase at the wall. Andy had words with me about the chipped plaster that had been appearing around the place and threatened to keep my deposit. I could have re-gifted the flowers but I needed them dead. So I emptied the case into the sink, boiled the kettle - made myself a cup of tea - and poured the remaining water over the flowers. I then emptied the bottle of bleach from under the sink over them.

I cleaned up the mess before anyone got home.

*It was really is over. This chapter was finally closed. I was over her. Then why does she insist on opening it?* I couldn't work out if this an apology or her poking the wound; making sure I didn't move on.

I chose not to think about it. I didn't want her fucking up my life again.

*I'll believe you. Many wouldn't.*

That night was a dark and stormy night - *Seriously, seriously James you can't think of any better adjectives, or are you attempting to be funny again?*

*Actually it's a Star Trek reference, now can I continue?* - and my dreams were intense and vivid. Emily was in this, but I was aware I was dreaming. She was seeking me out and the floors were a way of opening that door.

"They are, aren't they?" I asked her. Part of my unconscious body tried to yell. I could feeling my sleeping chest and throat straining in reality.

Emily didn't answer but growled and giggled and started moving towards me silently - I couldn't move. Her pupils dilated and twitched until they engulfed and whites; I could see the muscles in her arms and legs twitching and contracting: she looked like an animal.

I still couldn't move.

The rumble grew louder and her eyes... Her eyes were black pits in her face.

I still didn't move.

I woke up as she collided me: I sat bolt upright, pulling off my T-shirt to reveal long, deep wounds down my chest and arms, panting, exhausted and an overwhelming anger in inside of me - *How could she leave? And why did I care?* I felt the burning desire: an unquenchable fire and her eyes watching me from the corner of the room. *A hallucination?*

I kicked the sheets off and opened the window: the cool air felt soothing on my chest but the wounds looking worse in the moonlight. I closed my eyes and I could feel the light healing my wounds - physical, emotional and spiritual. That's when I started coughing.

The coughing grew worse until I was choking and retching. I doubled over trying to grab my bin to throw up into and as I covered my mouth I felt a viscous fluid with a copper taste fill my mouth. Coughing I saw my hands were covered in a dark liquid and shaking I tried to reach for my lamp to bring an end to this nightmare.

"I must be dreaming. I must be dreaming. I must be dreaming." I repeated. My head span and I collapsed back down onto my pillow and tried to will the spinning to stop, I gripped my chest as I convulsed and shook.

My vision went hazy and the salty tears streamed down my face as I opened my eyes to feel sunlight on my face, warming my skin as I slowly woke up. I awoke to clarity I didn't realise was possible.

"I'm alive?" I ran my fingers over my chests to test the sensitivity of my wounds. They were gone. I looked for the dry blood on my hands. There was none. Last night started to come back to me in pieces, the sheets were still damp and I could still feel the burning need and anger. *It was a dream.*

I watched a man and his dog walking down the street, wincing at the light. I squinted to shield my vision and for some reason I was disgusted at this man, I knew he did this every morning and it was his only escape from his mundane life. It gave him a chance to walk and think about what could have been.

I pondered on this as I noticed the ache in my chest, right on my solar plexus. I felt more alive than I ever had, the world was beautiful and bright I could smell the bread baking for two streets over.

*Oh fuck it.*

I knew had to leave this life, pack a bag and leave London. I knew I had to find her. I knew she wasn't in London any more. As fire attracts fire, I wanted to be burnt by her.

*"My bounty is as boundless as the sea / My love as deep; the more I give to thee / The more I have, for both are infinite."*

## 56

*I'm sure you're wondering why I have to find her? Isn't it obvious? I'm an emotional masochist, or an idiot. More than likely both.*

Printed in Great Britain
by Amazon